Timeless

Timeless

Roz Lee

DEDICATION

For everyone who followed their dream.

ACKNOWLEDGMENTS

This book is a work of fiction. Characters, places, and events are all figments of my imagination, though some might be inspired by real persons, places, or things.

Many thanks to Paul, Debbie, and Jessica Ritter, who own and operate Brook Hollow Winery. Your kindness and friendship inspired this book series.

I admit to taking liberties with the wine business. Any errors in regard to the production and marketing of wine are mine. I consulted an expert, then I *might* have twisted a few things to fit my story. I refer you back to the first sentence. This is a work of fiction.

I invite you to have a glass of wine, sit back, and enjoy the story.

Roz Lee

CHAPTER ONE

Sean Nightingale stood atop the crest of the rocky hillside, hands loosely resting on his hips. Rows of leafy vines hugged the curves of the terraced landscape like lace ruffles on a prom dress. He filled his lungs with hot, dry Southern California air, savoring the smell of the ripening fruit. Having grown up on a vineyard, Sean had always associated the heavy scent with obligation and hard work, but somehow, today, it was different. Today, it smelled like freedom.

He'd signed the papers on these 200 acres weeks ago, but obligations that had weighed him down his entire life kept him from beginning this new chapter until today. The sign above the gate bore his family name, Nightingale, but unlike the vineyard he was part owner of back in New Jersey, this one was all his. Purchased with funds he'd accumulated over the years through savings and shrewd investments. He'd put an entire continent between himself and his family, but he wasn't a fool. The Nightingale name meant something in the wine industry, and he aimed to add to his family's reputation, not exile himself from it. Like his older brother, Wade, who was the CEO of the family business, Sean wanted to put his own stamp on the legacy he'd inherited. Had it been necessary to put so much distance between them to do so? Maybe not, but he wanted to create something new, something extraordinary. Growing more grapes in the same soil and under the same weather conditions as they were already doing wasn't going to cut it. Nightingale Vineyard needed fresh blood, or new grape juice if you will, and that's what these acres represented. They were the future of his family's business, whether the rest of the Nightingales realized it or not.

They would come around. He'd already secured a guarantee from Wade to ship him some wine from this year's New Jersey harvest. Sean planned to blend grapes from their east coast vineyard with grapes from his west coast vineyard to produce new blends like no other on the planet.

Movement on the road that wound its way along the hillside connecting the various buildings drew his attention. Coming from the farthest point, the car could only contain one person. Angellica Capello. In the weeks he'd been gone, the woman had moved out of the main house, the only home she'd ever known, to the vintner's cottage. When he got around to hiring more help, he'd make sure they lived off-site. His previous life as the marketing director for Nightingale Vineyards hadn't offered him much in the way of privacy. He'd once craved the jet-setting lifestyle but had grown weary of the constant travel and parties. He'd put on a good show for years, but his last duty had drained him of his acting ability. A week aboard the erotic-themed cruise ship, *The Lothario*, followed by a tour of the island retreat opening later this year, cemented one thought in his mind. He was ready to settle down. He wanted a family of his own, and more than anything; he wanted to create his own legacy separate from the one he'd inherited.

The previous owner had attached one stipulation to the sale. Sean agreed to employ the man's daughter and allow her to live in the vintner's cottage for one year. Supposedly, Ms. Capello had been running the farm for the past three years. According to her father, she knew everything there was to know about the vines dotting the hillside and the wines aging in the cask room. Her father insisted she'd be an asset, but Sean saw her and her "expertise" as an insult to his own abilities. True, he'd yet to prove himself as anything but a savvy marketer in the wine industry, but you didn't grow up with grape juice in your veins without learning a thing or two about wine. He'd waited a long time for a chance to test his theories, and nothing—*nobody*—was going to stand in his way.

The phone vibrating in his pocket drew his attention away from his one full-time employee long enough to glance at the screen. *Damn it. Couldn't the woman take a hint?* He'd taken the supermodel out one time. One time! What had started out as a mutually beneficial public appearance had devolved into a quickie in the back of a limo on the way to her apartment. She'd spent the rest of the evening crying her eyes out over what they'd done in the car and wailing about her ex. Two months had gone by without a word from her, which suited him just fine. He never wanted to see her again. He'd ignored a dozen calls from her in the last week, so what was one more? He clicked a button on his phone, sending the call to voicemail. When he looked back up, the car he'd seen earlier sat in front of the blending room, and a woman was lifting a cardboard file box from the trunk. She proceeded to the security-controlled entrance, where she keyed in a code. Sean was too far away to hear the locks disengage, but when she put her hand on the knob and her shoulder to the heavy metal door, it swung open, allowing her entry. The self-closing hydraulic cylinder did its job, and the door clanged shut, sealing the woman inside.

Taking one last look at his new domain, Sean closed his eyes and silently asked the universe to give him strength. The next few years would be a challenge, not to mention a drain on his resources. He planned to use the funds from selling this year's harvest to finance the research and develop his new line of wines. After that, he'd bottle and sell off all the wine stored in the cask room. He wasn't about to put the Nightingale label on them since no one in his family had been involved in the processing. Instead, he planned to market them to collectors as limited editions bearing the previous owner's label. As the last of their kind, they'd command a premium price. Releasing one vintage per year for the next three years would maximize his cash flow and open up space in the cask room for his new creations. Once all the Capello wines were gone, he'd introduce the new Nightingale West brand to the world.

The wine business was all about patience. It took years for new vines to mature enough to bear fruit and years more to get a substantial harvest from them. The process from harvest to bottling couldn't be rushed either. It took someone with a keen pallet and infinite patience to turn ordinary grape juice into an award-winning wine. Sean had plenty of the former and far less of the latter, but enough, he thought, to make a go of it. He'd bided his time, saving his money, learning everything he could about the wine industry, and honing his pallet on every conceivable vintage. He was ready for this.

He examined a cluster of ripening Cabernet Sauvignon grapes. He estimated another week before they reached their peak. He separated one from its stem for a closer look. The texture and color of the skin were perfect. Squeezing it between his thumb and forefinger, he judged the firmness to be adequate. Sean popped the deep purple orb into his mouth and crunched down on it. Tart juice flooded his mouth, confirming his earlier thoughts. The extra time on the vine would allow the sugars to develop to an acceptable level. He'd had his eye on these vines since he first set foot in the vineyard. Grown in what amounted to desert soil, their sweet-tart flavor, when blended with the slightly sweeter New Jersey grape, would produce a unique wine. One he hoped would keep Nightingale wines at the top of every sommelier's list for decades to come.

"Two weeks," he said to himself as he gave the heavily laden vines one last look before making his way down the hillside to the blending room. It was time to set things straight with Ms. Capello.

CHAPTER TWO

Angellica set the heavy box on the desk in the office that had been her father's for as long as she could remember. A bank of dusty file cabinets lined two walls, silent witnesses to decades of success in an unforgiving industry. Shelves filled with plaques and trophies were proof her family's small winery had run with the big dogs. Industry standards labeled them a boutique winery. Nothing more than a hobby to some, but it had been everything to her father and her. Wine was all Angellica knew, and she had a Master of Science degree from UC Davis in Enology and Viticulture to prove it. Not that her academic achievements had made a difference with her dad. In his world, women took care of their men. They cooked, they cleaned, and they had babies. His old-school ways drove Angellica mad, but she loved him despite his faults. They'd argued for months over his decision to sell the family business to an outsider rather than turn the day-to-day operations over to her. Angellica had overseen the sale of their harvest to other wineries for the past three years, but it wasn't enough. Tomas Capello refused to believe she could run a full-scale operation.

Picking a framed photo of her father from the box she'd brought with her, she managed a weak smile before placing the memento on the far corner of her new desk. She'd won a minor victory when she convinced her father to negotiate a position for her with the new owner. One year wasn't much time to prove herself, but it was more than her father had ever given her, and she wasn't going to waste a minute.

The next item was a leather-bound notebook containing her notes and ideas for blending and aging the wines she longed to create. Like the previous three years, this year's harvest had been sold before the new owner signed the papers on the acreage. When all the grapes were in and the juice extracted, they would only have a few hundred gallons of juice left to work with. It wasn't much, but it was more than she'd been able to hold back over the last few years. With her father watching every transaction, it had been difficult to hide even a few extra gallons from him, but she'd done so, hiding the excess in the cask room. It was the one place on the property Tomas Capello wouldn't go. Too many memories, he'd said. He'd proposed to her mother in the underground room. Every year, they'd celebrated the anniversary with a candlelit dinner in the exact spot where he'd proposed to her with his mother's diamond ring.

Angellica twisted the diamond ring on her right hand. Upon her mother's death, her father had insisted she have it, and she'd worn it ever since. The design was elegant and timeless, just like their love had been. She knew her parents had hoped she would find the same kind of love they had, even setting her up with what they considered suitable gentlemen. Her father had been pushing her toward his best friend's son ever since they were both toddlers. Several months ago, he'd invited James over for dinner without telling her. As soon as James arrived, her dad remembered he'd agreed to meet with a potential buyer in town. It was a setup and a lousy one at that. She and James had laughed about his obvious charade but hadn't let it spoil the nice dinner she'd prepared. Both agreed they were better friends than anything else, despite what both their parents thought. James' family owned a vineyard on the other side of the Temecula Valley. They'd been in business almost as long as Angellica's family. James was the heir apparent, but unlike her, he wanted no part of his legacy. Having majored in Theatre Arts in college, her friend aspired to be on Broadway. She wished him well. Everyone deserved a chance to achieve their dream.

She was filling a chipped mug with all the pens and pencils her dad had left in the top drawer when the telltale squeak of hinges announced she was no longer alone. Since she hadn't heard a vehicle drive up, she assumed the new arrival had to be her employer, Sean Nightingale. Though he'd owned the property for almost two weeks, he'd only arrived the previous night to take possession. Rumor had it Sean was a bachelor, and as far as she knew, he'd spent the night alone in the big house she'd called home for her entire life. It was only a guess since she'd moved to the vintner's cottage and she hadn't bothered to welcome the man. The house and the two hundred acres surrounding it should be hers. She'd be damned if she was going to pretend being relegated to employee status didn't suck donkey balls.

Sean Nightingale's reputation as a playboy in the wine world was well documented. He attended gala events with an actress or supermodel on his arm, lording his wealth and family's status over everyone. Angellica had never met the man, but she knew his type. Too handsome for his own good, he traveled the world on his company expense account, pretending to be a wine expert. Her best guess? He knew nothing about the product his family had been making for two centuries. Why he was interested in Capello

Vineyards was something she couldn't work out in her mind. Her family's acreage, though substantial, was a hobby farm compared to Nightingale Vineyards. Angellica had hoped that one of the parties involved would come to their senses and cancel the contract before the sale became final. It wasn't until the work crews took down the Capello Winery sign and replaced it with one bearing the Nightingale logo and name that she lost hope. Hope was for fools, it seemed, as all her dreams had evaporated with the stroke of a pen.

The same day the sign came down, Angellica claimed it and stashed it away behind her new home. She spent the next 24 hours crying her eyes out. It was done. Sean Nightingale had cast a spell over Tomas Capello, making the newcomer the devil in her eyes. She'd work for him for the year her father had negotiated, but if the man thought she was going to make his life easier, he had another think coming.

CHAPTER THREE

Sean cringed as the squeaky hinges announced his arrival to the only other occupant of the building. The blending room was as dusty and outdated as Sean remembered from the brief tour the previous owner had given him over four months ago. Fortunately, Nightingales had recently updated their own facility. It hadn't taken much to convince Wade to ship their old equipment across the country. The used equipment would arrive in the next few days, leaving plenty of time to clean the place and get it ready to be modernized before the harvest began. But his first order of business was getting Ms. Capello out of his blending room. It didn't matter why she was there. She had to go. He'd waited too long to have a place of his own to work, and she had no place in his lab.

Following her footprints on the dusty floor, Sean stalked his prey along the short hallway. He paid little attention to the framed black and white photographs lining the walls. He had a million thoughts running through his head. Too many to pay attention to trivial matters. Angellica Capello wasn't a trivial matter, and the sooner he checked her off his list of things to do, the better.

As he'd guessed, the footprints led him to what had been the Vintner's private office back in the day when Tomas Capello had taken an interest in his wine. From the looks of things, it had been years since anyone had worked in the building. That was all about to change.

Rounding the corner, Sean stopped in the doorway to the only office in the building. A shaft of light through a grimy window sliced the room in half. Dust particles danced like fairies, refusing to settle again once disturbed. The fairy dust went unnoticed. Instead, the woman standing behind the ancient desk, calmly arranging items upon its pitted and scratched surface, claimed all his attention. His brain stuttered for a second, trying to make sense of the vision before him.

This is Angellica Capello? It couldn't be. Tomas Capello knew his wine, but there was a reason he remained behind the scenes, letting his product speak for itself. The man resembled a wine barrel in stature and had the face of a gargoyle. This. This *vision*, straight from a fairy tale, couldn't be his daughter. Anger, white-hot, spiked his temper. Clenching his fists at his side, he strode into the room, stirring a cloud of dust that nearly choked him as he closed the distance between himself and the woman. This was not the way he wanted to begin his day. Not giving a care about his language, he belted out, "What the fuck are you doing in my blending lab?"

"Good morning," the vision said as she rummaged through the box on the desk. "I guess my father forgot to tell you—you should wear boots in the vineyard."

Sean glanced at his dust-covered feet clad in expensive leather flip-flops, then back up at the woman. "It's my vineyard, and I'll wear whatever I damn well please."

The woman shrugged. "Suit yourself. But, if you insist on wearing those shoes, watch where you step. The rattlesnake population has increased over the years."

Rattlesnakes? "Are you saying they're a problem?"

For the first time since he'd entered the office, she raised her chin. Her brown eyes met his, and a hint of a smile tugged at her lips before she brought it under control. "That's exactly what I'm saying, Mr. Nightingale."

He chuckled. She'd gotten him good. A giant smile broke across his face. "Bravo, Ms. Capello. Bravo. You had me going there for a while."

"It wasn't a joke. But suit yourself. Just make sure you have 9-1-1 on speed dial next time you go walking alone, practically barefoot." She dug a small picture frame from the box and placed it on the edge of the desk.

Silence stretched between them as Sean contemplated her and her statement. Her long, dark hair was pulled back and held by a clip at her nape. Her attire was casual but elegant, if that was even a thing. A silk blouse with pockets and a row of buttons down the front was tucked into either slacks or shorts. He couldn't tell which since the desk hid her from the hips down. Likewise, it hid her feet from view. He thought back to the footprints he'd used to track her down, then glanced over his shoulder to refresh his memory. He involuntarily curled his toes under at the sight of the waffle-weave prints. Boots. The woman was wearing boots. And not the designer kind. The kind you would wear to hike a mountain. Swallowing his pride, he cleared his throat before speaking. "You really aren't kidding, are you?"

"No. I'm not kidding." She stuck her leg out to the side so he could see her footwear. "I saw one of our day laborers get bitten when I was about ten years old. Ever since, I only venture into the vineyards wearing hiking boots."

"Sensible," he said, sauntering over to take a seat in one of the old chairs facing the desk. "What other predators should I be watching out for?"

"Coyotes. We're a long way from the border here, so

I'm talking about the four-legged kind. Though we get the occasional group of migrants who set up camp on the property."

"What about mountain lions?" He'd heard of hikers being attacked by one on one of his previous trips to California.

"I've never seen one, but they have a wide territory. The coyotes keep the small wildlife population under control, so there are better places for the mountain lions to hunt than here."

"Won't they come after the coyotes?" It made sense to him.

"I have no idea. Why don't you go research that? I'm almost done here. Then I have to check the vines. It'll be time to harvest soon."

"Two weeks."

Her gaze locked with his. She twisted her bottom lip to the side and caught it with her upper teeth as she studied him. "What makes you say that?"

"I tasted one of the Cabernet Sauvignon grapes a few minutes ago. They're ripening well, but they need more time to develop their sugar content."

"The sugar content will be too high if we leave them on the vine that long."

"Why do you think I want them to stay on the vine longer?"

Her cheeks flushed with color, and she narrowed her eyes. "The wineries we've contracted with aren't expecting a high sugar content. They're expecting the same product we've been delivering to them for the last several years."

He glared back at her. She might be right about his choice of shoes, but when it came to the grapes, what he said was law. "Okay then. We'll harvest three-fourths of the grapes next week. That should be enough to fulfill the contracts. The rest will remain on the vine until they fully develop their sugar content."

"That's absurd. Why would you do something like that?"

No one other than Wade knew what he intended to do with the harvests from here on out, and he wanted to keep it that way. "It's good crop management," was all he said before heading for the door.

 CHAPTER FOUR

"Ugh." Angellica dropped into the desk chair, stirring up a cloud of dust. "The man is insufferable." Not that she'd expected anything else, personality-wise, but she hadn't expected the way her body reacted to him. She'd done her research. She'd seen hundreds of pictures of him on the Internet and knew he was sinfully attractive, but the photos didn't do him justice. They didn't convey the physicality of Sean Nightingale. Dressed like a beach bum, he still exuded confidence and virility. One glimpse of the guy and her ovaries perked up and did a do-si-so with her uterus. She'd dated her fair share of handsome men, and not one of them had caused such an instantaneous reaction. The tsunami of hormones had thrown her off her game at first, but she soon found that not looking directly at him helped. However, his voice. *Good lord.* She'd expected a heavy New Jersey gangster accent. Instead, he sounded like a late-night disc jockey. He had the sort of voice that kept women up at night, listening to song after song, imagining the disc jockey pounding them against the headboard and whispering dirty words in their ear.

He'd spouted some dirty words, all right. Well, he'd been about to before she cut him off mid-tirade and redirected his attention to his inappropriate footwear. He'd been on the cusp of ordering her to vacate the vintner's office. Like he belonged there. He knew nothing about grapes or when to harvest them. And what was he going to do with the ultra-sweet grapes he wanted to save for last? There wouldn't be enough to bottle. It made no sense.

Angellica dug through the tote bag at her feet for the water bottle she'd filled that morning. Relaxing back in the chair, she took a long pull, letting the cold liquid wash away the dust and the sour taste in her mouth following her encounter with the new owner. She'd waited years to test her ideas. She wasn't going to let some playboy from New Jersey derail her plans. This was her opportunity to show the world she was more than a pretty face meant to grace some man's arm and be his broodmare. Not that she was opposed to marriage and kids, but those had never been high on her priority list. She'd grown up expecting to inherit the family business and had done all she could to prepare herself to do just that. Then her mother passed away, and her father lost interest in his life's work. No matter how much she pleaded with him to let her take over the business, he'd insisted on selling it.

Looking around the dust-covered room, she supposed she should be grateful her father included this opportunity in the terms of the sale. No matter how dubious her position appeared to be, at least she wasn't wearing a paper hat and flipping burgers for a living. When the year was up, she'd take her skills elsewhere.

Stifling a sigh, Angellica resumed making herself at home in her new office. The sunlight coming through the east-facing window grew dimmer as the day wore on, and by the time she resorted to turning on the overhead lighting, most of the dust had been conquered, and she'd filled and emptied the trash bin multiple times. The place hadn't looked so good in years. And best of all, her new employer had stayed out of her way. Other than the brief appearance he'd made that morning, she hadn't seen or heard him all day. A good thing, she thought as she shut the door behind her and made her way to the main entrance. When she stepped out into the early evening, she was looking forward to a hot shower, followed by dinner and a glass of wine. The vintner's cottage was a short walk, but she'd driven her car this morning rather than tote the heavy box of office accouterments. Unless it was raining, there'd be no need to drive most days. She plopped her tote bag on the hood of the car and did a deep dive for her car keys.

"Have you been working on that office all day?"

The voice was unmistakable, but also unexpected. Angellica jumped and spun around, dragging the tote bag off the hood, causing the contents to scatter across the hard-packed ground. A very unladylike oath escaped her lips before she could stop it. Ignoring her belongings, she mustered her willpower and cast her gaze upon the man who was currently the bane of her existence. "Not that it's any of your business, but yes. I spent the day cleaning and organizing."

It was his business, but he kindly refrained from saying so. He pointed to the objects littering the driveway. "Need some help with that?"

"Nope. I'm good." She'd pick it up when he was gone. "Did you need something?"

A hint of a smile appeared on his face as he silently assessed her situation. "No. I was just heading home to clean up, then I thought I'd go into town for dinner." His gaze shot to a spot over her left shoulder, then back to her face. "Would you like to come along? My treat? We haven't discussed my plans for the business or what I see as your role in it."

It was her turn to look away. She focused on the corner of the building where she'd spent the day organizing for her new job. Or what she hoped her new job would be. She didn't have a clue what Nightingale expected of her. She'd been promised nothing more than a place to live and a job title. For all she knew, he expected her to sit on her ass and collect her pay until her contract expired in twelve months. The thought was unacceptable, and the sooner she let Nightingale know her intentions, the better. "Okay. There's a great Mexican place in town. Maria's. It's on Main, near the old theater. I'll meet you there in an hour?"

With a slight nod, her boss accepted her choice of restaurant and her decision to drive herself there before he turned and walked away. Angellica watched his tight ass until he rounded a bend and disappeared. Only then did she kneel and gather her belongings.

After seeing his vehicle traversing the long driveway to the main road, Angellica waited five minutes before she followed in her own car. They could have easily taken one car, but having a means of escape if their discussion became heated was good planning. Other than what she'd read about the man on the Internet, she didn't know what kind of person he really was. If he became verbally abusive, she was out of there. Not that it would do her much good since their houses were a short walk from each other, but walking out on him would send the message that she wasn't a doormat.

He stood when she approached the table. The man looked like he'd stepped off the page of GQ Magazine in a crisp, white button-down shirt tucked into tailored black slacks. The belt circling his trim waist probably cost more than her entire ensemble, not to mention his leather dress shoes. When he swept his arm out, indicating she should take the seat across from him, she glimpsed a leather watch band and a hint of shiny gold. She'd bet her last dime he wasn't wearing a Timex. He'd washed and combed his hair, yet it still looked fashionably unkept, adding a touch of reckless to his already sexy-as-hell appearance.

Angellica hastily slid into the booth. She felt underdressed in her outlet store sundress and a pair of sandals embellished with fake jewels. Hoping to throw him off his game so she might gain the upper hand in their discussion, she'd gone to a lot of trouble to look nice. But one look at him put an end to those thoughts. He'd dressed the part of the millionaire wine executive in a suit that probably cost more than her car was worth. Nothing in her closet could top that. The worst part was he'd looked equally good that morning wearing a Nightingale Vineyards T-shirt, cargo shorts, and flip-flops.

A short woman wearing a traditional Mexican frock hustled over to take their order. Angellica had known Maria Lopez for years, so it was a little annoying that the owner of the restaurant ignored her in favor of the man sitting across from her. "*Buenos noches*, Senor. Welcome. What can I get for you this evening?"

Nightingale's smile lit the room. "Thank you," his gaze dropped to her name tag, "Maria." He turned his attention to Angellica. "What would you like, Ms. Capello?"

The restauranteur glimpsed Angellica's direction, then refocused on Nightingale. "She'll have a strawberry margarita, like always." She raised her order pad and pen. "You don't strike me as a strawberry margarita kind of man."

Sean chuckled. "And what kind of man do you think I am?"

"You, Senor, are a Dos Equis man. Am I right?"

"Yes, ma'am. In the bottle?"

"Of course."

The two shared a conspiratorial look before Maria dashed off to fill their drink order. Angellica caught Sean's gaze and raised an eyebrow in question.

"What?"

"How did she know that?"

"She didn't. I just let her think she did."

"Do you even drink beer?"

"Absolutely. And Dos Equis is one of my favorites, especially paired with Mexican food."

Angellica shook her head. "You're smooth, I'll give you that." She met his gaze with her stone-cold one. "Just so you know. Your charm won't work on me. I'm immune to you, Mr. Nightingale."

His smile dimmed. "Sean."

She blinked. "What?"

A server placed a basket of tortilla chips and two small bowls of salsa on the table. Maria followed close behind with their drinks, vowing to return shortly to take their orders. Sean unwrapped his silverware and draped the napkin across his lap. "Call me Sean."

CHAPTER FIVE

Sean shifted in his seat. His trousers suddenly became uncomfortable, all because Angellica Capello was lecturing him. Again. That was twice in one day and more than any man should have to endure without retaliation. The woman needed a good spanking, which was exactly why his dick was hard as stone. It wasn't the first time he'd imagined her ass-up over his lap, her backside red from his hand, and he doubted it would be the last. The fantasy had reared its head that morning when she'd given him what for about his choice of footwear. She'd been right, of course, but it was her tone of voice, her attempt at bravery when he knew how unsure she was about her position, that got to him. He wanted nothing more than to show her exactly where he wanted her. But he couldn't do that. She was his employee first, and with her supposed knowledge of winemaking, she *could* be an asset.

By and large, women liked him, but if Angellica was as affected by him as he was by her, she sure wasn't showing it. She sat back in the booth, her warrior woman's countenance firmly in place. When it became obvious she wasn't going to acknowledge his attempt at being friendly, Sean straightened his shoulders and met her stern face with one of his own. "Let's get a few things straight. I'm perfectly capable of running the business on my own. I don't need you." Not in the way she thought he did, but that was a discussion better left for another time. "However, your father assured me you would be a valuable employee. Therefore, I'd like you to stay on for the terms of your contract."

"What, exactly, do you expect me to do for you, Mr. Nightingale?"

His thoughts weren't the kind voiced in public places, but he had to come up with something. "You can start by cleaning out the blending lab."

A fire blazed behind the woman's eyes, and her cheeks flushed. She was a volcano about to erupt, and he couldn't help but wonder if she'd bring the same passion to bed. He'd sure as hell like to find out. Letting her stew, Sean took a long pull from the ice-cold beer Maria had brought earlier. His dinner companion remained silent, which Sean took as a signal for him to continue. "After that, I need a complete inventory of every cask in the cellar. We'll be bottling them soon." Sean took another sip of his beer and waited for the woman to respond. He didn't have to wait long.

"You've got it all figured out, don't you, Mr. Nightingale? But what do you actually know about California wines? Nothing. That's what you know. However, I'm an expert on the subject, and no one knows Capello wines better than I do. I've spent my life learning everything there is to know about the land, our vines, and our grapes. I have a degree in Enology and Viticulture. While you were partying your way through life, I was learning all I could about winemaking." She sipped her drink. Carefully placing the glass on the table, she glared at him. One corner of her mouth lifted in a sneer. "You're nothing more than a glorified salesperson for a winery that's grown so big it's sacrificing quality for quantity. What are you out to prove, Mr. Nightingale? That you're a better winemaker than your father and your older brother? Well, you're not. You're nothing more than a playboy *playing* at being a vintner. Capello wine is my life. By all rights, it should be mine. Mine!" She snatched up her purse and leaned across the table, her gaze boring into him. "If you think I'm going to be your cleaning lady, you're sadly mistaken."

Sean remained in the booth long after Angellica left. He finished his beer and ordered another one. He'd lost his appetite and had both meals boxed to go. He'd imagined tonight going differently. Clearly, he'd underestimated his opponent. The woman was beautiful, well-educated, and vicious. The rattlesnakes in the vineyard had nothing on her. Hell, they could learn a thing or two from her. Like the serpent she was, she'd struck fast and without mercy. Her venom had hit more than one nerve. He *was* the second son, and he did have something to prove. And she was right about Nightingale wines, too. The change had been gradual, happening over a decade or more, but you only had to open a bottle from one of their earlier vintages to taste the difference. Sean had tried to tell his family, but no one wanted to listen. They still made a damn fine wine that was easy to market, but it wasn't as good as it could be. It was getting harder and harder to sell their product to high-end markets. The best only wanted the best, and Nightingale wines were slowly inching their way toward mediocrity.

One thing Angellica *had* been wrong about. Like her, he had grape juice in his veins. He didn't have the formal degrees she had, but he'd studied as much or more than her. He knew as much about the science of grape farming and winemaking as anyone in the business, and he knew superb wine when he tasted it. It had taken years for him to earn his Master Sommelier certificate, an achievement he'd kept to himself but one that had proven invaluable in his search for the perfect vineyard to purchase. Nightingale needed an infusion. Fresh blood, if the family name was going to remain synonymous with the highest quality wines. The Capello grapes were exactly what Sean had been searching for. The soil and growing conditions in Southern California brought out qualities in the grapes that couldn't be achieved in New Jersey with its milder climate, soil conditions, and shorter growing seasons. After some initial testing, Sean concluded that combining wines from the two vineyards could create something extraordinary. Something that would once again put the Nightingale name at the top of every sommelier's list. Now, he just had to convince his family that he was right.

The first step to doing that was to make a test batch on a larger scale than the two-bottle sample that had convinced him to make an offer on the Capello vineyard. As certain as he was of his conclusion, a hunch and a party trick wouldn't convince his family. He needed a wine that would shock their taste buds. Nothing short of a game-changer would do.

CHAPTER SIX

Angellica left the restaurant, her blood boiling and her heart aching. As much as she loved her father, his stubbornness and old-world values were to blame for her situation. She'd harbored foolish hopes that the new owner would at least hear her out, but nope. Sean Nightingale was as much of a Neanderthal as her father. No wonder the two had gotten on so well. To hear Tomas Capello talk, Sean Nightingale was the future of the wine industry.

If that was so, the industry was doomed. She'd heard of other wealthy people investing in vineyards. Movie stars and tech billionaires who wanted to brag about making their own wine, but most of them had the good sense to hire an actual vintner. Someone with knowledge and experience to run the place.

Capello's didn't stand a chance. Sean Nightingale didn't know the first thing about making wine. If he had any sense at all, he'd hand the place over to his brother or his dad. From what she'd read about the family, those two at least knew what they were doing. Their wine wasn't what it used to be, but they still produced an excellent product. She should know. Up until her dad had told her he was going to sell to Sean, Nightingale's had been her go-to wine when she wanted a change. She wouldn't touch a bottle now with a ten-foot pole.

Angellica parked in front of the blending room and went straight for the stairway leading down to the cellar, where the full casks were left to age. She headed straight for the oak barrel she'd had one of the farm workers muscle into the shadows right after her mother passed. The accumulation of dust testified to how long it had been since she'd been back there. She retrieved a crystal glass and a pipette from a plastic container she'd stashed nearby. The cork in the bunghole came out easily enough, allowing her to insert the pipette and fill her glass. As the deep burgundy liquid flowed into the bowl of the glass, Angellica inhaled, savoring the subtle notes of the decadent wine. After replacing the cork in the barrel, she gently swirled the liquid, observing the way it coated the sides of the glass. Even in the dim light, she could make out the legs—the thin rivers formed along the glass as the wine succumbed to gravity. Having allowed her special blend to breathe, she brought the rim of the glass to her nose and inhaled. The fruity scent brought a smile to her face. She'd been patient, allowing the wine to age without interference. But after tonight's disastrous dinner, she needed to bolster her confidence in herself. Bringing the rim to her lips, she tilted the glass up and allowed the wine to kiss her tongue.

Eyes closed, she concentrated on the flavor notes, picking up cherry and strawberry with a hint of vanilla. The whole concoction felt velvet smooth, easing the tightness in her throat when she swallowed. Touching the bowl to her forehead, she took a moment to savor the hint of chocolate left behind.

Heaven.

It was the only word to describe the custom blend she'd planned on serving to her father. But once he'd decided to sell, she'd known even a magic potion wouldn't convince him to hand the winery over to her, so she'd kept it hidden. For a split second, she considered telling Nightingale about her secret barrel, but then she remembered how he'd spoken to her at Maria's and decided he didn't deserve exquisite. He deserved vinegar. Which was what he was probably going to end up with. For the first time since seeing the Nightingale sign go up beside their driveway, she was glad the Capello label wasn't going to go on anything the man produced.

She'd have to bottle her magic potion in secret because when she left here a year from now, she was taking it with her.

Angellica allowed herself one more taste, then made her way up the stairs. She washed her glass and pipette and left them to dry beside the sink. Tomorrow, she'd put them back where she'd found them. She had a feeling she'd be returning to sample her magic potion many times over the next year.

The next morning, Sean Nightingale was waiting for her in her office. The arrogant jackass sat in *her* chair, his boot-clad feet resting on top of *her* desk. He was thumbing through the latest copy of *Wine Enthusiast* magazine like he had all the time in the world. Angellica stopped in the doorway and waited for him to look up.

"You're late," he eventually said, dropping the magazine to the desktop, right beside his feet. "And you left last night before we finished our discussion."

"Discussion? That implies an exchange of ideas. All I heard was you dictating my life when you have no right to."

"Regarding your employment, I have every right." He placed his elbows on the arms of the chair and steepled his fingers. "This is not your office or your desk. I want your things out of here by lunchtime today."

"Where am I supposed to work?"

"There's a closet down the hall. Clean it out. You should be fine in there. It's not like you're going to have time to sit around. Harvest will begin in a couple of weeks. Before then, you need to place the collection equipment at the end of each row. When that's done, make sure the crusher is clean and in working order. We need to inventory the IBC tanks on hand and make sure they're clean. I've arranged for tankers to pick up the mash and deliver it. I've contacted all the purchasers and assured them their shipments will go out as soon as possible. Questions?"

"What are you going to be doing while I'm working my ass off?"

"I hired a cleaning crew to scrub the blending room from top to bottom, so it'll be ready for the new equipment when it gets here."

"What new equipment?"

"My dad just renovated his lab. He's shipping his castoffs to me. Nothing is new, but it's a hell of a lot newer than what's here."

"What are you planning on blending? Most of this year's harvest is sold, and it'll be months before what we keep is ready to blend."

"That's none of your business, Ms. Capello." Nightingale dropped his feet to the floor and stood. She hadn't paid any attention to his attire other than to note his dusty hiking boots on her desk. She took in his light blue button-down shirt and pressed khaki slacks. "I've got business in San Diego this morning. I want you out of this office before I get back."

As he approached the door, Angellica stepped back, allowing him to leave the office. He turned toward the hallway, then stopped and looked over his shoulder. "The cleaning crew should be here in half an hour. If there's anything you want to keep, anything sentimental, I suggest you remove it before then. Otherwise, it goes."

CHAPTER SEVEN

She listened as Nightingale's steps faded down the hallway. The door opened and closed on creaking hinges before she let out the scream she'd held in since the moment she saw him in her office. His office. Though he hadn't come out and claimed it, he'd just said she couldn't have it. He was insufferable. Arrogant. Annoying. And probably the best-looking, sexiest man she'd ever laid eyes on. Why did the beautiful ones have to be gay or assholes?

Stomping off to the closet that was soon to be her office, she almost choked on the dust flying with each step she took. There had to be a winery out there somewhere in need of someone with her skill set. Even lacking any official work experience, the Capello name was well known in California. Anyone who lived on the land they farmed would recognize the value of having grown up on a vineyard, especially one with the reputation Capello's had. She could start as an apprentice. The starting salary would be practically nothing, but with the salary Nightingale had to pay her for the next year, she could survive. Especially if she lived rent-free in the vintner's cottage. A year was more than enough time to prove herself capable of running a winery. Then she could tell Sean Nightingale to go screw himself.

She'd almost talked herself into going on a job hunt. Then she opened the door to the storage room, and a dust storm nearly choked her. Fanning the air, she stepped carefully into the windowless room and fumbled along the door facing until she found the light switch. She flipped it to the on position. The single bulb in a spartan ceiling fixture cast a yellow glow over the contents of the room. Instead of the expected boxes, stretched canvases leaned against both side walls. An old workbench piled high with art supplies spanned the length of the back wall. A paint-splattered smock hung from a rickety coat rack off to her right. Next to it was an old wooden stool that looked as if it had been hand carved. Of all the things in the room, it was by far the oldest, but it was the paintings that drew Angellica further into the room. Picking up a painting, she used the corner of her T-shirt to wipe decades of dust from the canvas. Even in the dim light, the workmanship was obvious. Not a valuable masterpiece, but a competent likeness of a vase of pink peonies sitting on a round table. Needing to get a closer look, she carried the small painting back to the office she was supposed to vacate and laid it on the desktop.

She recognized the table and the vase. They'd been in the entryway of their house for as long as she could remember. Her father had sold the house fully furnished. As far as she knew, he'd taken his personal possessions with him to Italy and left everything else for Nightingale to do with as he pleased. So, unless the new owner had moved the items, they were still there.

Angellica grabbed a tissue from the box she'd placed on the corner of the desk the day before and gently cleaned as much dust as she could from the painting. The signature in the bottom right corner drew her eye. It was small and crudely drawn but unmistakable. Anna Capello. *Mom.*

The memory of her mother painting was a distant one, and she'd never been sure if it was real or something she'd imagined. Angellica had been more interested in the workings of the winery and learning everything she could about the grapes. Her mother's life had seemed dull compared to the fascinating world of winemaking, and Angellica wanted no part of the domestic lifestyle. Sure, she'd loved her mother, but it was her father she'd followed around and wanted to emulate.

The painting had a timeless beauty about it. The subject was simple, and the background blurred so as not to distract from what the artist wanted you to see—the flowers. The fragile petals were each a work of art that made you want to reach out and touch them or lean in to catch a whiff of their delicate fragrance. Angellica had never seen anything more beautiful. Her mother obviously had incredible talent, so why had she given it up? In the twenty-four years of Angellica's life, she'd never seen her mom pick up a paintbrush or even doodle. It made no sense.

Captivated by what she'd discovered, Angellica went back to the room repeatedly. She brought out another exquisite painting with each trip until they covered the once neat office. There were landscapes, still-life renderings, and a portrait of Angellica's father as a young man and another of Angellica as a toddler. Each one revealed a side of her mother she'd never known.

She was trying to wrestle a large canvas out of the storeroom door when the telltale creaking hinges stopped her in her tracks. She leaned the heavy painting against the door and brushed a strand of hair out of her eyes, mentally preparing herself to deal with her boss.

"What the hell?"

Angellica cringed. There was no avoiding the coming confrontation. She rolled her neck and shoulders to release the built-up tension. She marched toward her nemesis. "Mr. Nightingale," she said in her sweetest voice. "I didn't expect you back so soon." A glance at the clock she'd placed on a bookshelf made her gasp. Where had the time gone?

"I said I'd be back by noon. It's after one o'clock. Where the hell is the crew I hired to clean this place up, and where did these come from?"

"I haven't seen your cleaning people. And, if you'll recall, you told me to empty the storage room down the hall so I could use it as an office." She swept her arm around the room, indicating the vast array of paintings. "These were in the storage room."

Her boss stared at the first one she'd unearthed, the peonies in a vase. After examining it for a moment, he turned to face her. "This vase and table are in the entryway of my house." There was a hint of wonder and confusion in his voice. "Who painted this?"

"My mother."

"She was an artist?"

Angellica shrugged. "Apparently. These all have her signature on them, but she never mentioned painting, and I never saw her with a brush. As best as I can tell, these were all done before I was born, except one." She pointed to the portrait of herself.

Nightingale moved around the room, his gaze stopping on each painting as he came to it. "These are remarkable. Why the hell were they stuffed in a closet?"

She suppressed the urge to call him out on the use of the word *closet* in relation to the space he expected her to turn into an office, but his praise for the paintings and his disbelief at their handling overrode her anger. "They're exquisite. Not masterpieces, but not the work of a novice, either." Angellica huffed out a breath and joined her employer in front of a large ocean scape. "Why were they hidden away? I have a theory." One that pissed her off beyond anything she'd ever felt before.

"I'd like to hear your thoughts on the subject."

"Really?"

Nightingale's head swiveled and his gaze locked on her. "I've seen far worse than these in high-priced gallery showings. I'd like to know why someone stashed them in a closet." He swiped a finger over the top edge of the painting, stirring decades of dust. "Like they don't matter."

He'd unwittingly hit the proverbial nail on the head. "Okay. I'll tell you. You've met my father. To say he's old-school is a gross understatement. I think he saw my mother's painting as a hobby, but when I came along, her real life's work began. A woman's calling is to be a wife and mother. A homemaker."

"So, you think he forced her to quit?"

Angellica shrugged again. "I can't say for sure. Maybe painting was just a hobby for her. One she willingly gave up in favor of taking care of her new family."

"You don't really believe that. Do you?"

CHAPTER EIGHT

Sean watched his employee carefully as she contemplated her answer. This brief conversation had already provided more insight into the woman than all their other encounters combined. He was eager to see if her answer was what he expected. She bit the corner of her lower lip, her gaze fixed on the near-perfect seascape. The gallery-worthy painting called to his love of the ocean. He could almost smell the salt-tinged spray and hear the thunderous roar as the waves crashed into the rocky shore at the artist's feet. If he'd seen this in a gallery, he would have bought it no matter the price. Angellica's voice, tinged with anger, jolted him out of his thoughts.

"No. I think my father made her quit. His views on a woman's role are archaic."

"Like he sold the family business rather than let you run it."

She angled her body his way, and he mirrored her. Their gazes met and held for a fraction of a second. "Exactly."

Sean nodded, accepting the truth of her words. He

turned his attention back to the painting, giving himself time to think about her situation. Her animosity toward him made sense now. They weren't as different as he'd thought. Clearly, he hadn't experienced misogyny directed at him, but he knew what it felt like to be denied the work he craved. He'd struggled for years to get his father and older brother to listen to his ideas, but his pleas had fallen on deaf ears. His father thought the status quo was good enough, and Wade had his own problems expanding the family operations to include an event facility. His brother eventually prevailed, and the facility became an important revenue stream for the business.

"So, you went to college and studied the wine industry, expecting one day to take over the family business."

"I probably wouldn't have if I'd known about these paintings before."

"Because?"

"Because they represent hopelessness. Mom's talent meant nothing to my father. Her real talent was in being a wife and mother, and that's what he expected, expects," she corrected herself, "of me. He's been trying to fix me up with the son of one of his friends for years."

"You aren't interested?"

She rolled her eyes. "James is a friend. His family owns a vineyard on the other side of Temecula Valley. He's an only child and will inherit the business. A marriage between us would have eventually merged the two businesses. "

"And you were opposed to this?"

"It's archaic, don't you think?"

"Not if you had feelings for James."

She laughed. "Wouldn't matter if I did. I'm not his type. If you get my meaning?"

Sean smiled and nodded. "Gotcha. He bats for the other team."

"Yep. James is an actor. He doesn't want any part of

the wine business. Other than the obvious reason we can't be together, a marriage would make perfect sense. He could do his thing, and I could run both businesses. I think our parents all thought the same thing, only they saw James running the merged vineyards and me popping out babies and serving family dinners."

"Babies aren't your thing?" He didn't know why he asked that. It was none of his business.

"Not saying that I don't want children someday, but I don't think motherhood and a career have to be mutually exclusive."

"They don't. My mother has worked in our family business all my life. She's the head of our HR department."

"And your father allowed that?"

Sean shrugged. "I don't think he had any say in the matter. My mother has a mind of her own. I wouldn't dream of telling her she couldn't do something she wanted to do. I'm pretty sure my dad feels the same way. The woman is a force of nature." He was beginning to think Angellica Capello had a lot in common with his mother.

They both stared at the painting, the silence stretching between them. Eventually, Angellica sighed and moved to the door. "I'll get this cleaned up." She waved a hand to indicate the canvases scattered around the room. "I know my father sold you everything, lock, stock, and barrel, but would you mind if I kept a few of these?"

"They're yours. All of them. But would you allow me to hang this one in the house?" He pointed to the seascape. "I think it's extraordinary."

Angellica dipped her head, silently acknowledging his request. "Thanks. I'll move these to the cottage, then I'll finish cleaning the closet out."

"Leave the closet. If I ever find the crew I hired, I'll have them do the grunt work." He paused, thinking about what he was going to say next. "I've been thinking. You should keep this office. I have one in the house, and all I need in the actual blending lab is a desk and maybe a file cabinet."

Her smile was tentative. "Are you sure? It seems like a lot of space for someone whose job is picking and crushing grapes."

"About that." Sean studied the toes of his hiking boots. "I owe you an apology. I acted like an ass."

"If you're expecting me to deny your statement, you'll be waiting a long time. Like, forever."

He chuckled, glad to hear the humor behind her reply. "No, just gathering my thoughts. Look, the dust in here is killing me. Can we have this conversation somewhere else? Like Maria's? I haven't had lunch."

She leaned against the doorjamb; her gaze fixed on one painting across the room while she contemplated his offer. He studied the seascape, letting the imagery soothe his nerves. He'd yet to decide how much he was willing to tell Angellica about his plans, but the little insight into her life today had shifted his assessment of the woman.

Angellica straightened. Sean swiveled his head, awaiting her verdict.

"I'll go under one condition."

He felt a weight lift off his shoulders. He didn't even care what her demand would be. He'd decided to ask for her help, and he was going to go through with it. "What's that?"

"No more insults. I'm a grown woman, and I know my worth. I'd be an asset to any winery, but I don't want to go anywhere else. This is my home. I know these vines better than anyone, including my father. I don't have a clue what you wanted with our vineyard, but I aim to find out."

"Okay, then. How about we both clean up a bit and I'll meet you in front of the house in half an hour? We'll take one car this time."

CHAPTER NINE

Maria escorted them to the same booth they'd had the night before. They both ordered without looking at the menu. Once they were alone, Sean opened the discussion. "Again, I apologize for insulting you before." He washed the dust from his throat with a swig of ice water. "If it's okay with you, I'd like to start over."

"Seeing those paintings and wondering how much my dad's attitude influenced my mother's decision to quit painting did a number on me. She was a strong woman. A loving mother and a doting wife. I hate to think there was also an artist jailed inside her. No one should live like that."

"I know exactly what you mean." Sean shifted in his seat. "The person you think I am. The playboy? The screwup? That's not who I am. That man is nothing more than a persona I developed as a cover."

"Cover for what?"

"I'm a genius." At her smirk, he held his hand up, palm out. "No. Seriously. I've got the IQ test to prove it."

"You're a genius?" She wasn't buying it. Most people wouldn't. He'd gone to great lengths to hide his intellect.

"I swear on my sainted grandmother's grave."

"Okaaay." She dragged the word out. "Say I believe you? What does your IQ have to do with you buying my family business out from under me?"

"I'm sure you know this, but I have brothers. Two of them. One older, one younger. Nightingale Vineyards has been passed down through five generations—to the oldest son. With three sons and a brother of his own, my dad did what he could to bring the business into the new century. He broke the business into five equal shares, so we're all part owners of the company."

"That's admirable of him, but I still don't see a problem. You own a portion of a very profitable wine business."

"On paper, yes. But when it comes to the operation of the business, Wade and my dad are in charge."

"Let me guess, that big brain of yours has ideas, and no one will listen to you?"

Sean nodded. "Pretty much. Nightingales has been around for over two-hundred years. We're still making the same wine in the same way my ancestors did. Yes, it's excellent wine, above average, but the wine market is more competitive than ever. There are more and more wineries that don't grow their own grapes. They purchase the juice from vineyards that produce more than they can ferment and store or who, like Capello, have stopped their wine production. The market for those blended varieties is growing exponentially. If Nightingale's is going to stay relevant, they need to expand their brand."

"I still don't see what you need with Capello Vineyard. Why not just buy our juice?"

"Nightingales don't *buy* juice. We grow our own grapes. Always have. It's a standard no one in the family will compromise on. In the last few years, Wade has bought up every available acre of suitable farmland within driving distance of our facility. There's nowhere else for us to expand in New Jersey, and my uncle, who oversees the actual farming, is stretched thin. The only answer is to acquire land somewhere else and establish another branch of Nightingale Vineyards."

"Why Capello's?"

"Because the soil conditions give your product a unique taste that I think will complement Nightingale's flavor signature."

"You bought an entire vineyard because you *think* the two wines will blend well?"

"I don't think. I know."

CHAPTER TEN

That was the most ridiculous thing she'd ever heard. Who spent millions of dollars on a hunch? Only an idiot would. *Genius? I don't think so.* He obviously didn't know much about wine. Blending was an art. It required a lot more than guesswork to merge two or more distinct wines into something better than its parts. It took knowledge and skill, two things Mr. I'm A Genius didn't have.

"How could you know?"

He looked away, then back at the basket of chips in the center of the table. The lines of his face seemed frozen in place; his jaw tight. "I know, okay? Let's leave it at that."

"Okay." She physically distanced herself from him, squaring her shoulders and placing her hands in her lap. He didn't like to be questioned, something she'd be wise to remember in the future. "So, you know our wines will blend well. I still don't understand why you had to purchase the vineyard."

"Your father refused to sell barrels. He'd sell the fresh-pressed juice, but once it was fermented, he wouldn't budge until it was bottled."

"No winery I know will sell their wine before it's bottled. What's to keep someone from bottling it themselves and putting their own label on it? It's just not done."

"I get that. I offered to sign anything he wanted, stating that the wine wouldn't be bottled and sold under any label, but he wouldn't budge."

"So, you bought him out."

Nightingale shrugged. "I waited years. I'd given up hope of him ever selling, but then the place came on the market. It was an opportunity I couldn't pass up. Nightingale Vineyards needs this expansion."

"Don't you mean *you* need this?"

There was nothing friendly in his gaze when it met hers. "Yes. *I* need this. Winemaking is in my DNA. Everything I've done has been to advance the Nightingale name in the industry. This is the right step at the right time. Nothing and no one is going to stand in my way."

She was getting a clearer picture of her employer with every word he spoke. Setting the absurd genius remark aside, she could see that the man was on a quest to prove himself to his family. They had that in common, but unlike her, he had the means to do whatever was necessary to accomplish his goals. She'd been at her father's mercy, which turned out to be non-existent.

Their meals were served, and they both dug in. Neither spoke until the plates were cleared and the check delivered.

Angellica drank the last of her iced tea, then set the glass down. Hoping her new boss had sufficient time to cool off, she asked, "What's my role in your grand plan?"

"You say you know the Capello wines. I need you to tell me everything you know about the stored vintages. What makes each one different from the others."

"Taste them for yourself. If your palette is as good as you say it is, you should be able to tell all that."

"I have tasted them."

"When?"

His shoulders rose and fell. "Recently."

"Then what do you need from me?"

"You were here when the grapes were on the vine. I need to know about the growing seasons. What made each one unique? What nutrients were added to the soil? How long they were on the vine? I need to know everything."

"Why?"

"So I can determine the prime growing and harvesting conditions to produce the best wine blend possible and do it consistently. Consistency equals market stability. Nightingales need a blend they can produce year after year with consistent results. Wade is going to send me enough barrels to produce some test blends, but he'll never put the Nightingale label on something that can't be reproduced on a commercial level."

"We're a small vineyard. At best, we produce fifty thousand bottles a year."

"A blend could easily double or triple that amount, depending on the ratio of wines used. A superior blend with the Nightingale name on it, and, in a limited quantity, could sell for several hundred dollars a bottle. I know a few buyers who would buy the entire vintage if it's good enough."

She quickly did the math in her head. The numbers were staggering. No wonder he was willing to purchase an entire vineyard. Then reality set in. "Still, you bought Capello's on speculation. You have no empirical data to support your theory."

"Not true."

"Where's this data at?"

"The house."

"I want to see it."

"I'll show you under one condition."

"What's that?"

"If the data is convincing, you'll help me."

She wasn't sure the Nightingale name carried enough weight to launch a new blend at the price point he quoted, but if it could? It was something she wanted to be part of. After a brief hesitation, she held her hand out across the table. "Deal."

"Deal," he echoed as he slid his hand into hers.

A current of electricity hummed through Angellica's body at the casual contact. She quickly pulled her hand back and tucked it under the table, where she rubbed her palm over her denim-clad thigh. She'd heard of people experiencing that sort of thing, but it was new to her and more than disconcerting. It seemed as if every cell in her body instantly became aware of the man sitting across from her. Her hand itched to reach out and touch him again. Would it happen again, or was it a onetime thing? Deciding that the question should remain unanswered, she reached for her purse. "We should go."

"I'll get the check." He swiped the slip of paper Maria had left earlier and slid out of the booth.

Angellica followed him to the register at the front of the restaurant. "I'll meet you at the car." Once outside, she took a deep breath and tried to focus her attention away from her body's unexpected reaction to Sean Nightingale. Over the last few hours, she'd questioned everything she knew about the man, but one thing wasn't in question. He was her employer. A fact she found difficult to remember, given that she still lived in the same place where she'd grown up. The land still felt like it was hers. It was going to take a lot longer for her to adjust to being nothing more than a paycheck employee in her own home.

"Come on. It's getting late, and I still need to figure out what happened to the cleaning service I hired."

"I sent them away," she admitted as she slid into the supple leather seat of his Range Rover. Nightingale shot her an incredulous look. Angellica shrugged. "I was busy with the paintings. They would have been in the way." She clicked her seatbelt into place. "They'll be back tomorrow."

Sean cranked the engine and backed out of the parking space. "I'll help you move your mother's art in the morning. Do you know where you want to put it?"

"I suppose I need to rent a storage locker or something. I don't have enough room in the cottage, and I think it needs to be in a climate-controlled location."

He was quiet as he pulled into traffic and navigated toward home. "There's plenty of room in the house. You can store them in one of the guest rooms."

It was a generous offer and one she couldn't refuse. "Thank you. You're sure they won't be in the way?"

"It's a big house, and there's only one of me."

That was true. It still chafed that she'd had to move out of her home so this man could move into it. Her father's doing. Nightingale had legally purchased the property. It was his to do with as he pleased, reminding her, "I'm excited to see this data you claim to have."

He slowed to make the turn into the driveway marked now with the new Nightingale Vineyard sign. "Come to the house? It won't take more than a few minutes."

"Okay. Let's get this over with."

CHAPTER ELEVEN

He was going out on a flimsy limb. Only Wade knew about his blending plans, and he was skeptical. Still, he'd supported Sean's vision, agreeing to ship him enough barrels of the requested vintage to experiment with. In the meantime, Sean had everything he needed to convince Ms. Capello that he wasn't nuts.

He pulled around to the back of the house and cut the engine. The house was grand, as befitted an established vineyard, but it was too much for one person. He decided from day one to close off most of the rooms and only use the parts of the house he needed. So far, that comprised the main bedroom suite, the kitchen, and what had been Tomas Capello's office on the first floor. He'd barely seen the remaining rooms. They weren't the reason he'd purchased the property and held little to no interest for him.

He ushered Angellica in through the back door and switched on lights, illuminating the farmhouse-style kitchen. His mother would love the kitchen. It had acres of counter space and even more storage, as well as commercial-grade appliances. A large brick fireplace, brick floors, and warm wood accents made it feel cozy and inviting. Besides the office, it was his favorite room in the entire house. One of these days, he planned to cook a meal there, but he'd been too busy to do anything more than the basics. He had those covered. Coffee, cereal and milk for breakfast and midnight snacks, and wine.

He tossed his keys on the soapstone countertop. "Make yourself at home. I'll be right back." Not waiting to make sure she was situated, he hurried down the stairs that led to the private wine cellar below the kitchen. Tomas had left it well-stocked with Capello wines. Sean had added his favorites, including several cases of Nightingale's merlot. He knew exactly what he wanted and, in less than a minute, was back in the kitchen.

Angellica raised an eyebrow as he placed the two bottles on the island countertop. "I came here to see the data you claim to have." She waved a hand at the bottles. "This is not data."

"Oh, but I beg to differ." He opened a drawer, pulled out a corkscrew, and reached for the Capello wine first. "This is the best data. The only kind that matters to the drinking public." He popped the cork free. After removing it from the screw, he repeated the process with the bottle of Nightingale wine. "Grab a couple of glasses, will you?"

Angellica gave him a look he easily interpreted to mean she thought he was crazy before she turned and claimed two stemmed glasses from the cabinet behind her. The fine crystal clinked as she placed them on the counter next to the open bottles. Her task finished, she backed away until her hips met the cabinets lining the wall. Arms crossed, she raised both eyebrows, questioning his next move. "Okay, genius. I'm waiting."

Sean wasn't nervous. He knew wine and knew he was

right about blending these two. His concern resided in his ability to produce the same results consistently. It wouldn't be the end of the world if he failed. The Capello vines produced a quality grape. He could either bottle his own wine under the Nightingale label or sell the raw juice, as the vineyard had been doing for the last few years. Either option would earn him a nice return on his investment, but he was after more than financial gain. The money wasn't enough, and having the Nightingale name wasn't enough. Like his father and forefathers, he was a vintner and wanted to be recognized as one. The only way he was going to achieve his goal was to create something unique. Something worthy of the Nightingale label.

Lifting the Capello wine, he presented the label for her inspection. When she nodded her recognition of the variety and vintage, he poured a scant ounce into each glass. He repeated the process with the Nightingale merlot. Picking up the glass nearest to him, he swirled the dark liquid in the bowl before handing it to Angellica.

She waited until he'd prepared his own glass before she raised hers to the light and gently rocked the bowl, allowing the wine to coat the sides of the glass. Sean did the same, noting the rich color and the legs on the blend, things that would please any good sommelier.

Angellica's face remained passive as she brought her glass to her nose, closed her eyes, and discretely inhaled. He knew the exact second he'd caught her attention. Her eyelids twitched, then she went back in for a second sniff. His heartbeat raced as he awaited her reaction to the taste.

Eyes still shut, she brought the glass to her lips and tilted it up, letting a tiny sip roll over her tongue. Her wine-coated lips puckered, and her eyes popped open, her gaze locking with his as the flavor notes registered.

Yeah, I know. It's a kick in the ass, isn't it? He resisted the urge to smile as she swallowed the elixir and immediately went back for another sip. Was this scientific?

Hell no, but it was enough for him to risk the entirety of his fortune on it. It was enough to risk putting the Nightingale name on the sign by the road.

Sean sipped from his own glass, savoring the flavors he'd committed to memory. He could pick out a Nightingale merlot in a blind taste test every single time. He could do the same with a Capello Cabernet Sauvignon. Both had qualities that made them superb and unique. Together? They were magic.

"How did you think to do this? It's—" Her voice trailed off as she searched for the right word to describe what she'd just tasted.

"Magic?"

"Yes. Magic. How'd you know they'd blend like that?"

"I told you. I'm a genius," he deadpanned.

Her smile lit the room and lit something within him as well. He took another sip of his magic elixir and reminded himself to take it slow. No need to rush the woman.

She held her empty glass out. "Do it again."

He reached for a bottle. "One more, then we need to get to work."

"Yes." He set the Capello wine on the counter, and she picked it up, examining the label. "This is ten years old. Aged for five in the barrel." She nodded at the bottle in his hand. "What's that one?"

"Nightingale Merlot. Also, ten years old. Aged all ten in the barrel."

Her eyes widened. "You mean it hasn't been released yet?"

"Nope. It's scheduled to be bottled later this year. I convinced Wade to let me bottle some for my own consumption. He's shipping me ten barrels to experiment with. They'll be here sometime next week."

"The oldest we have in the aging room is six years."

"The age doesn't matter as much as the flavor notes.

We just need to determine which vintage is the closest to your ten-year-old cab, flavor-wise, and go from there. Who knows? Maybe there's a better blend out there we haven't discovered yet."

She swirled and then sipped from her refilled glass. "I doubt that."

"So, my data is convincing?"

"Extremely convincing."

"Can I count on your help? Tomas left all his records, but they're written in Italian. I speak it better than I read it."

"You speak Italian?"

"Si. And Spanish, French, German, and enough Mandarin to order a decent meal."

"How did you learn all those languages?"

He shrugged. "I've always had an ear for languages. Reading and writing them is something completely different. A different side of the brain, I think. It helps to sell to international distributors if you can speak their language."

"You must have been good at your job. What's Nightingale's going to do without you?"

"I left the marketing department in excellent hands. And Wade knows he can call on me if he really needs to."

Her shoulders grew a little tighter at his admission. "You aren't going to live here long term?"

"I love California. Always have. Once I establish the new blend, I can hire people to tend to the grapes during the growing season. And I'll need a full-time manager for the vineyard. It won't be necessary for me to be on the property year-round."

"I see." She carefully placed her empty glass on the counter. "You want me to use my knowledge of Capello wines to help you prove something to your family and maybe to yourself, then you plan to walk away? Let a bunch of strangers make the wine you say is so important to you. I get it. This is all a game for you. Rich boy plays at being a winemaker to get his parent's attention. I wish you luck." She stomped to the door leading to the front of the house. "I've got a storage unit to rent and a truckload of paintings to move. After that, I'll make sure everything is set up for the harvest. As for the knowledge I have up here," she tapped her temple, "that's exactly where it's going to stay."

CHAPTER TWELVE

"Hey! Wait!" By the time Sean reached the front door, Angellica was gone. Standing on the flagstone drive, he kicked a pebble, sending it flying in the direction of the vintner's cottage. It was hotter than hell out there, a perfect match for his temper. She hadn't given him a chance to explain about the house he rented in La Jolla and planned to make it his primary residence if things went well with the blend. It was a short drive from the vineyard and an even shorter trip by helicopter. The helo was a stretch, but if the blend turned out to be the hit he imagined it becoming, it wasn't out of the question. The point was— he'd be close enough to oversee the vineyard and winemaking process when necessary and still spend his free time surfing or lying on the beach. It was all part of the dream. He'd seen enough cold winters in New Jersey to last him a lifetime.

Sean stomped back inside, corked the open wine bottles, and washed the crystal glasses. Figuring he'd give Angellica time to cool off, he set out on foot to check out the harvest equipment for himself. The woman drove him nuts. She was so damned beautiful that he struggled to think straight when he was around her. Her short fuse didn't allow him any room to mess up, and somehow, he'd messed up—again. Sent her running. Only this time, she'd taken her toys with her. At first, he didn't think he needed her knowledge, but after spending a few hours trying to translate her father's notes, he knew he needed help.

He couldn't use the ten-year-old Capello vintage for his blend—that genie was already in the bottle. But he hoped to replicate the same flavor notes with one of the vintages not yet bottled. If so, he needed to know everything he could about the crop and the year it was harvested. He couldn't control the weather, but there were things he could control, like the sugar content at harvest and the steps taken during fermentation. No two vintages were exactly alike, but consistency was the key to gaining a loyal following. Wine connoisseurs didn't like nasty surprises. They liked a winery they could depend on to deliver excellent wine, no matter what the variables were in the production process.

That Angellica would think he'd turn a blind eye to his crop or to the processing of his wine was an insult beyond measure. Nightingales made wine. Some of the best on the planet, and he'd never do anything to tarnish their name or reputation. She was right about one thing, though. He had something to prove to himself and to his family.

As he passed by the blending room, Angellica gave him the evil eye as she hefted a large painting into the back of her car. He thought about helping her, but didn't think she'd accept his friendly gesture. Maybe later, after they'd both had some time to cool down. Sean continued to the old Quonset hut barn where they stored the crates for the harvest. Tomas had shown him the storage building on one of his exploratory visits. At the time, Sean had been more interested in the vines and the barrels of wine aging in the cellar to pay much attention. If they didn't have enough crates or if any of the equipment needed for the harvest needed repair, he was screwed.

The door slid open on well-oiled tracks, revealing a tightly packed interior space. Front and center sat a tractor with forks on the front, perfect for hauling stacks of crates to and from the vineyard. Enormous stacks of plastic crates lined both walls as far back as he could see. Sean climbed aboard the tractor. Finding the key in the ignition, he said a silent prayer to the farm equipment gods and then turned the key. The starter groaned a few times, then the engine fired off; the sound echoing off the walls of the old building. Sean smiled at his good fortune, then put the machine in gear and slowly eased it out of the building. It had been a long time since he'd worked this portion of the harvest, but he hadn't forgotten the lessons he'd learned during his teenage years. His uncle insisted that everyone in the family take part in the harvest as soon as they were old enough to do the simplest of tasks. As a child, he and his brothers had learned to scout the vines for grape clusters overlooked by the adults who were doing the actual harvesting. It wasn't unusual for a cluster to be hidden beneath a canopy of leaves. When they were old enough and strong enough to take part in the harvest, the boys were given gloves and pruning shears and put to work. As teenagers, they learned to drive tractors, hauling crates from the vineyard to the crushing room and back again. Harvest was a chaotic time with a lot of moving parts. Any breakdown along the chain could spell disaster for a crop. Choosing the exact moment to harvest could mean the difference between a mediocre wine and one that would become legendary. Like any farm, equipment failures could cause delays that risked the entire crop being ruined by bad weather. It was up to the farmer to make sure nothing went wrong. Sean never thought he'd see the day, but it had come. *He* was the farmer. The harvest was his responsibility.

He spent the rest of the day hauling the crates out to the vineyard, carefully placing them at the end of every row. Soon, workers he'd hired from the local co-op would fill them with grapes. From there, they'd be moved to the barn where the juice would be rendered and made ready for shipment to the established buyers.

Sean vowed that this would be the last year they would sell the crop to other wineries. If his plans materialized, next year's crop of Cab grapes would become part of his signature blend.

The sun had disappeared behind the rim of the valley by the time Sean called it quits for the day. He was tired, sweaty, and hungry. He cast a quick glance at the blending room as he passed by on his way home. Angellica's car was still out front, and light spilled through the windows. Even moving a few at a time, she should have moved all the paintings by now. He didn't consciously decide to check on her. His feet just turned in that direction.

She wasn't in the office, but the painting she'd agreed to let him keep was. Calling out her name, he went in search of her. He found her swiping a heavy mop across the floor of the now-empty storage room. With her back to him, and a set of old-fashioned headphones over her ears, she didn't notice his arrival. She wielded the mop like a boss, her hips swaying to a tune only she could hear. Her T-shirt and cargo shorts wore a significant amount of the dust and dirt that had recently coated everything in the room. Locks of her hair had fallen from her low ponytail and swayed in counterpoint to her hips. A streak of dirt ran from the back of her left knee to the scrunched-up sock peeking from the top of her well-worn hiking boot. She was so far from the actors and models he'd courted for the publicity that it wasn't even funny, but Angellica was real. There wasn't an artificial bone in her body. No Botox. No fake nails or lashes. He'd seen enough fake boobs to believe himself an expert on the subject. He couldn't be one-hundred percent certain, but he'd stake the last of his fortune on hers being real. One thing he *was* certain about. He wanted to examine every inch of the woman.

Backing out of the doorway, he leaned against the wall until he'd gotten his wayward libido under control. He needed her knowledge of Capello wines and the vines that produced them. The only way to access that information was to treat her with respect. It's what every woman in the workforce deserved. His mother would skin him alive if she found out he'd hit on an employee. She hadn't been a fan of his glamorous lifestyle marketing ploy, but after he assured her he never disrespected the women he dated, she'd accepted it. Every woman he dated knew the score. The publicity was mutually beneficial, or they didn't go. He never touched them inappropriately in public or anywhere else—unless that, too, had been agreed upon. He was nice, but he wasn't stupid. If a cover model wanted to sleep with him, who was he to turn her down? Call him crazy, but he'd much rather have a woman like Angellica beneath him than a stick-thin woman who waxed so much they looked like a department store mannequin.

A wet, sloshing sound followed by a loud screech jerked him back to reality. He quickly decided the sounds came from the old commercial mop bucket with the wringer on top that he'd noticed in the corner of the room. Figuring it was as good a time as any to show himself, he knocked on the jamb as he stepped into view.

CHAPTER THIRTEEN

Angellica nearly jumped out of her skin as the figure of a man appeared in the doorway. It took less than a heartbeat for her to realize it was none other than the jerk who was hellbent on ruining everything her family had spent over a century building. Painfully aware of how filthy she was, she jerked her headphones off and left them hanging around her neck as she waited for him to explain what he was doing there.

"Hi." He motioned to the mop she held in her hand. "You didn't have to do that. The cleaners are coming tomorrow, remember?"

"I remember, but there was too much of my mother's stuff in here. I wanted to sort everything out myself, and I really didn't want anyone else touching it. One thing led to another, and," she lifted the mop, then let it sink back into the filthy water, "here I am playing Cinderella."

"I guess that makes me the evil stepmother?"

She shrugged. "If the shoe fits."

He smiled at her quip but let the remark die

unanswered. "I got most of the crates put out for the harvest next week. I'll get the rest in the morning. I got a text from the shipping company. The equipment for the blending lab will be here tomorrow afternoon. If the cleaning people get here before I'm back from putting the crates out, will you get them started in the lab? I'll help them move the old equipment out when I'm done."

"I can finish with the crates." It was one of the few jobs he'd initially assigned to her. Did he think she couldn't run the tractor?

"That's unnecessary. I started the job. I can finish it." His gaze slipped to the mop bucket, then back to her face. "It's late. Why don't you call it a night? The cleaning people can finish this tomorrow."

"I'm almost done," she countered. "I'll close up when I leave."

He stared at her for a moment like he wanted to say something but wasn't sure if he should. Then he pushed off the doorjamb and nodded. "Okay. Goodnight, Angellica. I'll see you in the morning."

Angellica waited until she heard the front door open and shut before backing up until her shoulders met the wall. She slowly sank down until her butt hit the floor. She didn't need a mirror to know how awful she looked. Her Cinderella remark wasn't far off. She was dirty and sweaty and stank worse than the nasty mop bucket.

Sean Nightingale hadn't been any cleaner. Sweat and dirt had caked his face, and his hair had been matted to his head where he'd worn a hat most of the day. He'd apparently forgotten sunscreen, and tomorrow he was going to have a hell of a sunburn on his arms and the back of his neck. If she cared anything about the man, she'd advise him to wear a hat with a brim all the way around instead of the Yankees baseball cap he favored. It wasn't doing him any favors.

Despite all that, he still looked like a million bucks.

Looking back over her day, she could hardly believe she'd discovered her mother's paintings that morning. It seemed like she'd lived a week when it had been less than twelve hours. Emotionally, she'd been up and down, and physically, she was worn out. Forcing herself to stand, she pushed the ancient mop bucket to the restroom, where she'd found it. She washed up in the sink and then headed to her secret stash. She rarely went there, so two nights in a row said something about the stress she was under. Limiting herself to a tiny sip, just enough to remind her she had more to offer any winery, she was walking up the stairs to the blending room when her phone rang. Pulling it from her pocket, she smiled at the familiar face displayed on the screen. "Hey there, girlfriend," she said cheerily as she pressed the phone to her ear. "What's up?"

"You're asking me what's up? You're the one with the news. Spill, Jelly. What's he like? Is he as good-looking in person as he is in all the photos?"

Angellica cringed at the use of the nickname Lexie had given her on the first day of third grade when they'd been assigned side-by-side seats in the classroom. Alexa and Angellica. Alphabetical order inadvertently launched a lasting friendship between the girls. Lexie had gone to school for cinematography and now worked as an assistant producer on a popular reality show. The very show Angellica planned to catch up on as soon as she had a shower and got some food in her. She reached around the doorjamb to turn off the lights in the office, but the big leather chair behind the desk seemed to call her name. "And here I thought you were calling to see how I am." She plopped down in the chair and propped her feet up on the corner of the desk while her best friend prattled on.

"I am calling to see how you are, silly girl. You know I'm concerned about the way things worked out with your dad, but you've met Sean Nightingale! The Executive Producer of my show would do anything to snag him as the next bachelor! So, spill. What's he really like?"

"He's an ass. A handsome-as-sin one, but still an ass."

"Oh." Lexie's voice held none of the exuberance from before. "I was afraid of that. Guys that rich and good-looking are usually full of themselves. I should have known, but I had high hopes for him, and for you."

"What are you talking about?"

"Sue me for caring about you, but I kind of hoped the two of you would hit it off. What better way to get your hands on your family legacy than to marry the owner?"

Angellica removed the phone from her ear and stared at it for a moment before resuming the conversation. "You can't be serious, Lexie."

"Hey, it was just a thought. You know me. I believe in happily ever after and love at first sight. Why do you think I stay where I'm at? I keep hoping the couples that match up on the show will make it work."

"Well, that's not going to happen here, so get that thought out of your head. Okay?"

"Okay, but what are you going to do?"

"I have a year to find a better position. In the meantime, I've got a few things to take care of around here."

"Like what?"

"Like figure out what to do with a room full of paintings I found today."

"Paintings? Valuable ones?"

Angellica brought her friend up to speed regarding her discovery. "I took them all to the cottage, and now I seriously need a shower and some food. Then I'm going to get caught up on this season of your show." They talked a little longer, then someone yelled for Lexie and her friend ended the call with a promise to pick up where they left off soon. Angellica tossed the phone on the desk and closed her eyes for a moment. She couldn't help but smile at Lexie's fanciful thinking. Ever the optimist, and a true romantic. Her stomach grumbled, reminding her it had been ages since she'd eaten. Sher swung her feet off the desk. Her right foot caught the edge of the wastebasket next to the desk, sending trash across the floor.

"Criminy," she mumbled as she kneeled to scoop the old papers and dried up pens back into the bin. The cleaning crew could empty it when they arrived.

Angellica made sure the lights were off and the door locked before getting into her car and driving past the old barn to the vintner's cottage. It was the original homestead built by her grandfather when he first arrived in California from Italy. Prior to her moving in, it had sat empty since her mother's death. Her father had let all the farm hands go, including the manager. If it weren't for Angellica's determination to keep the place running, the vines would have died a long time ago, and there wouldn't have been anything to sell to Nightingale.

After a long, hot shower, Angellica fixed a sandwich and a tall glass of ice water. She ate sitting in front of the small flat-screen television she'd brought over from her room in the main house. Reality shows were her guilty pleasure, and she had several episodes of *Love at First Sight* to catch up on. She was deep into the first recorded episode when a knock on the front door sent her heart rate into the stratosphere.

Angellica grabbed the only thing handy, an unopened bottle of Capello wine she'd left sitting on the kitchen counter, and approached the door. Her breath caught in her throat as she realized the door wasn't locked. She'd been so tired when she got home that she had forgotten to throw the deadbolt. It was a mistake she'd never make again—if she lived to see another day.

Tightening her grip on the neck of the bottle, she raised her makeshift weapon to her shoulder. Her voice quivered as she called out, "Who is it?"

"It's me. Sean. Nightingale."

Holy crap! What's he doing here? She took stock. She wore an old UC Davis T-shirt that had more holes than a golf course and a pair of pink satin sleep shorts she'd owned for so long she couldn't tell if they were pink or gray. Her hair was clean but hung in tangles from where she'd towel-dried it after her shower. Why did he always catch her at her worst? "What do you want?"

"I tried to call you. When you didn't answer, I thought I'd better check on you."

She patted her hips like she was going to find her phone in a non-existent pocket while she frantically glanced around the room, looking for the device. It was nowhere to be found. Then she remembered she'd left it on the desk in the office. "Sorry. I'm fine. I left my phone in the office."

"Can you open the door? I had something I wanted to talk to you about. And I'd like to see for myself that you're okay."

"It's late, Mr. Nightingale. Can't we talk about this in the morning?"

"We could, but I still want to make sure you're okay."

Angellica leaned against the wall then groaned. Her boss beat a fist against the door.

"Angellica! Are you hurt?"

Shit. He heard that. "I'm fine. Please. I'll see you in the morning."

"Is there a house phone out here?"

"No."

"You can't stay out here alone without a phone. I'm going to get yours. I'll be back in a minute."

Shit. Shit. Shit! His boots crunched on the gravel as he strode back the way he'd come. She'd been too involved in her program and hadn't heard him walk up. Hurrying to the bedroom, she pulled on a pair of cargo shorts and a Capello Vineyards T-shirt. After attempting to brush her hair, she gave up and wrestled the tangled strands into a high ponytail. The ancient window air conditioning unit was losing the battle against the heat that had built up during the day, but the cooler air still felt good on her exposed nape.

Returning to the main room, she collected the remnants of her meal and dumped them in the sink. Just as she picked up the remote to pause the episode, she heard Nightingale returning. Hopping up, she quickly threw the deadbolt. Just in case. As a woman alone in a remote location, she knew better than to assume she knew the person approaching her front door. A soft knock sounded on the door.

"Angellica. It's me. I've got your phone." She considered asking him to leave it on the porch, but no sooner had the idea entered her head than he spoke again. "Open up. I just want to see that you're okay."

She flicked on the exterior light, then twisted the deadbolt and pulled the door open. Sean Nightingale stood on the other side wearing shorts, hiking boots, and a T-shirt from a famous surf shop. His hair was wet, and a drop of perspiration trickled from his hairline to his jaw. He looked ridiculously sexy and pissed off. He handed over her phone. "I don't think I'm comfortable with you staying out here all alone."

"I don't think that's any of your concern," she countered.

"You're my employee, Ms. Capello, and you live on my property. That makes me responsible for your safety." He leaned in, and his gaze swept the room behind her. "There's no house phone? Is there an alarm system?"

"No. We've never needed either before."

"You never had a single woman living here alone. In the next few weeks, there are going to be a lot of strangers on the property. Workers helping with the harvest and the pressing. Anyone can access the property on foot from the road. I don't like the idea of you going about alone after dark, and I especially don't like you alone out here without even an alarm system."

"I appreciate your concern." She really didn't. She was a grown woman and could take care of herself. Sort of. She made a mental note to remember to set the deadbolt whenever she was home. "I don't have anywhere else to go, Mr. Nightingale, and according to our contract, this house is mine for the next year."

He stepped backward off the porch and looked around at the front of the house. "There aren't even any motion lights to scare intruders away."

No, duh, Sherlock. She'd had enough of this conversation. "Is there a reason you were trying to call me?"

His brows furrowed as he processed the change of subject. "Oh, yeah. I wanted to tell you there's a documentary on tonight about Napa Valley wineries and how they're coping with the severe weather issues they've been facing. I bet you don't have cable out here, do you?"

"Actually, yes. I have cable, and though the documentary sounds fascinating," not, "I'm in the middle of watching something else."

"Yeah? What did you find to watch?"

"Uh. Just an old movie." No way was she telling him what she was really watching. She'd never hear the end of it. Men didn't understand a woman's fascination with love stories. Only a few seasons of the show had ended with the bachelor finding his soulmate, but it was enough to keep hope alive for millions of women that they, too, could find that one person they could share their life with. Call her a sap, but she'd seen the love her parents shared, and she wanted that for herself, even if her understanding of the dynamics of that union was shifting. Angellica had no intention of giving up any of her interests just to please a man.

"Really? Which one? I love old movies." He craned his head around her, trying to get a look at her television screen. Angellica moved, blocking his view of the room. "I set the documentary to record. We can watch it some other time."

We? What we? Is he angling for an invitation to watch TV with me? "Look, Mr. Nightingale—"

"Sean," he interjected.

"Look, Sean, I'm tired, and all I want to do tonight is watch a little TV, then go to bed and maybe read a little before I go to sleep."

"Is that one of your mother's paintings?" he asked, pointing at the only thing visible in the sliver of space between her hip and the door frame. "I didn't see that one before."

If hints were clothes, he'd be naked by now. She threw the door open wide. "Come on in, but I guarantee you'll regret it."

He went directly to the painting and crouched down to get a better look. "This is incredible. Your mother had a remarkable talent."

After closing and locking the door, Angellica joined him. She'd stored the rest of the canvases in the second bedroom, but couldn't bring herself to hide this one away. Her mother had captured the beauty of the vineyard with the last rays of sun illuminating the fruit-laden vines— everything from the hawk overhead searching for a tasty snack to the veins of the leaves in the foreground was captured in minute detail. The colors were rich and vibrant. If you stared at it long enough, you could almost feel the late afternoon heat rising off the hard-packed ground. "Yes. I think this must have been one of the last ones she painted." She pointed to a line of eucalyptus trees barely visible off to one side. "Those were cut down shortly before I was born. Our Pinot Noir grapes are there now."

Sean leaned in for a closer look. "You're right. And these are the Cab grapes," he said.

"This is the only painting she titled." Angellica picked

up the canvas and turned it around to show him the single word written on the back.

"Timeless," he read.

"Fitting, don't you think?"

CHAPTER FOURTEEN

Seeing the name inscribed on the painting sent a tingle up Sean's spine. *Timeless.* "It's perfect," he said. Absolutely perfect. He could see this painting as the backdrop of the new label, and he couldn't think of a better name for the new blend. Timeless said it all. "This should hang in the tasting room when we open it."

"You're going to open a tasting room?"

"Of course, we are. Why wouldn't we? Tasting rooms are a key marketing tool. People come in. They taste. They fall in love and leave with a few bottles. When they get home, wherever that is, they buy more Nightingale wine from their local store, or they order it online to be shipped to them. Not to mention the auxiliary sales. Souvenir items can generate significant income." Something his soon-to-be sister-in-law, Serenity, had recently reminded him of.

He could see it now. This painting reproduced on postcards and T-shirts, and many other products. He could practically hear the cash register dinging. They'd cross-promote—selling items on both coasts to encourage people to stay loyal to the brand. Buying the right to reproduce the image would cost him a fortune, but it would be well worth it.

"I thought you just wanted the vines."

The confused look on her face stopped him short. "What? Did you think this was a hobby?" Sure, she did. She'd hinted at it more than once. "The vines are why I bought Capello's, but this will be a full-scale vineyard and winery operation before long. Nightingales don't dabble at making wine. We go all-in, or we don't go at all."

He glanced around the room, noticing the paused image on the television screen. "Wait. Is that *Love at First Sight*?" Before she could stop him, he grabbed the remote control off the coffee table and put the show in motion. "Is this the current season?"

"Yeah. I think this is episode two. Why?"

"I know one of the women on this one. Janette. She works for *Wine Enthusiast* magazine. She interviewed me last year for an article on the popularity of New Jersey wines in Europe."

Angellica plopped down on the sofa. "Let me guess, you dated her."

"If you call taking her to dinner following the interview a date, then yeah. She told me about this that night. She'd already been cast and couldn't get involved with anyone until after the taping was over." He tossed the remote aside and joined Angellica on the sofa. "Have you seen her yet?"

"Blonde hair? Big boobs? Nice smile?"

"That sounds like her."

"They didn't name the magazine she works for when they introduced her. Just said she was a journalist. Lives in New York?"

"I honestly don't remember where she lives. I'm not sure she told me. We met up at an industry event in Chicago. I was her last interview of the day. Thus, the reason we had dinner together. We were both starving."

They watched the segment until it went to commercial. "Holy cow. It's hot in here. Don't you have air conditioning?"

"There's a window unit in the bedroom."

"This is unacceptable, Angel. Why didn't you tell me? I could have had the place fixed up before you moved in."

"It's the original homestead. It's fine the way it is."

"Maybe so, but there's no reason for you to suffer if you don't have to. Next commercial, we're going to the big house. We're taking that painting with us. It should be in a climate-controlled location. Did you bring them all here?"

"I couldn't find a suitable storage place in town."

"I'll help you move them all to the house tomorrow. They'll be safe there until you can figure out a long-term solution."

She opened her mouth to argue, but the commercial break was over, and Janette appeared on the screen. Sean grabbed the remote and increased the volume, effectively ending their conversation.

He'd given her no choice; he thought later that night as he lay in bed. But he'd had no choice either. He should have given more thought to where Angellica was going to live once he moved in, but he'd been busy in the weeks between closing on the property and showing up to take possession. There was no reason she couldn't remain in the home she'd grown up in. There were more rooms than he could use. Once he got the business enterprise on solid ground, he'd take up residence in La Jolla. It would be good to have someone living in the house, and who would be better than Angellica? He'd only just met her, but in those few days, he'd learned a great deal about her. She was intelligent and strong-willed, and she knew more about the vineyard than anyone other than her father. It made sense to keep her on as the farm manager.

He tried to forget the quiver in her voice when he'd

knocked on her door the first time this evening. Knowing only the two of them were on the property, she hadn't expected any company. She'd been afraid, but no way was she going to admit that to him. To do so would be to admit a weakness, and he couldn't imagine her doing such a thing. She'd powered through tonight, doing her best to convince him she didn't need his help. Thank goodness for those paintings and the ancient window air conditioning unit. If not for those two things, he would never have convinced her to spend the night under his roof.

Thinking about her down the hallway, safe in her own bed, was a road he didn't need to go down. No matter how loudly his body protested, he wasn't going to make a move on the woman. If she found him irresistible and flung herself at him, well, that would be a different story. He was only human, after all. As a male of the species, he came pre-programmed to notice the opposite sex, especially when they were as beautiful as Angellica Capello. He'd never get the image of her mopping the floor out of his head. Seeing her ass swaying to the music only she could hear had unleashed something primal inside him. He'd wanted her, dirt and all. He'd envisioned stalking up behind her and imprisoning her in his arms, sinking his teeth into her neck. When he had her weak and at his mercy, he'd strip her down to those sexy-as-hell hiking boots. Then he'd press her against the wall and take her from behind. *Christ!* He would never get to sleep if he kept thinking of all the ways he wanted to fuck his only employee. Sitting up, he dropped his feet to the floor and, gripping the edge of the mattress with both hands, inhaled deeply. On the exhale, he willed his unwanted erection to go away. If he was at the house in La Jolla, he'd take a walk on the beach and let the ocean breeze wipe his brain clean. Since that wasn't an option, a cold shower was the best he could do.

The frigid water proved nothing more than a temporary solution to his problem. As soon as he was back in bed, his mind went right back to where it had been before, and after enduring the torture of desire for as long as he could stand it, he took matters into his own hand. He'd been with his share of beautiful women, and in times of need, like this, there were a few images that regularly popped into his head to spur him on, but that night, only one image popped up. Angellica Capello, filthy from head to toe, dancing with a mop.

Sean hadn't slept well. Dreams of Angellica had surfaced every time he closed his eyes. He'd woken several times aching for her but stubbornly told himself once was once too many and instead made mental lists of all the things that still needed to be done before he could turn his new property into a money-producing enterprise. Thinking of the sorry state of his bank accounts cured his physical problem, but did nothing to help him get back to sleep. Thus, he felt like shit as he walked into the kitchen the following morning. The sun was hours away from making an appearance, but his brother would already be at work on the East Coast. After making himself a cup of coffee, he opened his laptop and placed a video call to Wade.

"Hey, bro. Isn't it a little early out there?"

Sean rubbed his eyes and scratched his morning beard. "It's still dark. I don't know if that qualifies as a late night or an early morning."

"Did you just get home from a party?"

"Nope."

"Then it's early."

"If you say so." He sipped his coffee, wincing at the bitterness of the grocery store brand. "How's it going there? How's Serenity doing in her new job?"

"I wish I could say everything is running smooth here, but not everything is. However, Serenity is fabulous. She might even be better than the guy she replaced."

"Hey! I'm the guy she replaced!"

Wade laughed. "I thought that would get a reaction. But seriously, she's doing great. She loves the job and has come up with some new marketing campaigns that are genius, in my opinion, but she said she wanted to run them by you."

"She wants the opinion of a genuine genius. Smart girl."

"Okay, smartass. Enough about my fiancée. What has you awake in the middle of the night? Problems with the vineyard already?"

"Not with the vineyard. With an employee."

Wade scrunched his eyebrows together in thought. "Last time I heard, you only had one full-time employee. Angela? The daughter of the former owner? Let me guess. She's dumber than a box of corks, and her face could stop a freight train."

"Nope, and nope. Her name's Angellica, and she's fucking gorgeous. And brilliant. She's got multiple degrees from UC Davis's viticulture program."

"So, what's the problem? You could use someone like her to help you get the place off the ground."

"The problem is," he paused and listened to make sure she hadn't snuck downstairs without him knowing. "She's got me tied up in knots. I can't sleep for thinking about her. But she's my employee, and if there was one thing Dad drilled into our heads when we were teenagers, it was that our employees were off-limits."

"That didn't keep him from marrying mom, and it didn't keep me from getting together with Serenity."

Sean took another fortifying sip of coffee, then shook his head at his brother. "Those were different circumstances."

"I don't see how. Mom worked in the tasting room. That's how she and Dad met. And Serenity was working for us when I fell for her. How is that different?"

"For starters, you've known Serenity for most of your

life. And Mom and Dad only saw each other during the summer for the first couple of years after they met. Angellica is living under the same roof as me. She was dancing with a mop last night, and I damn near lost my mind watching her."

"Wait a minute. I thought she'd moved into another house on the property."

"She did, but she couldn't stay there. There's zero security and almost no air conditioning. The place needs a major upgrade I can't afford right now. Everything I've got has to go into the vineyard for the foreseeable future."

"I could lend you some money."

"No! Hell, no. I'm doing this on my own, so if it fails, it won't financially compromise Nightingales."

"We've discussed this, Sean. You *are* a Nightingale. Dad might not agree with your assessment of our situation, but we all support your vision. And, I hope you succeed. Since you left, Serenity has been going over our sales figures for the last few years, and though our sales are up, sales to high-end customers are down. You were right. We should have listened to you when you told us we needed to rethink our product line. If you need money, you've got it. We're in this together."

"I appreciate your support, but I need to go this alone." He ran his fingers through his hair. "As soon as this place is up and running on its own, I'll move to La Jolla, and proximity won't be an issue."

"If she's *the one*," he emphasized the words with air quotes, "it won't matter how far away you are. Distance isn't a cure for desire or genuine attraction. And if you love her, a day away from her will feel like an eternity, and a mile will feel like an ocean."

"She's not *the one*." Sean rolled his eyes as he, too, used air quotes.

"How do you know?"

"Because I don't believe there is a *one* out there for

me. I've been all over the world, Wade, and dated hundreds of women. I think I would have found *the one* by now if she was out there."

Wade shrugged. "All I'm saying is, in all those years, and after dating hundreds of women, your words, not mine, this is the first time you've called me for advice on how to stay away from one. I think that says something. Don't you?"

Everything his brother said was true. He'd never felt so out of control around a woman before. He couldn't get Angellica out of his head. He wanted to know everything about her. He wanted to protect her. He wanted to make her his in every way. Sean rested his elbows on the countertop and dropped his head into his upturned palms. "Fuck, Wade. I'm screwed."

"Depends on your point of view, I suppose. If you aren't ready to give up your playboy lifestyle, then yeah, you're probably in for a world of heartbreak. But if you're open to finding a partner to share the rest of your life with, then this might be the opportunity of a lifetime. She's right there. Spend time with her. Get to know her."

"How do I know if she's *the one*?"

"If you can't imagine your life without her, then I'd say that's a pretty good clue." Wade glanced at something off-screen. "Look, I've got a mountain of work to do today. The tanker is supposed to be here in a few minutes to load the vintage you requested. Do you have containers to offload into? If not, I can have some shipped to you."

Glad for the change of subject, Sean shoved thoughts of Angellica out of his head. "There are plenty in storage here. I ran across them yesterday. I'll get them out and make sure they're clean and in good condition."

"You sure 600 gallons will be enough?"

"It's more than enough to experiment with, but thanks for asking."

"I've got your back on this, Sean. We all do."

"Thanks, bro. That means a lot to me."

They said their goodbyes and signed off. Sean's thoughts immediately went back to the woman sleeping upstairs. Wade was right. He'd never been so messed up over a woman, but no matter what his brother said, anything beyond a business relationship with Angellica was out of the question. A sexual harassment lawsuit or any accusation of impropriety could ruin not only his new endeavor but the entire Nightingale operation. It was a risk he wasn't willing to take.

CHAPTER FIFTEEN

Just as she had for most of her life, Angellica woke with the sunrise slicing across the foot of her bed. The room was familiar, but it lacked the personal touches that had made it hers—when it had been hers. Now the room and the entire house belonged to Sean Nightingale. That was a truth she still couldn't get used to. And no matter how hard she tried; she couldn't stop thinking about the man. Granted, some of her thoughts involved murder, but most them involved the two of them naked together. How was it possible to want to strangle him one moment and want to jump his bones the next?

Unable to make sense of her mood swings, she dressed in the one clean outfit she'd brought with her last night when insufferable Sean had insisted that she return to the house with him. "It's not safe," he'd said. "It's too hot," he'd said. But living under the same roof as the man was both unsafe *and* dangerously hot. Knowing he was just down the hall from her had kept her awake, then plagued her dreams when she finally dropped off to sleep. Did he sleep naked? She'd heard a lot of men did. He seemed like the type to do something like that. Arrogant. Confident. Self-absorbed. Cocky.

Hoping to avoid Sean, she went down the front stairs rather than the back set that ended in the kitchen, where he was likely having breakfast. She needed coffee badly but would make her own when she got back to the cottage. The less time she spent with her new boss, the better. Besides, she had a million things to do to earn her keep. The harvest was less than two weeks away, and all the equipment had to be checked out and cleaned. Sean had said the new equipment for the blending lab would arrive that afternoon. She still hadn't gone through all the things her father and grandfather had left behind. It might all be junk, but she might find some things that had sentimental value. She'd almost reached the bottom of the stairs when a voice she'd come to know called out. "Angellica! In here. Now!"

What's he on the warpath about so early? Stifling a sigh, she changed course for the kitchen. Sean Nightingale sat at the table in the breakfast nook, a laptop computer open in front of him and a coffee mug sitting nearby. He wore another T-shirt bearing the famous surf shop logo, tan cargo pants, and hiking boots. A scowl marred his otherwise flawless face. "You bellowed?"

"I didn't bellow. I raised my voice to be heard in the front of the house before you snuck out."

"I wasn't sneaking. I've got a lot to do today. No time to dawdle."

"At least you got that part right. Have you seen the weather forecast for the rest of the week?"

"No." It was her turn to frown. Farmers always had to be on top of the weather. "What's going on?"

"The Pineapple Express, that's what. He grabbed his coffee mug and stood. "We're moving the harvest up. We'll start tonight." He put a fresh pod in the coffeemaker and pushed the button. Hot, fragrant liquid dribbled into his cup. "I've called the co-op, and they promised to send over as many workers as possible, but everyone from here to Napa is clamoring for laborers. There aren't enough to go around."

Pineapple Express was a slang term for an atmospheric river—a weather event that begins near Hawaii and crosses the Pacific. They bring torrential rainfall once they hit land and can cause flooding and crop damage. "What are the chances it's going to affect us?" Angellica selected one of her favorite mugs from the cabinet. When Sean retrieved his filled cup, she put in a fresh pod and watched the dark brew flow into her cup.

"According to NOAA, one hundred percent. They're saying we could get five or more inches of rain later this week."

The National Oceanic and Atmospheric Administration was rarely wrong about such things. That kind of rain when the fruit was so close to harvest could devastate the crop. The grapes were plump, making the clusters tight. Pockets between the grapes trap water and allow mildew to grow if not dried properly. The drying process was slow and didn't guarantee success. The best solution to the problem was to keep the clusters dry. Which meant harvesting earlier than planned.

"How did we not know about this sooner? Are we the last to know?"

"The people I spoke with at the co-op said they hadn't heard anything about it until one of the other growers called late yesterday to change their harvest date. Then it was one after another calling. We weren't the first, but we weren't the last, either. We'll get some workers, but not enough."

"I know some people I can call. We'll have to show them what to do, but they'll learn quickly."

"That's good. As soon as I hung up with the co-op, I called my brother. He's going to see who he can round up from our crew. We've got our own plane, so they can be here tonight if he can get them moving fast enough."

"You've got your own plane?" *Seriously?*

"*Nightingales* has a plane. Not me, personally. Wade has his own plane, but it's small. I think it seats four, including the pilot."

She was still trying to process how wealthy her employer had to be to own a plane, much less two, when he waved a hand in front of her face. "Earth to Angellica."

"I hear you. Just processing." She took a sip of coffee. The caffeinated brew seemed to hit her bloodstream instantaneously. She was suddenly awake and firing on all cylinders. "How long before the storm hits?"

"Forty-eight hours. Maybe a little more if the system stalls off the coast."

"If it stalls, it'll just be bigger when it does come ashore."

"That's what they say. We need to take advantage of every minute between now and then. I still have to call and arrange for the tanker to come earlier. We don't have enough IBC totes to hold the quantity of juice we'll produce in the next few days."

The food-grade plastic containers were widely used to hold water and other liquid food products. They kept a few to temporarily store juice before the fermenting process began. "We have two dozen, I think. They'll need to be hosed down, along with all the crushing and pressing equipment."

"Wilson at the co-op said he'd send a couple of hands this afternoon to help us with that kind of work. They don't know anything about harvesting grapes, but they know how to use a water hose and scrub brush."

Angellica nodded, then took another fortifying sip from her mug. "That's good. What time do you want to start harvesting tonight? I'll make some phone calls and see whose arm I can twist to come help."

"We'll start as soon as the processing equipment is

ready to go, even if it's just you and me out there. We don't have a minute to waste if we're going to salvage this crop."

Angellica left Sean to make his phone calls while she ran to the cottage, where she downed a power bar and fixed herself another cup of coffee. She made a quick list of friends she could count on and began making calls. Her first call was to Lexie, who said she'd try her best, but that they were in the middle of taping the next season of her show and didn't know if she could get off or not. After hanging up with her best friend, she continued down the list she'd made. In half an hour, she'd contacted three friends from college who lived in the area and had gone on to work on the sales side of the wine industry. They promised to call their friends and put the word out on her behalf. Within an hour, she had six volunteers and was feeling a lot better about the upcoming harvest.

She was returning to the house to see what kind of progress Sean had made when the truck carrying the new equipment for the blending lab came down the driveway. She waved them in the right direction and then opened the building for them. "Just put it anywhere," she said, showing them the already cramped area. Arranging the room and throwing out the old equipment would have to wait until after the harvest. She idly wondered when the cleaning service would show up as she watched impatiently as the men emptied the delivery truck and carried everything inside. The vintner in her wanted to check out every box, but there was no time for that. As soon as they were through, she signed the delivery ticket and sent them on their way. They hadn't left the property when a pickup truck pulled up next to the panel truck. A trio of teenage boys exited the cab.

"We're looking for Florence Nightingale," the tallest of the bunch said, smiling at his joke.

Not in a joking mood, Angellica glared at the teen, whom she guessed to be sixteen or seventeen. His buddies appeared to be about the same age. "*Sean* Nightingale isn't available right now. I'm in charge of the vineyard. How can I help you?"

"My uncle, Jerry Wilson, said you needed some help today. My name's Scott. This is Dennis and Tyler." The two friends nodded as he introduced them, but kept their mouths shut. Angellica returned the gesture and then addressed the self-appointed leader of the group.

"It's nice to meet all of you, and thanks for coming so quickly. Your uncle is right. There's a giant storm rolling in, and we had to move our harvest up. There are a lot of things that need to be done, none of which are fun or glamorous. We'll pay minimum wage plus a bonus for a job well done. You can work as many or as few hours as you want, but I'd appreciate it if you didn't leave in the middle of a project."

Scott silently questioned his buddies. Dennis and Tyler nodded again. "We've got school tomorrow, but we can help for a while," Scott said. "Show us what you need."

She had to give the boys credit. They didn't even flinch when she showed them the equipment in the barn and told them what needed to be done. While they sorted through the cleaning equipment, Angellica used the tractor to move the crushing and pressing machines into the center of the barn. Scott assured her he'd taken part in harvests since he was ten years old and knew exactly what to do. Nevertheless, she hung around until she was certain they could handle the job.

She met up with Sean as he was leaving the house to look for her. "Did I see a delivery truck earlier?" he asked.

"Yep. The new equipment is here. I had them put it all inside. By the way, I haven't seen that cleaning crew you hired. It's still a mess in there, but organizing that building is way down on the priority list right now."

"Absolutely. We've got to get all the grapes in, not just the Cabs. The weather service says this thing might last for a week or more. If it was just a few days, I'd opt to leave the rest of them on the vine, and they'd dry out naturally once the sun comes back out, but seven days of rain will ruin them all. We'll have to harvest and hope it's not too soon for whatever we have to leave."

"This is a disaster."

CHAPTER SIXTEEN

Sean couldn't agree more. He focused on the pickup parked in front of the blending room. "Whose truck?"

"Mr. Wilson at the co-op sent his nephew and a couple of his friends to do the grunt work. They're scrubbing the crusher as we speak. I told them we'd pay minimum wage plus a bonus for a job well done. I hope that's okay?"

"It's fine. How long can they stay?" This change of plans was going to cost him a small fortune, but it couldn't be helped. The grapes had to be harvested before the storm hit or they'd lose the entire crop, and that was unacceptable.

"A few hours. Hopefully, enough to get the equipment clean. I've got six friends coming later to help with the harvest. Some can stay all night, but not all of them."

"Wade found ten workers willing to take a California vacation. They'll work around the clock if necessary."

"How soon can they be here?"

"They'll be here before sundown today."

"What are we going to do for lights?"

"I found a rental place that has lights on trailers, the kind they use for construction work on the highways at night. They're bringing out enough to illuminate a football stadium. At least that's what they promised."

"We'll need to feed the harvest crew."

"I called Maria and told her what was going on. She's sending her niece out to cook for us, along with enough supplies to feed a small army. We won't starve."

"It sounds like you've got this under control. I'm impressed."

Sean stifled a sigh. "I know you think I'm an idiot, but this isn't my first rodeo or my first harvest."

"I bet it's the first time you've had to work all night to get a harvest in."

"You'd lose that bet," he said as he walked off toward the barn. "Let's see how these kids are doing. If they've got it under control, you and I can start picking grapes."

He couldn't fathom why her lowly opinion of him mattered one iota, but it did. He'd worked his ass off all morning and not once thought if his actions would impress her or not. He'd simply done what needed to be done. She'd expected him to fail. Thus, her need to say he'd impressed her.

Truth be told, she'd impressed him, too. She'd jumped in and done her part as well. She'd rounded up help from among her circle of friends and then handled the equipment delivery without interrupting his workflow. As they rounded the corner and caught sight of the barn, he saw she'd accurately assessed their new hire's skill levels as well. The crusher gleamed like new, and the press was getting a good scrubbing as they approached. "You moved these out yourself?" The machines had been crammed into a corner behind a stack of IBC totes. He'd planned to come out earlier and move them himself, but the unexpected weather report had put an end to his plans.

"I learned to drive a tractor when I was seven, I think."

She shrugged. "I was too short to work the pedals, but Dad let me sit on his lap and steer. Who do you think put these machines away last year?"

He raised an eyebrow. "You?"

"For the last three years, actually."

"I'm impressed."

She met his gaze. "This isn't my first rodeo, Mr. Nightingale. Or my first harvest."

CHAPTER SEVENTEEN

Sean couldn't hold back his smile. She'd thrown his words back at him, effectively putting him in his place. She'd delivered the line like a practiced actor, then walked away, mimicking his own behavior. The woman was driving him crazy. She'd proven his earlier assumptions wrong at every turn, leaving him reevaluating all his plans. He'd been prepared to make a go of his new venture all alone. Hell, he'd been looking forward to it. He'd been dancing to the tune of his family obligations his entire life. Moving to California might seem drastic to some, but it was the right thing for him. And purchasing the Capello vineyard was the right thing for Nightingales, too. The family might not see it yet, but they would once he perfected the blend. But first, he had to save this year's harvest. Contracts had to be fulfilled, and he needed the income from the sale to make the improvements required to bring the vineyard and winery up to Nightingale standards.

As he watched her sexy ass walk away, he wondered if he was making a mistake keeping her at arm's length.

"Good work, guys," he said as he entered the barn. "I'm guessing you've done this before?"

"Yes, sir." The tallest of the bunch stepped away from the work and, after wiping his hand on his shorts, stuck his hand out. "Scott Wilson. These are my friends, Dennis, and Tyler." The other two kept working but waved and muttered something that resembled a hello.

Sean waved back, then shook hands with Scott. "Sean Nightingale."

"It's nice to meet you, Mr. Nightingale. You're related to the Nightingales from back east?"

"My family. I guess you can say I've got grape juice in my veins."

Scott chuckled. "I can't say that I do, but I know my way around a vineyard. I've pretty much been doing everything but drinking the wine since I was just a kid."

He was still a kid, but Sean didn't think it prudent to point that out. The young man was earnest and mature for his years. "I can't thank you enough for answering my call for help."

"There aren't many jobs around here for teenagers, except flipping burgers. We're grateful for the work."

Sean nodded at the crusher, gleaming like new. "You guys did an excellent job on that. Better than I would have done." He snickered, recognizing the truth in his statement. "There's a lot still to be done around here, even after the harvest. If the three of you want jobs, you've got them."

All three stood practically at attention. "You mean that?" Scott asked.

"Every word. I'll take however many hours a week you can give me. But let me be clear. Your schoolwork comes first. I expect you to keep your grades up if you want to work for me."

Scott glanced at the other two, whose broad smiles and enthusiastic nods said it all. "I guess you've got yourself three new part-time employees, Mr. Nightingale."

"Please, call me Sean. We'll make this formal after we get these grapes in. I'll have time then to do the paperwork." Sean slipped his phone out of his back pocket and put in his password. He handed the device to Scott. "Put in your contact information so I can reach you. I'll text you back, so you'll have my number."

The young man entered his contact information and handed the phone back. Sean immediately sent a text. "There. We're all set." He motioned toward Angellica, who had been watching their interaction from the sidelines. "Ms. Capello knows more about this operation than I do, so if you have questions, you can ask her. How long can you stay today?"

Scott shrugged. "A few more hours?" His cohorts confirmed with nods.

"Use your best judgment. Tomorrow's a school day. But if you're around later, we've got someone coming to cook for us. You're welcome to stay for free food." All three brightened at the idea. He recalled being constantly hungry at their age and figured all teenage boys went through the same thing.

"Thank you, Mist…Sean. We won't stay too late, but we won't leave you hanging, either. We'll get the work done."

"I can see we're going to get along just fine," Sean said. He shook Scott's hand again and, with a nod to the others, he exited the building. Who said today's youth were lazy? Maybe he'd accidentally stumbled across the only three with ambition and a work ethic he could admire, but he didn't think so. When Angellica caught up to him halfway between the barn and the blending room, he asked, "Does the local high school have an agricultural program?"

"They do. Why?"

"Call them. See if they have any students interested in viticulture. If so, offer to hire some to help with the harvest. Minimum wage and on-the-job training provided. Tell the teacher I'd be interested in a co-op situation with their program in the future."

"Why don't you call them? I've got shit to do."

Sean stopped so fast the toes of his boots kicked up a cloud of dust. "I've got shit to do, too, Ms. Capello. That, and the fact you probably know these people better than I do, is the reason I'm asking you to make the call."

"Getting students out here on such short notice probably isn't going to happen."

"Maybe. Maybe not. If even one comes, that'll be one more person harvesting, and we need all the help we can get." He resumed his trek to the first row of Cab grapes. "Oh, and be sure to invite the teacher. What's his name?"

"Mr. Hanson."

"Invite Mr. Hanson to come out and see for himself that the offer is legitimate. I'd like to meet him."

He left Angellica fuming in the midday heat as he donned gloves, then pulled a pair of pruning shears from the pocket of his cargo shorts. The sooner he got started, the sooner the grapes would be safe inside the barn.

Angellica joined him almost an hour later. "What took you so long?"

"After I called Mr. Hanson at the high school, I called one of my professors at UC Davis. He said he had some students who could use some extra credit and some hands-on experience. He wasn't sure how soon he could get them out here, but he's going to make some calls." She shrugged and, working the row ahead of him, said, "It was a good idea you had. I just took it a little further."

They might end up buried up to their eyeballs in inexperienced volunteers, but he'd take that over losing most of the crop. "Thanks. I hadn't thought about enlisting college students. I probably wouldn't have thought of the high school program if it wasn't for Scott and his friends. They seem eager to work. Who knows, they might go on to study viticulture in college."

"Like me?"

"Like you," he acknowledged. Tires crunching on the gravel driveway drew his attention toward the house. A minibus, the kind used to shuttle small groups from one place to another, kicked up a cloud of dust as it came to a stop in front of Sean's new residence. The folding passenger door opened, and a familiar figure stepped out. Sean smiled and pocketed his shears. "The cavalry is here," he said. "Come on. I'll introduce you."

Sean hailed his brother. "Wade!" Drawing nearer, he asked, "What are you doing here? Who's running the show at home?"

Other familiar faces slowly filed out of the bus behind his brother. He recognized several Riverside locals who regularly helped with their harvest. At least he wouldn't have to tell them what to do. Hand them some shears and they'd do the rest.

The elder Nightingale brother stretched his arms above his head and swiveled his upper body like a swimmer getting ready to compete. God, it was good to see him. The brothers had always been close, and though Sean was a hundred percent committed to his relocation to California, he was going to miss spending time with Wade and Ian.

"Hey, bro." The brothers embraced. "Dad and Serenity are in charge back home. Mostly Serenity since Dad's bottling his three-year-old Chardonnay. You know, the one he thought would age better in the bottle?"

"I'm not sure I agree with him, but he's never been wrong before."

"My thoughts, exactly. He's got a sixth sense about wine. Must be something you learn because I sure as shit didn't get that gene."

"You got the business genes. I got the winemaking genes." He shook his head and shared a conspirator's smile with his older brother. "I'm not sure Ian is ours. He didn't get *any* of the Nightingale genes."

Wade howled with laughter. Ganging up on the youngest brother was as instinctual as breathing for the two oldest. "Damn straight. The little do-gooder has been nothing but a pain in the ass since the day he was born." He didn't mean it, of course. When Sean got together with Ian, they threw shade on their older brother, and no doubt those two slung arrows at Sean when he wasn't around. But they were family, and that meant a lot to the Nightingale clan.

Wade drew Sean in for another hug. "Damn glad to see you, bro. But did you really think I'd leave you hanging in the wind?"

"I knew you'd send help. I just didn't expect to get you away from your fiancée. Serenity driving you crazy with the wedding plans?"

"Every. Fucking. Day," he said, then a giant smile broke across his face. "But it's all worth it, man. She's everything. You know?"

He did know. Serenity Granger had been Sean's best friend since their first day of first grade. He'd also known she was the perfect partner for his big brother. It had taken nearly three decades to get them together, but he'd finally done it this past year. With his plans already in place to move to California, his window of opportunity to make the couple see what was right before their eyes had been closing fast. It had taken some doing, but the two lovebirds had eventually seen what he'd known all along. "I'm happy for you, Wade. And for Sen, too. She's one of a kind."

"Don't I know it? She sends her love, as do Mom and Dad."

"Not Ian?"

"Didn't have time to tell him where I was going. He's working on some big case. Hush-hush stuff."

"He's not in danger, is he?" Ian was a deputy sheriff—an ongoing source of worry for the entire family.

"No more than usual."

CHAPTER EIGHTEEN

Dear God. Angellica stood a safe distance away, watching the bus empty. It wasn't the army he'd brought with him that stunned her. It was Wade Nightingale himself. He was maybe an inch taller than his younger brother, but the men could pass for twins. She couldn't help but wonder if these two had commandeered all the good-looking, sexy-as-hell genes and left all the ugly-as-sin ones for their youngest brother. Either way, it wasn't fair to the rest of the male population.

One worker stepped out of the bus and into her line of sight. It was the reality check she needed to get her feet moving again. As she approached the group, her thoughts scrambled to process the situation. Where were they going to put all these people? Even working around the clock, they'd eventually need places to sleep. She'd have to alert Rosa to the change in numbers. More food supplies would need to be brought in, and the poor girl was going to need help in the kitchen. Not that Angellica wasn't grateful for the new arrivals, but their presence created a logistical nightmare.

There was pride and genuine affection in his voice when Sean noticed her presence and waved her over. "Angellica. Come meet my brother." A few steps brought her into their realm. "Wade, this is Angellica Capello. Angellica, my big brother, Wade Nightingale."

Wade turned a dazzling smile her way and presented his hand to shake. His palm was warm, and his grip strong. "It's nice to meet you, Ms. Capello. I've been a fan of Capello wines since I became old enough to drink."

"He's lying," Sean interjected. "He was sneaking wine from our family cellars long before he reached the legal drinking age. And as far back as I can remember, we always had some Capello wine in the rack."

"You did?"

Sean nodded. "Yep. Our parents keep an eclectic cellar. Always have."

"That's…I don't know…I'm just amazed, I guess."

"Capello wines have a great reputation in the industry," Wade added. "I was sorry to hear you'd closed your winery."

The sincerity in his words warmed her heart. She'd always known that Capello wines were good, but to hear it from a Nightingale brought on a wave of emotion she wasn't prepared for. Her father had given up and sold without giving her a chance to carry on the family legacy. She choked back tears. "Me, too." Squaring her shoulders, she glanced at the men and women milling about. "I wasn't expecting such a crowd."

"All I did was mention a free trip to California, and the plane filled up fast." Wade called for everyone to gather in, then began his introductions. "Everybody, listen up! This is Angellica Capello. If you need to know where something is, ask her. You all know my idiot brother, Sean." Wade and Sean joined in the ensuing laughter. When everyone had settled, he continued. "We've got roughly thirty-six hours before this monster storm hits. You all know how this works. Harvesters, follow Sean. This is his vineyard, so do what he says."

Sean took a few steps back. Most of the group moved his way, but a few stayed behind. Wade introduced Dott and Trisha. Angellica shook hands with the two women. "They're here to help in the kitchen. Sean said he'd recruited a chef?"

"I don't know if I'd call Rosa a chef, but she knows her way around a kitchen. I'm sure she'll be grateful for the help."

Wade stopped her before she took her first step toward the house. "Once you get them settled, come back? I'm going to pick a few grapes, then I'd like you to give me a tour of the place. Just a quick one. Then I'll get back to the harvest."

As grateful as she was for the help Wade had brought all the way from New Jersey, she didn't appreciate being ordered around by anyone, especially someone who, in her mind, had no right to tell her anything. Engaging him in a battle over her role here wasn't in anyone's best interest, so she gave him a curt nod and led the two helpers toward the house.

"Don't mind Wade," the elder of the two said once they were out of hearing range. "He doesn't know when to turn off being in charge. He's been domineering since he was a kid."

"You've known him that long?"

"All his life. I'm Dott, by the way. I own Dott's Diner in Riverside." She swept her arm out, encompassing the vineyard. "You've got a nice place here. This is my first trip to California, but from what I saw on the drive from the airport, I can see why Sean loves it here. I never heard anyone complain about snow the way he does."

She couldn't help but smile at the woman's remark. "He's not a fan of winter?"

"Not at all. Can't say that I am either, but it's a fact of life in New Jersey. You either accept it or get the hell out." She shrugged. "Apparently, Sean has chosen the latter. Can't say I blame him."

"I guess you've figured out that Dott will talk your ear off if you let her," the younger woman said. "I'm Trisha. I own a shoe store a few doors down from her diner. I've known the Nightingales my whole life. Sean and I were in the same graduating class."

Angellica was curious how both these business-owning women had managed to hop on a plane and fly across the country to assist with the harvest, but those questions would have to wait. Trisha provided a great opportunity to find out more about her new employer. "Sean claims to be a genius. Do you know anything about that?"

"That's no lie. He could have skipped a few grades in school, but his mother wouldn't hear of it. He tested out of a lot of college classes, though."

Okay, so maybe his claim was true. That didn't mean he knew anything about making wine. "I'm surprised he bought Capello's. From what I saw of him on the Internet, he's more of a playboy than a serious vintner," she prodded.

"Don't let his lackadaisical attitude fool you. It's a cover, an act he puts on, so no one suspects he's paying attention. He could run Nightingale's blindfolded, and everyone, including Wade, knows it. Sean absorbs knowledge like a sponge. You'll see. Give him a few weeks here, and he'll know everything there is to know about this operation."

They'd reached the back door that led into the kitchen. Angellica ushered the new arrivals inside and introduced them to Rosa, who gushed with enthusiasm at having help. "We're going to need more supplies," Dott said, taking stock of what was on hand. "Is there a car I can use to go to the grocery store? Wade gave me his credit card and said to spare no expense." She placed a hand on her chest. "Words I took to heart."

They all laughed at her fluttering eyelashes and exaggerated delivery. "My car is at the vintner's cottage. Wade wants me to take him on a tour of the property. I'll bring the car back with me."

"Perfect!" the diner owner enthused. "Okay, ladies, let's make a list. Anyone know how many we're cooking for?"

"Two dozen?" Angellica supplied. "Some of those are teenagers, so factor that into your calculations."

"Oh, yeah," Rosa said. "I know those boys. They can put away the food."

"Okay then," Trisha interjected. "Food for three dozen!"

Angellica left with a smile on her face, but it vanished quickly as she neared the vineyard. Wade saw her coming and slid his gloves and pruning shears into the back pockets of his shorts. "Everyone settled?"

"Yes. Thanks for thinking of kitchen help. With all the other vineyards in the area hustling to get their grapes in too, it's nearly impossible to recruit enough short-term help."

"Don't give me credit where it isn't due. Sean suggested I try to find someone willing to cook for a crowd. I was having breakfast at Dott's Diner with my fiancée and her best friend, Trisha. Dott overheard the conversation, and before I knew it, she'd signed on, and so had Trisha. I wasn't about to tell them they couldn't come."

Angellica ambled up the hill toward the vintner's cottage. She figured they'd begin the tour there by picking up her car. Wade followed along. "Rosa welcomed the help." She wasn't sure how to broach the subject, but curiosity was eating at her. "Dott said you gave her a credit card to buy groceries?"

"I did."

"Why?"

"Because Sean is my brother, and even though I hate that he's moving to California, I believe in him. He sank all his available cash into purchasing this land. I'm sure he could afford to finance a traditional harvest, but the expense of a spur-of-the-moment operation like this could put him in a hole he might not dig himself out of. Nightingale's stick together."

As an only child and considering her father's recent desertion to pursue his own agenda, Angellica couldn't help but envy Sean's situation. One phone call and his brother came running. "Did Sean tell you why he bought Capello's?"

"He did."

Wade didn't elaborate as they approached the cottage. Angellica related the story of how her grandparents had built the small structure and planted the vines they'd brought from Italy over a hundred years ago.

"I didn't realize your family had been in the wine business that long. It must have been difficult for your father to let it go."

She wished that was the case, but Tomas Capello hadn't blinked an eye at selling their family legacy out from under her. "I suppose," she said as she ushered her guest to her car. They stopped at the barn, where Wade quickly but thoroughly inspected every piece of equipment. When he had seen enough, he got back in the car without a word to her. Angellica fired up the engine and took him to the only other building he hadn't seen—the blending room. "It's a mess right now. We were going to remove my father's old equipment this morning before the shipment you sent from New Jersey arrived. Then we got the weather forecast and had to shift our priorities."

Wade weaved his way past the newly arrived shipment to the small space where her father had spent so much of his time while she was growing up. "This is a nice space," he said. "My dad would love it."

"You think so?" She envisioned Nightingale's New Jersey operation to be much grander and certainly more modern. The used equipment cluttering the front of the building was light years newer than what her father had worked with.

"I know so. He complains all the time about the stainless-steel tables, white walls, and fluorescent lighting. Says the place has no soul."

"Sean said he'd just renovated his lab. That's where all this came from." She indicated the newly arrived furnishings with a sweep of her arm. "Did he replace this stainless steel with something else?"

"More stainless," Wade said with a smile. "I tried to talk him into Quartz or Granite countertops, but after a decade working with the metal surface, he'd come to appreciate how easy it was to keep clean. He still complains about it, though."

"I don't see the point in renovating. Everything he sent seems in like-new condition."

"It is. He renovated because he knew Sean wouldn't accept a new blending lab if he offered it. But it would be impossible for him to turn down used equipment. Sean hates waste, and all that stuff up there would have been hauled to one of our storage buildings and left to collect dust."

"Your dad spent I don't know how much on a renovation he didn't need just so he could help Sean?"

"I told you. Nightingale's stick together."

Angellica led the way to the cask room. At the bottom of the stairs, she flipped on the overhead lights.

"Holy smoke!" Wade stood with his hands on his hips, his gaze sweeping the enormous underground room. "These are all full?" he asked, lifting his chin at the racked oak barrels.

"Yes."

The elder Nightingale brother shook his head. "Incredible. Sean's sitting on a gold mine here."

"They've aged longer than normal. The oldest vintage here is nearly six years old. They could be vinegar by now." She knew better, but no need to tell Wade she'd kept a close eye on the wines, hoping her father would eventually allow her to bottle and sell them.

"Neutral barrels?"

His knowledge surprised her, but she quickly realized whom she was talking to. The CEO of Nightingale's would know the proper way to store wine for any length of time was to use "neutral" barrels that no longer had any flavor to impart to the wine. "Of course."

"Then you've got nothing to worry about. Centuries ago, wines never left the barrel until they were going to be consumed. If they've been stored properly, which it appears these have, they're fine. Maybe better than fine."

She shrugged. "Maybe. We'd better get going. Dott needs my car to go into town and we've got grapes to harvest."

CHAPTER NINETEEN

"Where have you been?" Sean asked when Wade finally joined him in the row. "I was about to send out a search party."

"Ms. Capello gave me a tour of the property." He put on his gloves and produced pruning shears from a pocket in his cargo shorts. "This is quite the operation. I didn't know Capello's was as old as it is."

Sean clipped a heavy cluster off the vine and carefully laid them in the plastic crate at his feet. "It's one of the more well-established vineyards in the area. I was lucky to get my hands on it before one of the larger operations swallowed it up."

Wade pointed out a cluster Sean missed, then snipped it off the vine himself. "The place has potential," he said, "and its share of challenges."

"Have you ever known me to shy away from a challenge?"

"Never."

"I'm going to make a go of this, Wade. I'm not out to

disgrace the Nightingale name."

"Never thought you were. Mom and Dad are taking your relocation hard. They're behind you, one hundred percent, but they miss you."

"We own a jet. They can visit anytime they want."

"And you can go see them."

"True. But until I have this place running on its own, I'm not going anywhere."

"Help is yours for the asking. You know that, right?"

"Yeah. I know, and I appreciate it, but I want to do this on my own."

"I get it. You've always loved the stories about how the first Nightingale on this continent started with nothing and built an empire. It makes sense that you'd want to start something of your own."

"You saw the sign out by the road, right? This is a Nightingale vineyard. My name might be the only one on the deed, but the vineyard belongs to the family. You know as well as I do, Nightingale wines need to evolve if we're going to stay relevant." He gestured to the expanse of vines surrounding them. "This is how we're going to do it."

The brothers looked up as a couple of trucks made their way down the driveway. "More help?" Wade asked.

"Looks like we've got lights so we can harvest throughout the night. Don't know who's in the van. The local co-op is supposed to send us some workers."

"Better go see who it is. I'll take over here."

Sean jogged down the row, arriving in front of the house as the two vehicles came to a stop. The bed of the large truck leading the way was packed full of generators and light standards. The passenger van trailing behind came to a stop, and half a dozen people spilled out. *Tourists.* He stifled a groan. He didn't have time to deal with this. Every minute he spent in the driveway was a minute wasted. Signaling the delivery driver to hold on for a minute, he headed toward the unwelcome newcomers. He was almost close enough to yell at them to get back in their van and leave when he spied Angellica heading their way, a giant smile on her face.

He held back as she threw herself into the arms of the tall guy who'd climbed out of the driver's side door. The guy picked her up like she weighed nothing, swung her around in a circle, then planted a kiss on her lips. Sean clenched his jaw. *What the hell? Who is this guy, and what right did he have to kiss Angellica?* As quickly as he'd scooped her up, the guy lowered Angellica to the ground. The two broke apart, and she greeted the rest of the group like they were long-lost friends. *These must be the friends from college she said were coming to help harvest.* Still, the embrace and kiss looked like more than friendship. Just because Sean had spent way too much time thinking about how her lips would feel beneath his didn't mean he had any business being jealous. The delivery driver approached with a clipboard. "Looking for Sean Nightingale."

"You found him. Sorry. I thought they were tourists, and I was going to get them out of here before they impeded the harvest. Looks like one of my employees knows them."

"No problem. I need you to sign the delivery ticket for these, then tell me where you want them. I've got a forklift to position them with. If you need to move them, you'll need something with a trailer hitch."

"Got it covered." Sean looked over the rental agreement and tried not to have a heart attack at the dollar amount as he signed for the equipment. He handed the paperwork back. Pointing up the hill behind him, he gave instructions for the initial placement of the lights. They'd need to be moved several times, but their presence would make a world of difference that night.

The sun was dipping low before Sean returned to the rows of grapes. He's spent most of the afternoon putting people to work on the various tasks as van after van of volunteers arrived. By the time he fired up the generators to power the lights, the vineyard was as busy as a hive of bees. For the first time since he'd received the weather report that morning, he thought he had a chance to save the harvest.

Starting with the workers who'd been on the job the longest, Sean cycled the entire crew through the buffet line Rosa and her helpers had set out. They'd found some pop-up shade covers somewhere, along with a couple of long tables and plastic chairs. He'd have to inquire about those later and thank whoever had donated them to the cause. Angellica's former high school teacher had put out the word, and it seemed like everyone from the freshman cheerleader squad to the janitor had come out to help. Sean put them all to work. The youngest volunteers handed out water bottles and flagged full crates on the rows so the football players would know to pick them up and empty them into the larger containers at the end of every row. The high school principal volunteered to drive the tractor, ensuring the full crates of grapes got delivered and stacked in the barn. It was a genuine community effort. Sean had wondered how he'd fit in to the community, but no longer. Thanks to Angellica, he'd been accepted with open arms. Nightingales had been a part of the fabric of their New Jersey community for generations. It was a tradition Sean silently pledged to uphold on the West coast. His heart swelled with pride. Like the first Nightingale to till the land in New Jersey, Sean had found his home. His community. His future.

CHAPTER TWENTY

It was a long night, and as the sun rose and the smell of fresh coffee wafted from the kitchen, Sean breathed a sigh of relief. They weren't done, but if the momentum continued, they'd get most of the grapes under cover before the storm made its way inland.

"You did good, Sean."

Sean glanced at his brother, who hadn't taken more than a few minutes of break since he'd arrived the previous afternoon. Wade looked like hell, but he had a cup of coffee in his hand and a smile on his face. "I owe these people. Big time."

"You do, but I don't think they expect anything from you. You've won the community over, little brother. They won't forget."

"Angellica deserves most of the credit. These are her friends. People she grew up with. I'm the outsider."

"Not anymore. You could have brought in machines to harvest the grapes, but you didn't. You reached out for help and didn't turn anyone away. Were those cheerleaders handing out water bottles, or was I getting delusional from lack of sleep?"

"Those were cheerleaders. I promised to contribute a case of wine to their next fundraiser in return for their help. They'll be back after school today."

"Glad I wasn't hallucinating."

"Me, too. Did you get some sleep?"

"A cat nap. How about you?"

"Not yet. I'll sleep when the grapes are in."

"You sound like Grandpa. That man never knew when to quit."

"True, but shit got done when he was around."

Wade laughed. "It sure did. Didn't matter how young, old, able, or unable you were. He'd put you to work."

"I still have calloused hands from when we were kids, and he'd make us help with the harvest, but he said we were too young to use the sharp clippers, so he gave us dull ones. My hand would hurt for weeks afterward."

Wade flexed his right hand. "Thank God for the invention of cordless electric clippers. I didn't know if you had any or not, so I brought a box full for our crew."

Sean had found several of the new electric clippers in the barn, but nowhere near enough for all the people presently working the vines. "I don't think I've told you how much I appreciate you coming out to help. It's one thing to round up some hired hands to do the grunt work. It's something else entirely to leave your job to pick grapes."

"You needed experienced people. Like you said, I've been doing this since I was old enough to operate a pair of dull clippers."

Sean's gaze swept over the hillside, taking in all the vines yet to be harvested.

"Something wrong?" Wade asked.

"Nothing. Just not enough caffeine yet." He took a long sip of his cooling coffee. It tasted bitter, but it was exactly what he needed to jump-start his brain. Twenty-four more hours to go. They'd brought in roughly a third of the harvest in just over twelve hours. It was crazy fast, but exactly what was called for. "I need to go check the weather forecast again. If we're going to run out of time, I'll have to prioritize. Deciding which grapes to leave on the vine and which to save isn't going to be easy."

"It never is. Remember Hurricane Irene? Came through right at harvest several years back. We couldn't save every variety, so Uncle Stephen decided to leave the Chardonnay grapes on the vine. After everything dried out, about half the Chards had survived, so he harvested them. Dad swears the reserve he made with those grapes is some of the best Nightingale has ever produced."

"I remember. And Dad's right. That 2011 Chardonnay is excellent."

"See? Nothing to worry about. Anything you leave on the vine might turn out to be special."

"I doubt I'm that lucky, but we'll see." Sean finished his coffee. "I'm going to check the weather one more time, then I'm going to turn the crank on this day. See if I can get it moving. Where are you starting at?"

"We got the Cab Savs in last night. Merlot next?"

"Yeah. Sounds good. I think we'll save the Pinot Noir for last."

Wade gave him a mock salute, then wandered off toward the vineyard. There wasn't much pep in his brother's step, but he was a Nightingale. He'd collapse between the rows before he'd give up on a vintage.

His decision to sacrifice all or part of the Pinot Noir harvest didn't sit well with him, but then again, abandoning any fruit on the vine went against everything he believed in. He could call some of the neighboring vineyards who used mechanical harvesters and see if they'd finished their harvest. Maybe he could rent one for long enough to get the last grapes in before the rain hit. No sooner had the thought occurred than he dismissed it. The machines were quick and efficient, but they mangled the vines. That, on top of a late-season torrential rain, might be too much trauma for the vines. Safeguarding the vines so there'd be a harvest next year, and the next was more important. Hand-picking the grape clusters was the safe way to proceed, even if he lost a significant percentage of grapes.

Sitting at the desk where Tomas Capello had spent so much of his time, Sean opened his laptop and accessed the latest weather reports. The storm had stalled offshore overnight but was still predicted to come ashore later that day. The stall had bought him a few more hours. He rocked back in his chair and stared at the ceiling. He should roust everybody and get them back out there right now. If he did, they'd probably beat the storm and save the entire harvest.

But at what cost? Everyone was dead on their feet when they stumbled into the house after completing the last row of Cabs. They deserved a few more hours of rest, even if it meant losing the Pinot Noirs. Besides, the high schoolers would be back this afternoon to take up some of the slack.

He needed more coffee and something solid to sop it up before it ate through the lining of his stomach. Dodging people who'd fallen asleep on the floor in almost every room of the house, he made his way to the kitchen. Rosa, Dott, and Trisha were hard at work preparing for another busy day. Dott saw him first and mumbled, "Good morning," before turning back to her work. The others did the same. No need to disturb them. The island was piled high with traditional breakfast items, plus sliced fruit and various pastries. Some looked store-bought, but others he pegged as Dott's work. Riverside residents flocked to Dott's Diner for her home-baked goodies. He grabbed a paper plate from a stack on the corner of the island and then piled it high with bacon, sausage, and scrambled eggs. He poured gravy over the whole thing, then topped it off with one of Dott's cinnamon rolls. It was a mountain of food, but he couldn't recall the last time he'd eaten an entire meal, and he wasn't sure when he was going to have the time to sit down for another one. No one was using the single-serving coffee maker, so he helped himself to a cup of his favorite brew and took it all back to his office.

CHAPTER TWENTY-ONE

Angellica woke exhausted. A quick glance at the clock revealed the reason. She'd closed her eyes at three a.m. It was six now. Flopping back against her pillow, she stared at the ceiling, her mind stuck on the one subject she had no business thinking about. Sean Nightingale. She had to hand it to him; he knew what he was doing in terms of the harvest. Every aspect of the operation had run as smoothly as could be expected, considering the entire thing had been thrown together at the last minute, and only a few of the makeshift crew had any experience. Still, they'd managed to harvest all the Cabs. A seasoned crew would have been hard-pressed to accomplish that in the same number of hours.

She'd half expected Sean to hide in his office, but he'd spent every minute of the day instructing and directing, making sure everyone had a task and knew how to do it. When he wasn't helping one of the volunteers, he was picking grapes himself or moving the giant lights so the harvest would continue without interruption. It was hard to equate the hard-working, organized leader she'd seen yesterday with the jet-setting playboy depicted in the celebrity magazines. She had no use for the latter, but the former intrigued her. It didn't help that he was gorgeous and sexy as sin. Groaning, she shook her head. He'd won the cheerleaders over with nothing more than a smile. It was a wonder he didn't drown, given the number of water bottles they delivered to him throughout the afternoon. He'd handled their adoration with grace and aplomb, something she hadn't expected from him. Again, not the playboy she believed him to be. Which made her wonder. Who was Sean Nightingale? His brother had nothing but good things to say about him and clearly didn't hold his cross-country move against him. By all appearances, Sean had the weight of the Nightingale family behind him and his new venture, even if he didn't realize it.

She wondered what that would be like. Her parents had been supportive, to a point, but her dad's backing had only gone so far. Education? Yes. Run the family business? Absolutely not. If she'd gone out on a limb the way Sean had, her father would have left her out there on her own.

After staggering through a shower, she made her way to the kitchen, where the trio of volunteer cooks were hard at work. "I didn't expect to be the first one awake today," she said as she helped herself to a cup of coffee.

Rosa briefly looked up from the potato she was peeling. "You're not. The boss came through about fifteen minutes ago.

"The boss? You mean Mr. Nightingale?"

"He's the boss, right?"

As much as it galled her to admit it, he was the boss, and a damned good one at that. "Did he say where he was going?"

"No. He filled a plate and took off. I think he was afraid we'd put him to work." She laughed at her own joke.

Angellica smiled and filled a plate of her own. "Holler if you need anything today," she said as she went in search of a quiet place to eat. Her first thought was her dad's office, but she should have known Sean would beat her to it. He sat at her father's old desk, his open laptop and an empty paper plate in front of him. His hair didn't look as if it had seen a comb in days. Dark circles beneath his eyes testified to either stress, fatigue, or both. He hadn't bothered to shave, and the resulting scruff only made him look sexy instead of unkept.

"Hey," he said as she moved on in search of a place to eat in peace. "Come on in." He hastily cleared a place on the corner of the desk. "Put your plate down here and pull up a chair. I wanted to talk to you."

"About?" Angellica stepped inside the room. His gaze seemed to track her every move as she situated herself across from him. Her skin heated at the intense scrutiny. It was almost like he was checking her out. *That's ridiculous. He puts up with you because he has to. The man dates supermodels and actors. Look at yourself, Angel. You're no supermodel.* In fact, if she had to describe herself that morning, she would have gone with *haggard farm girl,* given the dark circles under her own eyes and the sore muscles it would take weeks to revive.

First, I was wondering if you could run the crusher today. We need to empty some of the crates so the pickers can fill them up again. I know it's a lot to ask, but you know what you're doing, and we can spare the time to teach and supervise a newbie.

Angellica nodded. "I'll ask Kevin to help me. He can feed the hopper, and I can drive the tractor to keep the crates moving."

"Can you and Kevin handle the tanker when it arrives, too? It's not scheduled to be here until late."

"Sure. I'll need the paperwork for the buyers, so I know how much to load into each tanker section."

"I'll leave it here on the desk for you."

"Okay. What else did you want to talk about?"

"The grapes. The weather has been in our favor so far, but it's not going to last. We're going to have to leave some on the vine." He tapped a few keys on the laptop and then studied whatever was on the screen. "I'm thinking we leave the Pinot Noir. What do you think? Is that the best choice?"

"You're asking me?" She had to have misheard. Her father would never have asked her opinion on anything, much less something as important as which grapes to sacrifice to the weather gods.

His smile was weak but dazzling, nonetheless. "Yes. You've been here throughout the growing season. If anyone knows these grapes, it's you. I was thinking the Pinots might rebound better than any of the others. Their sugar content is low. They could use another week to ten days on the vine. If this weather pattern clears, and we get enough dry days on the back end, they might survive. We'd have to go through and reposition every cluster to maximize the drying potential, but if it worked, not only would we save the Pinot crop, but we'd have the potential to produce a better product in the end."

"Have you forgotten that crop is sold?"

"No, but I think I have a solid argument for postponing delivery to the buyers. What do you think?"

She bit off a bite of bacon and chewed. She'd come to a similar conclusion last night regarding the harvest. They were going to have to leave grapes on the vine. That was a given. The easiest thing to do was write those off as a loss, especially since they'd been earmarked for another winery. Not delivering would equate to lost revenue, but it would be a minor loss compared to losing the entire harvest. "Why not leave the Cab Blancs?" That was a smaller crop and would minimize the financial loss.

"I checked their sugar content last night. They're ready to harvest today. If we leave them on the vine another week, they won't be good for anything."

"You tested sugar levels last night?"

He raised one eyebrow. "Did you think I'd play Russian Roulette with my livelihood? I need to sell this crop. I need the cash to finance the future of this vineyard. I'm not leaving anything to chance if I can help it."

"Leaving the Pinot Noirs on the vine isn't leaving anything to chance?"

"No. We stand a good chance of saving them after the storm. Everything else needs to be brought in today."

"If you've already decided, why did you ask my opinion?"

"Like I said, you know these grapes. Can we save the Pinots, or should I call the buyer and give them the bad news?"

She popped the last of her bacon into her mouth and chewed while she thought about her answer.

"I've got to have more coffee." Sean grabbed his mug. "I'll be back."

As soon as he was out of the room, Angellica dropped her forehead to the desktop and groaned. All of her preconceived thoughts about Sean Nightingale were going up in smoke. Playboy or not, he knew the wine business. Even in crisis mode, he'd taken the time to assess every aspect of the crop in order to make an informed decision. It would be easy to just harvest the rows in the order they were planted. Finish one row, move on to the next. The Pinots weren't the last ones to be harvested if they held to that plan. The Cab Blancs were.

"Fuck!" A firm hand landed on her shoulder. "Are you okay?"

Angellica sat up quickly, nearly bonking her head into Sean's nose. He sank to a knee beside her. "I'm…" Her gaze met his concerned one, and she couldn't look away, even when his eyes dropped to her lips and stayed there. "Fine," she said with a hushed breath.

"Angel," he breathed. His hand caressed the back of her neck, sending tingles down her spine. "This is such a bad idea."

No argument there, but her good sense seemed to have flown out the window. Anticipating the feel of his lips on hers, she leaned toward him ever so slightly.

"Sean. Where the hell are you?"

At the sound of Wade's voice in the hallway, Sean abruptly stood and stepped away from her. Angellica straightened, and their gazes met. For that brief moment before his brother appeared in the doorway, she saw the fire in Sean's eyes before he blinked, and it was gone. Cold reality cooled the heat on her cheeks. She grabbed her plate and made a break for the door. "I'll leave you to it," she said as Wade stepped aside to allow her to exit.

"Wait!" Sean called out. "What about the Pinot Noirs?"

"Leave them. We'll either save them or we won't," she called out as she fled toward the kitchen.

Holy moly! What had they done? It was the stress. It had to be. Sean Nightingale couldn't possibly find her attractive. Not in her present state. Hell, not even at her very best. But Heaven help her—he was the sexiest man she'd ever laid eyes on. But kissing him was out of the question. He was her boss, for crying out loud! And no matter what he said, she knew he wasn't going to stay around. Once he had the winery and vineyard running to his satisfaction, he'd be out of here. If she wanted to land the job of head vintner, she needed to keep her distance from the man in charge.

In her absence, the kitchen had filled with people who paid her no mind as she scooted out the back door to find a place to eat. She claimed a spot beneath the Jacaranda tree her mother had planted next to the patio. They'd picnicked many times under the violet spring canopy. A few purple blossoms clung to life, but soon would become collateral damage from the storm. One by one, members of the temporary work crew filed out and took seats around the outdoor tables that dotted the patio. Everyone looked a little worse for the wear, but they were up and moving, preparing for an even longer day than the previous one. Kevin exited the kitchen, his gaze sweeping the area until it landed on her. He smiled and wove through the nearly silent group until he reached her.

"Rosa said I'd find you out here. May I join you?"

She wasn't in the mood for company, but Kevin was a good friend. "Sure. The ground's hard, but the shade is nice." The temperature was rising quickly. They'd have to make sure everyone stayed hydrated today. The cheerleaders wouldn't be back until later in the day, so she'd need to assign someone else to pass out water bottles to the harvesters.

Kevin sat cross-legged with his back against the trunk of the tree. "This is nice," he said as he balanced a full plate on one knee. "What are we doing today?"

"I was hoping you could help me in the barn today. We need to crush the grapes that were harvested yesterday or we're going to run out of crates. And, we have a tanker coming this afternoon. We need to ship out as much as possible before the heavy rain hits." She motioned toward the hard-packed ground. "Once the driveway gets soaked, it won't support the weight of a full tanker. They'd get bogged down and be stuck until it dries out again."

"Yeah, I could see how that would be a problem." Kevin hung his head, letting the conversation die away.

Angellica finished her coffee, letting the awkward silence draw out. Kevin was a good friend, but he still had feelings for her she couldn't reciprocate. He'd made it plain yesterday, greeting her with a full-on kiss, that his feelings hadn't changed. She'd once thought they had something special, but as his feelings grew, hers hadn't. She'd eventually broken off their relationship, hoping he would move on and find someone who could return his love. But that hadn't happened, and though they'd remained friends, she probably shouldn't have called him to help. It might have given him false hope. Given what had almost happened between her and Sean a few minutes ago, she knew she wasn't going to change her mind about Kevin. "Kev. I'm sorry if asking for your help made you think I've changed my mind. Just to be clear, I haven't."

He held up his free hand. "Don't, Angellica. You don't have to say it. I was out of line yesterday. I was just so happy to see you, and I got carried away."

"I know. I thought as much, but I needed to be sure we agree. We're friends. That's all."

"We are. And I'm glad you felt like you could call on me to help. We were friends before we were anything else, and I'd like to think we'll always be friends."

Her smile was genuine as she reached out and squeezed his hand. "Always, Kev. I'm truly sorry it didn't work out between us. You know that. Right?"

"I do. I've been dating recently. No one special yet, but I have high hopes." He sipped his coffee. "How about you?"

She shook her head. "No. No one special." But as the words left her lips, an image of Sean Nightingale popped into her head. *Criminy.* What was she going to do?

CHAPTER TWENTY-TWO

This Kevin guy could be a problem. Sean discreetly watched the couple from the office window. Sipping his coffee, he noted every subtle shift in body language between the two. He wished he could see Angellica's face, but she had her back to the window. Kevin's expressions said quite enough. The man was in love with Angellica.

Shit. Right now, he had more urgent matters to attend to. If he didn't deliver the promised product, he'd go bankrupt.

If Wade hadn't needed the key to the tractor, Sean would have kissed her. It was too soon to start a physical relationship with Angellica. They barely knew one another.

Damn. It was hard to watch Angellica interact with Kevin. Seeing her reach out and take his hand in hers lit a blaze in Sean's gut. It was all he could do to keep from bounding out there and telling Kevin to keep his hands to himself.

He stepped away from the window. Kevin would be gone soon. After the grapes were in, there'd be no reason for him to hang around.

Sean checked the weather radar every ten minutes. The radar looked like a kindergartener had spilled paint on the map. A large red blob would be directly over them soon. He'd sent a cheerleader into town to purchase an air horn and several extra plastic tarps. His plan was to keep the harvesters picking grapes until the last minute. They'd made it through the daylight hours and had brought in more produce than he'd thought possible. The first tanker pulled out an hour ago, and a second one had just pulled up next to the barn where Angellica and Kevin operated the crusher like seasoned professionals. Some clouds had rolled in late in the afternoon, but so far, the rain held off. At his signal, the harvest would officially end, and the pickers would rush to cover the crates of harvested fruit.

He was repositioning one of the rented light standards when the first raindrop landed on his head. Lifting the air horn, he reluctantly pressed the button. The ear-piercing sound put an end to his first harvest. He helped the nearest workers to cover the crate at the end of their row, then sent them running to the barn. Some stayed to help with the crushing, but most of the locals headed home. Wade and the crew from New Jersey stayed overnight to help bring the last of the crates to the barn and help Rosa clean the kitchen. Sean saw them off the next morning.

Later that afternoon, Angellica shouted over the deafening sound of rain on the barn's metal roof. "We did it!" She pumped her arms in the air as the second tanker truck pulled onto the main road and disappeared from sight. After a long night and day of processing the grapes, Sean and Angellica were officially alone.

Sean smiled at her enthusiasm. "We had a lot of help, but yeah, we did it." He eyed the single IBC left behind. Two hundred fifty gallons of crushed Cabernet Sauvignon grapes. It wasn't much to work with, but it would have to do. "And we got to keep something for ourselves."

"Is that going to be enough?"

"It has to be." He faced the open barn doors. The storm was everything the weather forecasters said it would be. It had come ashore almost eighteen hours ago and brought the entire Pacific Ocean with it. Torrential downpours and heavy winds showed no signs of abating. Wade had called it a mini hurricane, and Sean couldn't disagree with his brother's assessment. They'd been fortunate to save as much of the crop as they had. He had his doubts about the Pinot Noir grapes still on the vine. Losing the sale of those grapes would hurt, but he'd survive without the additional income. He eyed the Cab Sav in the container. "I'll start the fermenting process tomorrow. I'm too tired to concentrate on anything right now, and there's no room for error."

Angellica joined him in the doorway. "It can wait. We need to get some rest."

"There's just one problem with that."

"What?"

He made a show of looking around the area. "No car. We're going to have to walk to the house."

"Not walk," Angellica said. A wicked smile broke across her face a split second before she sprinted into the rain. "Run!"

"Hey, wait for me!" Sean darted out the door. The ground was a muddy mess, and puddles had formed in the ruts the heavy tanker had dug into the soggy driveway. Dirty water splashed up with each step while rain soaked his clothes and slicked his hair into his eyes. He finally caught up with Angellica at the front door, where she'd stopped to kick off her muddy shoes and wring water from the long braid that ran down her back. When she turned to face him, his heart lodged in his throat. Water ran in rivulets down her smiling face, and laughter bubbled from her with each heaving breath she took. Her wet blouse clung to her figure and did nothing to hide the lace bra she wore underneath or her protruding nipples. With the outside temperature hovering in the mid-fifties, she had to be freezing.

"I won!" she said as she playfully shoved him on the shoulder, bringing his attention back to her face. "Loser has to build a fire."

Who needs a fucking fire? Another word out of her mouth, and he might spontaneously combust. His gaze locked with hers, and try as he might, he couldn't bank the heat overwhelming his body. He took a step closer. And another. Her smile morphed into parted lips that called out to be kissed.

He should back off. Should run back out into the rain until the cold brought sanity with it. She was his employee. Seducing her was all kinds of wrong, but at that moment, he didn't give a shit about anything but making her his. "I'll keep you warm." He took another step toward her.

"Sean?"

His name on her lips sent a fireball straight to his groin. Every cell in his body screamed for him to take what he wanted, but he'd never been that guy. He preferred his women willing and all in without coercion. He fingered a lock of hair that had escaped her braid and fallen over her shoulder. Her earthy scent captivated him in a way no expensive perfume ever had. Rain-soaked and mud-splattered, she was tantalizingly real. A vision sent from the heavens to tempt the devil inside him. "The next move is yours, Angel."

My move. Such a gentleman. But Angellica didn't want a gentleman any more than she wanted to be an angel. Not tonight. It had been a long time since she'd been attracted to a man, and it had never been like this. Overwhelming and all-consuming. She'd been shivering a moment ago, but Sean was so close she could feel the heat radiating off him in waves, drawing her in. A cool breeze found its way beneath the portico. Angellica shivered, whether from the cold or the scent of virile male mixed with rain, she didn't know. And didn't care. Another shiver racked her body. She recognized it for what it was—desire. Straightening to her full height, she leaned in, so her breasts brushed his damp shirt. He sucked in a ragged breath but remained still. What would it take to shatter his control? Rising to the tip of her toes, she wrapped both hands around the nape of his neck and tugged his face down until his lips hovered a fraction of an inch above her own. "I'm no angel," she whispered right before her lips met his.

He kissed her back, taking control of the kiss with all the expertise she expected from a player. Warm hands closed around her waist, lifting her. Her back slammed against the door, then his hands were on her ass. She wrapped her legs around him and held on as he greedily explored her body. When his fingers delved beneath the hem of her shorts, her breath caught in her lungs. Breaking the kiss, she dropped her head to his shoulder.

"Tell me to stop, and I will.," he growled.

God, his hands felt good on her bare skin. Surrounded by his strength and his scent, she wanted nothing more than to continue. To see where this could go. But she already knew the answer to that. Nowhere good. She let her feet drop to the ground but remained pressed up against his solid form. It would be so easy to take what she wanted, but tomorrow the sun would come out and shine its light on their insanity. Sensing her withdrawal, Sean placed his hands on the door as if he needed the support to remain standing. "I'm sorry—"

"Don't be," he interrupted. "You're in charge of your own destiny, and I respect that."

"Can we talk about this inside? I'm freezing." His body had cooled along with her ardor. He stepped back, and her hands dropped to his shoulders, then away.

Sean reached for the door handle. "Put on some dry clothes. I'll get a fire started."

Angellica raced up the stairs. Once inside her room, she pressed her back to the door and sank to the floor. Her teeth chattered, not from the cold but from the loss of Sean's heat. She shouldn't have kissed him. It was reckless and stupid, and proof beyond a doubt that she was falling for the man. None of that stopped her from wanting to do it again.

Taking her phone from her pocket, she hastily dialed a familiar number. Lexie answered on the second ring.

"Hey, girlfriend. Sorry I couldn't make it down there to help with the harvest. How did it go? Did you get it all in?"

Typical Lexie. Once she got started talking, it was hard to get a word in. "We got most of it, but I need your help with something else."

"Anything. You know I'm always here for you."

Angellica closed her eyes and rested the back of her head against the door. "I did something stupid."

"How stupid are we talking? Robbed a bank stupid or had a few too many at dinner, stupid?"

"I kissed my boss stupid?" She cringed just saying the words. "And I want to do it again, stupid?"

"You kissed the ass? Jelly. You've got some explaining to do."

"I know! Sean is an ass. Sometimes. But he also knows his way around a vineyard, and he knows wines." She didn't want to get into the man's plans to blend east and west coast vintages. That had nothing to do with her present dilemma. "He's sexy as hell, Lexie, and we were all wet—"

"Backup a second. How did you get wet?"

"It's still raining, and we had to run to the house. We were laughing, and wet, and cold, and then he was there looking sexy and smiling. God, he's got the greatest smile.

And his voice! Oh, my god. It sends tingles down my spine, Lex."

"Then he kissed you?"

She bit her fingernail. "I kissed him." Before Lexie could respond, Angellica barreled on. "I know. I know. It was stupid, and I realized it as soon as my lips touched his, which are awesome, by the way. And he knows how to kiss. God, does he know how to kiss. But I came to my senses and pushed him away. Sort of. Then I ran upstairs to change, and he said he'd start a fire—"

"Whoa! Back the wagon up! I thought you were living in the cottage."

"I was, but he said it wasn't safe and insisted I move back into the house."

"Where are you now? Where is he?"

"I'm in my old room and he's downstairs. I think."

"What do you think is going to happen if you go back down there?"

"I don't know," she whined, "but I want to find out. Talk me out of it. Please, Lexie?"

In the end, Angellica promised Lexie she wouldn't leave her room that night and that she would call if she felt herself wavering. It was the right decision. She knew it was, but it didn't stop her from reliving every second of their kiss and wishing things could be different between them.

CHAPTER TWENTY-THREE

Sean stood at his bedroom window and silently cursed the weather gods. Rain fell in sheets that obscured visibility and dampened everything, including his mood. Last night had been a disaster, and he had no one to blame but himself. He should have kept his distance from Angellica, but damn, she was everything he never knew he wanted in a woman.

Angellica was sitting at the kitchen island when he made it downstairs. A steaming cup of coffee and a muffin sat in front of her. She'd dressed for the workday in jeans and a UC Davis sweatshirt. Thick socks adorned her feet. After last night, he'd expected to see distance in her gaze, but her smile seemed genuine and welcoming. She really was an amazing woman. She could have any man she wanted, as well as a career in the wine industry.

"Morning." He slid a mug under the spout of the single-serve coffee maker and waited for it to dribble out a hot, caffeinated beverage. "It looks miserable out there."

"That's one word for it, I suppose." She sipped her

coffee, then set the mug back on the quartz countertop. "Looks like you'll have to ferment in the barn. It's too wet to move the IBC to the blending room. The tractor would sink in the mud."

Sean opened the plastic container their volunteer chefs had left behind and selected a cinnamon roll. He took a giant bite and chewed as the coffee dribbles slowed. He grabbed his mug and joined her at the island. "The blending room is a mess anyway. I'll add the yeast to the mash first, then I'll get to work on the blending room situation."

"I'll help. The sooner we get things squared away, the better."

He wasn't about to turn down her help, but he still owed her an apology. "About last night."

She held up a staying hand. "Nope. Do not apologize. If anyone's to blame for crossing the line, it's me. I shouldn't have kissed you."

"Please don't apologize for the kiss. I liked it. Too much, I'm afraid."

"You aren't mad?"

"Why would I be?" He took a fortifying sip of his coffee, then his gaze met hers. "I know we shouldn't enter into a physical relationship given our situation, but we're both adults. It's your call, though. I firmly believe in a woman's right to choose her own path."

She cocked her head to one side and studied him. "Who are you, and where did you come from?"

Sean shrugged. "I'm a Nightingale. We like our women to have a mind of their own. Makes things more interesting." *In bed and out.*

"Hmm." She pinched a piece off her muffin, popped into her mouth, and chewed. Sean couldn't take his eyes off her lips, nor could he forget how perfect they'd felt beneath his. "I need some time to think about this. Last night aside, I'm not usually an impulsive person."

"Neither am I." He took a bite of his cinnamon roll.

"Take your time. I'm not going anywhere."

"Are you sure about that? I know you said you were going to stay in California, but how do I know that's true?"

"You'll have to take my word for it, I guess. My family is important to me, Angellica. If they need me, I'll be there for them. Same as Wade was there for me this week. But California is my home now. I want to put down my roots here. Have a family of my own someday." *With you.* The revelation hit him with the force of a boulder rolling down a steep hill, knocking the wind out of him. Angellica was *the one*. Wade had said Sean would just know it when he found the woman he wanted to spend his life with, and he'd been right. He could see his future, clear as day. The two of them years from now, having breakfast in this very kitchen surrounded by little monsters. Three boys and a baby girl who looked just like her mother.

Sean's heart raced and his toes and fingers were numb as he stared into the coffee cooling in his mug. *I know. She's the one. We're going to create a family together.*

"Sean? Hey!" Someone nudged him in the shoulder, and he looked up into Angellica's concerned eyes. "Are you okay?"

"I'm," he searched for a suitable lie, "fine. Just tired."

"You should get some rest today."

He miraculously lifted the mug to his lips without dropping it and took another sip of coffee. The bitter liquid helped snap him out of his daydream, or whatever it was. They had work to do. Lots of it. Sitting around hallucinating wasn't going to cut it. She was right, though. He needed rest, but sleep would have to wait. "Since it's still raining, I think I'll work on the blending lab this morning. See if I can put it in some kind of order."

"I'll help. I'll meet you over there. I need to go to the cottage and get some work clothes."

Sean took a moment to assess the situation and decided there was no good way to go about putting the place to rights. The lab looked like a tornado hit it, but a solid day of hard work was exactly what he needed to get his mind off making babies—four of them—with Angellica. The delivery people hadn't bothered with organization. Boxes were everywhere. On tables. Under tables. Anywhere they'd fit. "One thing at a time," he whispered to the inanimate objects occupying every square inch of space. The outer door squeaked on its hinges. Help had arrived.

"What's the plan, boss?" Angellica said as she joined him in the cluttered lab. Mud caked her boots, and water dripped from a folded umbrella dangling from her hand. Sean's first inclination was to chastise her for making a mess, but then he remembered the task at hand and decided one more mess wasn't going to make a difference.

"If we stack all the boxes in one spot," he pointed to where one sat on the floor all by itself, "we can move the new tables to one side. That will give us room to pull out the old stuff. As soon as the storm passes, I'll have someone come and haul the old tables away. In the meantime, we'll cram as much of it as possible into the storeroom you cleaned out the other day."

"What about the testing equipment and glassware?"

"We'll set it aside for now. Once we get the boxes unpacked, we can use them to box up the old stuff. If you want to keep anything, stick a note on it or something."

"I see some things. You move boxes. I'll get some sticky notes from the office."

He resisted the urge to turn and watch her walk away. She was enough of a distraction as it was. He didn't need the image of her ass in those cutoff jean shorts to add to it.

It took several hours, but when they were through, the lab was a picture of modern functionality. Angellica had convinced him to keep an antique display case which she filled with vintage testing equipment, beakers, and pipettes. The old pieces served as a reminder of the winery's origins.

"What do you think?" he asked as they stood back to

admire their work.

"It looks like something out of a spaceship."

Sean chuckled. "It does, doesn't it?"

"I like it, though. I can't tell you how many times I told my dad we needed to bring this place into the twenty-first century."

"Why didn't he modernize?" They'd had the money. He'd seen the books and had them looked over by an accountant he trusted before he agreed to purchase the place.

"If there's one thing that's true about Tomas Capello, it's that he's old school. He believes in the old ways, sometimes to his own detriment."

"Your dad turned out some spectacular wines using that old equipment. There's something to be said for the old ways."

"Easy for you to say. Your family embraces change."

Sean shook his head. "You're wrong about that. Wade embraces change. My dad, not so much."

"But he updated his lab and sent you all this equipment."

"Wade's doing. Trust me. My dad is supportive, but Wade has fought him for every change he's made since he took over as CEO. It took years to convince dad to build the event center. Wade still sweats every earnings report, and the place has turned a profit every time. Dad's still chairman of the Board, and he's not one to hold his tongue about anything."

"It sounds like he and my dad would get along just fine."

He imagined the two older men together and decided she was right. "Yeah, the two of them probably would get along. Maybe they'll meet sometime."

"Maybe."

She didn't sound convinced, but he knew better. *They'll meet at our wedding.*

Sean checked the time on his phone. "It's getting late. We missed lunch." His stomach growled as if to emphasize his point. Rain still drummed down on the roof of the building. "I'll give you a ride back to the house, then we can get cleaned up and decide on what we want to do for dinner." He was all for going into town. The less time he spent alone in that house with Angellica, the better. It was one thing to ignore his desire for her when they were both sweating and covered with layers of dust. Sharing dinner all alone in a cozy house was another thing altogether. Temptation lurked around every corner and behind every door. And no matter what kind of future he saw for them, she wasn't there yet. No. He needed to take his time. Not force the issue. They'd be together for the rest of their lives if he didn't fuck up and scare her away.

"Rosa and her crew left a bunch of food. It'd be a shame to let it go to waste." She gathered up the rags they'd used and tossed them into a plastic trash bag. "I don't mind heating them up, if you don't mind eating them."

She had a point. They could probably exist for a month on all the leftovers in the refrigerator and freezer. He'd have to suck it up and behave like a gentleman. It wouldn't kill him. Maybe. "Works for me. Come on. I'll give you a ride to the house."

"What'll it be?" Angellica surveyed the contents of the refrigerator. "Looks like there's a stack of grilled burger patties," she paused to examine something, "a container of chicken salad and enough cold cuts and sliced cheese to make sandwiches for an army." Peeking around the open door, she asked, "Any of that sound good? There's other stuff, but it's buried underneath. We'll have to take some of this out to see what else is in there."

"I could go for a burger. We can pop the cooked patties in the microwave. Right?"

Angellica hauled a plastic bag out and dropped it on

the island. "Burgers it is. See if you can find the buns. I'll find the fixin's." Sean went in search of hamburger buns. From the pantry, he could hear his roomie rummaging around in the fridge. "Mustard? Ketchup? Please don't say mayonnaise. Every kind of cheese imaginable. Lettuce. Pickles?"

"Yes, to pickles. Mustard for me. The plain yellow stuff. If you see a tomato, I'll take one of those, too." The sound of bottles clinking on the soapstone countertop rang out. "Voila! Found a package of buns."

Returning from the walk-in pantry, Sean opened cabinets until he found plates. The two of them worked together microwaving the meat patties, then assembling burgers. As they sat down at the island, Sean couldn't help thinking how domestic the scene appeared. If he didn't know better, he'd think the two of them had worked together countless times. Just like the harvest, and today, cleaning and organizing the blending lab, they expected each other's moves and didn't get in the way.

"Thanks for this," he said, popping a potato chip into his mouth and chewing. "I didn't really want to go into town tonight. Between this constant rain and my sore muscles, all I can think about is getting a good night's sleep." A few other things had crossed his mind, but he really was exhausted. He was self-aware enough to admit he wanted Angellica in his bed, but he also wanted to bring his A game when he did. He wanted to take his time with her, not shag her fast, then fall into an exhausted sleep.

"You and me both, boss man." She took a sip of wine—a recent Nightingale vintage Wade had brought with him as a gift to his brother. "You did good. With the harvest, I mean. You handled the situation like a pro."

"I told you. It wasn't my first rodeo. Remind me sometime to tell you about Hurricane Irene. Nightingales narrowly escaped catastrophic loss that year. So yeah, I've had a little experience with inconvenient storms."

"Experience pays off, I guess." She finished the last of her wine, then stood, taking her empty plate to the sink. After rinsing and placing her plate in the dishwasher, she rested her hips against the counter and crossed her arms over her midsection and surveyed the mess they'd made. "It's times like these that I wish I could afford a housekeeper. Rosa made cooking look easy and kept the kitchen clean at the same time. All we did was warm leftovers, and the place is a wreck."

Sean scanned the cluttered island, then laughed. "You're right. But we made the mess together, so we'll clean it up together." He stood and took his plate to the sink. Once it was in the dishwasher, he gathered an armful of condiment bottles and began stuffing them into the fridge.

"You don't have to do that." Angellica rescued the mustard container from the crook of his elbow. "I can clean this up." Her fingers brushed his bare arm, sending a tingle of electricity zinging through his body. She must have felt it too, because she froze, her fingers clasping the yellow plastic bottle still nestled close to his body. Her scent, enhanced by a day of hot, sweaty work, tickled his nostrils. Her clothes were dirty, her hair disheveled, and yet…he wanted her. Wanted her naked. Wanted to immerse himself in her. Wanted to taste her. Wanted her more than he wanted his next breath. He snapped his gaze from her hand to her face. When it landed on her lips, they parted. That simple movement that said nothing but everything at the same time transfixed him. He forced his gaze to her eyes. Her heated look fueled the fire already blazing inside him. His pulse roared past his ears, drowning out the rain drumming the pavement outside the kitchen. They were alone within an invisible bubble. No one would know if they crossed the boundary between employer and employee. Just this once. *It's inevitable.*

"We shouldn't," he whispered, unwilling to break the

thin walls of their bubble with fully voiced reason.
"Probably not."

CHAPTER TWENTY-FOUR

Time stood still. Their breaths mingled in the vacuum surrounding them. *I've lost my mind.* It was the only explanation for what she was about to do. With Sean Nightingale, of all people! But she was through denying the obvious. She wanted him. Any way she could have him. She'd never been attracted to a dirty, sweaty man before, but this one? Holy cow, the scruff on his jaw, the disheveled hair he'd run his dirty hands through countless times that day, the tangy scent of dried sweat and virile male? They combined like some kind of witch's brew that set her libido on fire. Then there was the way he looked at her, like he was starving, and she was the only meal he wanted. She was sick of denying her attraction to the man. Sick of fighting it, too.

Her heartbeat rocketed and her lips parted as her lungs fought for air.

"Ask me, Angel. Ask me to kiss you." The words were whisper-soft, but she heard the need behind them. Damn Sean for being a gentleman when what she needed was a man who took what he wanted, but she wasn't going to let that stand in her way.

"Kiss m—"

His lips, powerful and insistent, crashed against hers. When his tongue met hers, her head spun, and her legs gave out. Sean hauled her limp body up against his sturdy one, holding her securely while his lips and tongue said everything about what he wanted.

The mustard container hit the floor with a heavy thud. Her feet left the floor at the same time the refrigerator door slammed shut. Her ass met the cold soapstone counter. Her legs instinctively spread, and Sean's imposing form filled the space. Angellica clung to his broad shoulders as their kiss morphed from hot to just plain carnal. It was everything she'd expected the night before after their mad dash through the rain, and they'd kissed on the porch. She'd looked like a drowned rat then. Her hair dripped down her back. Her clothes were soaked and clinging to her dirt-streaked body. She'd felt the mud splatters drying on her legs, and she'd been cold. So cold—until the heat of Sean's body had set her on fire. Then Sean came to his senses and backed away. It had taken her a moment longer, but upstairs in the shower, she'd thought maybe he had been right to end things when he did.

Only her body didn't agree. And that bit of physical contact had sparked a fire inside her only Sean Nightingale could extinguish.

Suddenly, he wrenched his lips free of hers, but before she could protest, they were back, tracing a line along her jaw and down the slope of her neck. Angellica arched into his touch, silently pleading for more. More of his touch. More of everything.

He nibbled at her earlobe, then flicked it with his tongue. Angellica let out an unladylike groan and dug her nails into his scalp. His chuckle tickled her ear. "Like that, Angel?" He did it again, and she turned her head and returned the favor. His big body shuddered as he buried his face in the crook of her neck. "Fuck me," he breathed.

"Yes. Fuck me," she whispered in his ear, causing his body to quake again.

They remained wrapped up in each other for the space of several heartbeats. Angellica prayed he wasn't about to change his mind. Sean raised his head and his gaze met hers. His lips quirked up on one side. "That wasn't a question, Angel, but who am I to deny a woman what she wants?"

"You'd be a fool, Mr. Nightingale."

"Need I remind you I'm a genius?"

That. Again? Though he'd said it with a smirk on his devilishly handsome face this time. "But what do you know about female anatomy, genius?"

"I aced all my biology classes."

She didn't doubt he'd done that *and* aced his continuing studies outside the classroom, but she wasn't about to bring up his playboy days. Not when she was moments away from finding out for herself what he could do in bed. She met his smirk with one of her own. "Show me."

His expression shifted to serious. His gaze met and held hers. "This is a bad idea, Angel. An all-around bad idea, but for the life of me, I can't talk myself out of this."

She nodded. "Don't." She slid her hands down to cup his jaw, her thumbs stroking his cheeks. "We're adults. We can do casual and still work together."

"You're sure?"

"Positive."

The air between them grew heavy, and Angellica found it hard to breathe. Sean's gaze lingered on her eyes, then shifted to her lips. "I'm going to kiss every inch of you." The deep timbre of his voice sent a shiver down her spine. "Starting right here." He slid his hand across her nape, lifting her hair out of the way. Applying gentle pressure to her skull, he tilted her head down and placed his lips on the back of her neck. It was a simple kiss, but the manner of delivery was sensual and the most erotic thing she'd ever experienced. Angellica melted as he made good on his promise, kissing every inch of that side of her neck, then angling her to do the same to the other side. She was a quivering mess. Putty in his hands. Fingers tangled in her hair, he drew her head back, exposing the front of her neck. He kissed his way to the center, then to the open collar of her shirt. And down.

Holy mother of God. The man was thorough. He didn't miss a single inch of skin. And it was driving her mad. "Please," she begged.

"Nope," he said, barely raising his lips from her skin while he deftly undid the top two buttons of her shirt. "Trust me. The prelude will only make the main event better."

At the rate he was destroying her brain cells, she wouldn't live to experience the main event. "You're killing me, Sean."

His lips curved into a smile against her skin. "Nice way to go, isn't it?"

She had to hand him that. "Yes, but I'd hate to miss the main event."

He jerked his head up. His gaze met hers. "Trust me?"

"You know I do."

"Then let me do this my way. I promise you won't miss a thing."

The sincerity in that sexy voice of his convinced her. "Okay, but if I expire before the main event, I'll come back and haunt you until the end of time."

"Consider me suitably warned. Now, can I take this blouse off you? It's hampering access and I need to brush up on my anatomy lessons."

"I thought you said you aced your exams."

"I did, but every test is different. In order to do well,

one must study the subject in great detail. Learn everything there is to know. Then, and only then, can the student show their mastery of the subject."

He was already a master of the subject, but who was she to stand in the way of higher education? "By all means, Mr. Nightingale. You have my permission to remove any article of clothing that stands between you and your studies."

His eyes twinkled as he reached for the next button on her blouse. "You won't regret this, Angel. I give you my solemn word." His gaze held hers until the last button popped free, revealing her torso. With patience she didn't have, he brushed the edges of the blouse to the sides. It was then that she remembered what she'd put on that morning and attempted to cover herself.

"Uh uh," he said, pinning her hands to the counter beside her hips.

"I'm sorry. It's a work bra. I mean…I have nice ones, but I didn't think…"

"Anyone would see it?"

She nodded. "Yeah. This is…unexpected."

"It's sexy as hell," he said. "Lace is overrated." His gaze locked on her sensible cotton clad breasts. "May I touch?"

"Yes, please."

He grasped her left breast, his touch searing her skin through the layers of fabric as he massaged the mound gently at first, then harder. She moaned and arched into his touch. "You like that?"

"God, yes!"

He squeezed her other breast, and she cried out at the stimulation. "You'll tell me if it's too much." It was a statement, not a question. "Let's get this off." He swept her shirt off her shoulders and, with the skill of a pro, flicked the back clasp of her bra open, baring her to his gaze. He grasped both her wrists and planted her hands, palm down, behind her on the counter. She felt a little uncomfortable with her breasts on display, but then she noticed the fire in his eyes, and her embarrassment went up in flames.

"You're so fucking beautiful, Angel. I'm going to eat you up."

He touched her breasts, kneading and squeezing. As before, he started out gently and increased the pressure, gauging her reaction as he went. "So fucking beautiful," he repeated right before he bent and sucked her right nipple into his mouth.

Angellica cried out as he drew hard on one nipple while simultaneously pinching and pulling on the other. No one had ever handled her with such expertise, and God help her; she loved it. Reveling in the sensations coursing through her body, she dropped her head back and let him feast on her body. He'd lavished attention on both breasts, then began a slow exploration of the rest of her. He kissed his way across her ribcage, then along the waistband of her shorts, before slowly making his way back up to nuzzle at her breasts. Frustrated, she grabbed her breast and offered it up to him.

"Not the way this works, sweetheart." Removing her hand, he intertwined his fingers with hers, then moved both their hands back to the counter. He did the same with her other hand. Then he went right back to toying with her breasts. Every suckle. Every swipe of his tongue. Every scrape of his teeth fed her need until she thought she might come just from this. It had never happened before, but she'd never been with anyone as experienced as Sean Nightingale, either. The man knew what he was doing. That was for sure.

Desperate for more physical contact with him, she tried to extricate her right hand from where he had it pinned to the countertop. He squeezed her hand tighter, then let go of both her hands. Before she could reach for him, he held up a staying hand. "Not yet, sweetheart. I told you I was going to eat you up, and I've only had the appetizer." He slipped his fingers beneath the waistband of her shorts. "It's time for the main course, don't you think?"

"Yes," she breathed. *God, yes.*

He worked the snap, then the zipper on her shorts with enviable efficiency. Angellica lifted her hips, allowing him to slide her shorts and panties down to her ankles. He yanked them free of her feet and sent them sailing over his shoulder. At any other time, the move might have been humorous, but his expression as he gazed at the juncture of her legs put a different spin on his actions. He wasn't trying to be funny. He just wanted the garments out of his way. Fast. So he could get to what he really wanted. Her.

"Spread 'em, sweetheart. Let me see you."

The command in his deep voice sent a thrill skittering across her skin and set her core on fire. For a fleeting second, she thought she should be embarrassed at exposing herself to him so willingly—and on the kitchen island, no less, but his next command shattered her inhibitions into a million pieces. She wanted this man more than she wanted her dignity.

"Now, Angellica."

She complied, opening her legs so he could step between them again.

"More, sweetheart." His hands were suddenly at the back of her knees, lifting her legs and spreading them wide. "That's better," he said, placing her bare feet on the edge of the counter. "Lie back if you need to. This is going to take some time."

Hands on the back of her thighs, he bent and placed his mouth on her tender flesh. Sensation rocketed through her body, and her arms refused to support her any longer. She collapsed onto the countertop and tried to remember the basics—like breathing. As he'd done with her breasts, he alternated the use of his lips, teeth, and tongue, leaving her grasping for sanity one minute and begging for release the next. He was relentless. Driving her up the peak, then letting her crash back down, unfulfilled, only to push her back up the hill again. He teased her over and over until she moved her hips, rocking her core against his face in a futile effort to bring about the climax she so desperately needed.

CHAPTER TWENTY-FIVE

Fucking hell. Angellica Capello was going to be the death of him. The lyrics to an old song flitted through his brain as he devoured her pussy. *Wonderland. Your body's Wonderland.* Hers wasn't the first pussy he'd tasted, not by a long shot, but it was the first he thought he could become addicted to. Christ, she tasted better than any wine he'd ever had, and he'd sampled the best the world offered.

And her tits. They were real. And she had curves in all the right places. He'd dated rail-thin fashion models with no tits to speak of, and he'd dated lingerie models with enormous fake tits and curves as hard and sculpted as granite. There was absolutely nothing fake about Angellica's body. He suspected there wasn't anything fake about her at all. And that intrigued him more than anything as she rocked against him, chasing her orgasm.

Sean listened for her verbal cues, fine-tuning his strategy to focus on the methods and actions that gave her the most pleasure but never pushing her over. Her frustration was apparent in the way she fucked his face, but he knew that delaying her pleasure would make the climax that much more powerful in the long run. She'd thank him later.

Making a woman come was a challenge he gratefully accepted and took seriously. He gave her the flat of his tongue, licking her like a lollipop, then went back to focus on her tender, swollen clit. He'd taken her to the peak several times, then backed off. She'd cursed him more than once because of it, too. But he was aching, needed to be inside her soon or he was going to come in his pants. He hadn't done that since he was a teenager watching porn on his laptop, and he had no intention of doing it again. Not when Wonderland was his for the taking.

Sean flicked her clit with his tongue. Once. Twice. Then he latched onto the engorged bud with his lips and sucked hard. Angellica shouted out as she came, her hips bucking, her pussy flooding. As she settled back to Earth, Sean lapped up her come like the desperate man he was.

When she stilled, he placed a kiss on each of her thighs and then stood to look down at her body, sprawled across the island like the timeless beauty she was. He'd never seen anything more beautiful in his life. Her cheeks were flushed, and her eyelids closed as small puffs of air escaped her parted lips. She lay with one arm stretched over her head, the other lay to her side, her hand resting on her stomach. Thighs spread; her legs dangled limply over the edge of the counter.

Sean dug his wallet out of his back pocket and said a silent thank you to the universe when he located the small packet. He tossed the wallet on the counter, where it landed with a *plop* that startled Angellica. Her eyes popped open. "What?" she asked, frantically glancing around.

"Sorry. I was just getting a condom out of my wallet." He held up the neat square and raised an eyebrow. "Ready for round two?"

Her hand slid to the juncture of her thighs, where she

rubbed her pussy. Sean's gaze locked on the erotic tableau and refused to move. "I'm aching, Sean." Her hand delved deep, and he thought he saw her middle finger dip inside where his tongue had been a few minutes ago. He licked his lips, remembering the way she tasted. "Make the ache go away. Please?"

He could finger fuck her. Make her come again, but seeing her finger herself was more than he could bear. "I'm aching too, Angel. I need you."

Her shoulders rose off the counter as she dipped her middle finger deeper. "I need you, too. Hurry. Please?"

He had his shorts and underwear off, and his cock sheathed in record time. Then he grabbed her hips and repositioned her so her ass hung off the edge. "Let me in, sweetheart. I need to be inside you. Right now."

Angellica obligingly moved her hand. Sean lined his cock up and then with a powerful thrust of his hips, buried his cock to the hilt inside her. Angellica gasped at the sudden invasion of her body while Sean closed his eyes and dropped his head back, trying desperately to keep from coming right away. He didn't dare move. Not yet anyway. "Christ," he breathed. "You feel good. So. Fucking. Good." It was an understatement if he'd ever heard one, but it was all his lust-addled brain could come up with.

Her inner muscles clenched around him, and he saw stars. "Don't. Don't do that or this is going to be over before it even starts."

He felt her fingers around the base of his cock, and he instinctively grabbed her wrist. His gaze met hers. "What are you doing?"

"Feeling you. Inside me. God, you're so big." She struggled to rise on one elbow so she could see the point where their bodies joined. "I can't see. Help me sit up?"

No one had ever wanted to watch him fuck. He wasn't opposed to it. Hell, it *was* hot. He couldn't deny that. Somehow, her interest helped him back away from the edge. With one hand braced on the counter for support, he placed the other on her back and lifted her so she could see everything. She stared at her fingers as she stroked his cock and her stretched lips. He watched in wonder, too. Seeing them joined like this felt almost…sacred.

"You're perfect," he said. "Like you were made to take me, and only me." He glanced away to see her gaze still fixated on their union.

"I know. I feel it too." Then she looked up, capturing his gaze. "I want this to last."

He didn't know if she meant the moment or their relationship. Not that they really had a relationship. But he wanted everything with her. He desperately needed to move inside her, but doing so would mean a quick end, and he never wanted to leave her. "Me either," he whispered. Then he bent and took her lips in a kiss that he meant to be sweet, but that turned carnal in an instant. She still had one hand between them, stroking their joined flesh. Sean reached between them and thumbed her clit. Angellica moaned against his lips. He was determined not to come until she did. Once that happened, all bets were off.

It didn't take long. After just a few strokes of her clit, her body tensed. He increased the pressure on her nub, and she came hard, her inner walls spasming around his cock, milking him. She broke their kiss and dropped her head back. The guttural sounds coming from her throat sent a lightning bolt to his groin. His balls drew up tight. He lost control of his own orgasm, as white-hot pleasure jettisoned him into outer space.

Their bodies joined in the most intimate of ways; he couldn't distinguish her heartbeat from his as they clung to each other in the aftermath. He never wanted to let her go. Never wanted to break the connection between them. He belonged inside her. He belonged *to* her. He needed to fuck her again. And again. And again. Once would never be enough.

It took him a few seconds to realize the ringing in his ears wasn't from the sex. It was from his phone that he'd tossed on the countertop when he was digging through his pockets for his wallet. It took a few more seconds before he realized it was the ring tone he'd assigned to his older brother.

The discordant sound crash-landed Sean back on Earth, and reality set in. As good as the sex had felt for him, it couldn't have been that good for her. He'd never come that way before—without moving inside the woman even once. *Shit.* She had to think he was a one-pump chump when that was as far from the truth as it could be. He prided himself on satisfying the women he slept with. Angellica challenged him from the beginning. He had to admit, as he remained buried deep inside her, his cock spent yet still hard—being with her was nothing like any of his prior experiences. And that scared him more than the prospect of being unable to go the distance. There were drugs for premature ejaculation, but there wasn't a medication in the known world to keep a man from feeling the way he did at that moment. Like he'd simultaneously disappointed Angellica while still having the best sex of his life.

The phone stopped ringing, then immediately started up again. If Wade redialed instead of leaving a message, then it had to be important.

Mortified at coming like an over-stimulated teenager, and terrified to see the disappointment on her face, Sean refused to meet her gaze. Instead, he uttered the only excuse he could think of for leaving her. "I've got to get that." Anchoring the condom, he hastily withdrew from Angellica's sweet sheath. The retreat reminded him what he'd missed out on, what they'd both missed out on, but the last thing he wanted to talk about with Angellica was what had just happened. Until he understood it himself, he'd best stay far, far away from Angellica Capello.

Sean hastily disposed of the condom, then yanked his shorts and underwear up. Remembering his manners, he picked Angellica's clothes off the floor and tossed them onto the counter beside her. The ringtone stopped, then started up again. *Fuck.* He spotted the device behind him on the counter next to the refrigerator. The screen came to life showing a photo of Wade he'd snapped a couple of months ago on the night his brother had proposed to Serenity. Wade had made a complete fool out of himself that night. It was a good memory. Hitting the answer call button, he brought the phone to his ear. "What the hell is so important, asshole? I was in the middle of something."

He'd never admit how grateful he was for the excuse to escape having any kind of discussion with Angellica about what had just happened.

"It's Dad, asshole. He's been shot."

A pit opened up in his stomach and his knees went weak. He grabbed the edge of the counter for support. "What happened? Is he going to be okay?"

"Ian called me. He said Dad had gone to the bank to deposit the receipts from the tasting room when someone took a couple of shots at him. He got hit twice, and another bullet grazed the side of his head. Dad's in surgery. Mom's at the hospital. Uncle Stephen is with her. Ian's leading the investigation."

He broke into a run, headed for the staircase to pack a bag. "How bad is it?"

"Ian said he saw Dad before they loaded him into the ambulance, and he said it was as bad as anything he'd ever seen. "

Sean's feet felt like cement blocks weighing him down as he ran through the house. "I'll be on the next plane out."

"We *are* the next plane out. Get your ass to the French Valley Airport. We're about to leave San Diego. We'll pick you up there."

Sean hit the top of the stairs and ran down the hall to

his room. "I thought you left this morning."

"Everyone was exhausted, so we decided to stay tonight and go home tomorrow. Obviously, change of plans."

He randomly tossed clothes into a carryon bag he'd logged thousands of hours of flight time with. "Packing now. I'll be there as soon as I can."

"Don't be reckless. Our pilot says we'll have a tailwind all the way there. We'll make up the lost time in the air."

Sean zipped the case shut. "On my way."

CHAPTER TWENTY-SIX

Angellica clutched the wad of clothes to her chest as her head spun. What had just happened? Sean moved away from her like his ass was on fire, causing a cold draft that made her body temperature nosedive from sub-tropic to arctic in a split second. Barely registering Sean's conversation, she realized something was terribly wrong. She wasn't talking about the way he'd gone distant the instant he'd come—*they'd come*, she amended. She'd never had a simultaneous orgasm with a guy before and would have liked to have talked about it. Not a big discussion, but a little recognition that the sex had been beyond fabulous. He'd rocked her world, and she hoped she'd done the same for him, but clearly not. He couldn't get away from her fast enough.

In his defense, the phone kept ringing and ringing. Nobody did that these days. If they didn't get an answer, they left a voicemail or tried back later.

She continued to eavesdrop as she separated her clothes, then pulled her shirt on. The bra could wait. The basics were all she needed. Just enough to preserve some shred of dignity while she listened in on what was certainly a private conversation.

"How bad is it?"

Angellica pretended to be interested in the buttons on her blouse. Sean stirred up another draft as he sped past her.

"I'll be on the next plane out."

What? She hopped off the counter and quickly stepped into her shorts. *He's leaving? Now?* Hastily zipping up her shorts, she followed Sean, stopping at the foot of the stairs as he sprinted toward his room at the end of the upstairs hallway.

Angellica plopped down on the bottom tread and waited. He'd have to come back this way, and she'd find out what was going on then. She didn't have long to wait. In a matter of minutes, Sean ran down the stairs, a backpack slung over one shoulder. It was get out of his way or get mowed over. Angellica moved. "Where are you going?"

"Home," he said, grabbing his keys off the table beside the door. "Take care of the place for me."

"When will you be back?" she yelled at his back as he climbed into his car. "What about the wine?"

Sean paused, one foot on the driveway, the other inside the vehicle. A mask of indecision marred his perfect face. He shook his head. "I don't know. Do something with it. I don't care."

Angellica stood in the open doorway until his taillights disappeared into the night. Gone. He was really gone. With no indication of when he would return—if ever. Her whole body shook as a sudden chill formed in the pit of her stomach. How many times had she wished Sean would just go away and leave her alone? Dozens? Hundreds was more like it, but that was before she knew what it was like to be with him. Truly *with* him. Some might say they'd just had sex, but she knew better. She'd had "just sex," and it had never been as intense as what they'd shared. When he was inside her, she felt…complete. Like he was a part of her she never known was missing. When he pulled away, the emptiness inside her became a physical ache.

Barefoot and still clutching her bra and panties, Angellica glanced around the foyer. The table and vase from her mother's painting remained where they'd been all her life. The staircase. The wallpaper. The original wood flooring and elaborate chandelier were just as she remembered them. Nothing was different. Yet everything had changed.

She wasn't the same person she'd been that morning or even an hour ago. Her reality had shifted in a way she couldn't comprehend. All she knew was that she'd never be the same. Her body felt different. Empty yet full at the same time. She'd experienced something she'd never known was possible, and now that was a part of her. *Sean* was a part of her. And whether he realized it or not, he'd taken a part of her with him. That, and the ache between her legs, explained the dichotomy of feelings swirling around in her head, and her heart, if she was being honest with herself. But being honest meant labeling all those feelings, and she was too tired and too confused to unpack all that baggage.

"Maybe tomorrow," she mumbled to herself as she trudged up the stairs to her room, where, exhausted, she fell face-first onto the bed.

Still dressed in yesterday's clothes, Angellica leaned heavily against the kitchen doorjamb as she rubbed the sleep from her eyes. The kitchen was every bit the disaster she thought it would be. Dirty dishes littered one end of the island, while much of the soapstone countertop was mysteriously clear of clutter. A mental image of how she must have looked as she lay sprawled naked on the island popped into her mind. The image brought back the strange feelings she'd experienced the night before. "Too early for this," she muttered, and, pushing away from the doorjamb, headed straight for the coffeemaker. Her bare toes collided with something that skittered across the floor. Pain signals rocketed to her already throbbing head as she bent to pick up the mustard container that had started everything.

"Coffee first," she said to the yellow plastic container before she plopped it down on the counter. "I'll deal with everything after coffee."

Once the pod was in and the life-saving liquid was dribbling into a mug, Angellica turned and braced her hips against the countertop. Her gaze landed on the bare spot on the island, and once again, images of how she must have looked to Sean from his angle made her groan with embarrassment. He'd seen it all. Every little detail. Up close and very personal. Her breasts and her lady parts throbbed just thinking about the expertise with which he'd made her come. Twice.

She gave her head a tiny shake. "Not before coffee." She spun on her heels just as the last drops plopped into the mug. She usually liked a little cream in her coffee, but today was an exception. Taking her first sip of the restorative brew, she sighed in relief. Straight up was the way to go today. Mainlining caffeine was the only way she was going to make it through the morning. The next few sips helped clear her head enough to wander back upstairs. Before heading to the shower, she texted Lexie.

"Need to see you. 9-1-1. Can you take off work? How soon can you be here?"

Not waiting for a response, Angellica headed for the shower. The hot water felt good on her skin, and as she washed, she remembered what she'd done the night before. How Sean had filled her, and how empty she felt when he'd retreated from her body. She didn't need to close her eyes to recall the feel of him inside her. It was indelibly stamped upon her memory. Based on Sean's reaction in the immediate aftermath, she hoped the longing she felt to experience those sensations again would fade with time.

Donning the old robe she'd left behind when she moved to the cottage, she stepped out of the ensuite and came to an abrupt halt at the sight of someone lying on her bed. "Holy shit, Lexie!"

Her best friend sat up and dropped her feet to the floor. Her smile was anything but apologetic for scaring Angellica. "You texted 9-1-1. Did you expect me to drag my feet? And I was hoping there would be some leftover pastries."

"How did you get here so fast?"

"We were supposed to shoot outdoors today but there was a mudslide, so change of plans. I came down last night to see my parents. I let myself in." She waved her keys in the air. "I was afraid the ogre had changed the locks, but apparently, he hasn't. Where is he, anyway? Is he here?"

"He's in New Jersey. He left last night."

"Oh? Do tell."

"It's a long story, best told over breakfast." Angellica crossed to the nightstand, where she'd left her coffee. Picking up the cup, she frowned. "What the hell? You drank my coffee?"

"It was getting cold. You should thank me for saving you from having to drink it."

Angellica shook her head as she glanced at the old alarm clock she hadn't bothered to take to the cottage. "Wow. Sorry. I didn't think I was in there that long. Let me throw some clothes on and we can raid the kitchen." She opened a dresser drawer and selected a pair of sweatpants and an old UC Davis t-shirt. Another drawer provided a pair of gray panties that used to be white and a bra that had lost its support long ago. "To answer your question, there are enough pastries down there to feed half of Temecula."

"I knew I came to the right place. Hurry up. I'm

starving, and whatever this emergency is, I don't want to hear it on an empty stomach."

CHAPTER TWENTY-SEVEN

"Give me a minute." Angellica returned to the bathroom, where she dressed and tamed her wet hair into a high ponytail. She'd been avoiding thinking about last night, but seeing her reflection in the mirror and the pain in her eyes brought it all back. *Don't cry. Don't cry.* Tears wouldn't solve anything. *If* there was anything to solve.

"Hurry up! I'm starving."

Lexie's plea snapped Angellica back to reality. "Hold your horses. I'm coming." She dabbed at the corners of her eyes with a tissue, then smoothed a couple of disobedient strands of hair into place. Her best friend stood as Angellica stepped out of the bathroom.

"It's about time. What took you so long?"

"Give me a break, will you? I had a traumatic night. I'm entitled to a little breakdown."

Lexie wrapped her in a big hug. "Of course you are. You're also entitled to a decadent breakfast and all the chocolate you can eat."

Angellica smiled at her friend's affirmation. She could

always count on Lexie to understand and not pass judgement. "I'm starving. Let's get something to eat and I'll tell you everything."

"You screwed him, didn't you?" Angellica's silence was all the answer she needed. "You lasted less than twenty-four hours, Jelly!"

"Please. No lectures."

"What happened to keeping your distance from the man? To not getting involved with your boss?"

"It's complicated."

"Well, I want to know everything. And by that, I mean. Every. Detail."

Angellica rolled her eyes, then led the way to the kitchen. She waved an arm toward the island as they entered the room. "Stay away from there. We can eat at the table."

"Why would I—oh! You did it on the island? Please tell me you did it on the island." Lexie's voice vibrated with excitement.

Angellica carried a box of pastries to the small table in the breakfast nook as memories flooded in from the night before. "Yes. We did it on the island. I haven't scrubbed it down yet."

Her friend slid into a chair and grabbed a croissant from the open box. She tore a piece off the pastry and stuffed it into her mouth. Her eyes twinkled with merriment. "Spill, girlfriend. I want details. Were you both naked? Were condiments involved? Please tell me he made you come. He did, didn't he?"

Angellica grabbed a croissant and bit off a piece as she crossed to the counter and popped a pod into the coffeemaker. She talked as she grabbed a mug and placed it under the spout, then pushed the button to start the machine. "I was naked. He wasn't. No condiments were used, but he used a condom, and yes. He made me come. Twice."

Lexie sighed and pretended to swoon. "Twice? So, what's the problem? Why text me a 9-1-1?"

"Because the second time was…different. We sort of came at the same time, but…" She placed a full mug in front of Lexie, then returned to the counter to make herself another cup.

"But, what? Coming at the same time is awesome. You have to really be in tune with each other for that to happen."

Angellica filled her mouth with a generous bite of croissant and watched the coffee drip into her mug. She thought about how to describe what had happened with Sean. How he hadn't moved inside her, but came hard, if she was a judge of such a thing. Taking her full cup to the table, she sat across from her friend. "Have you ever had a guy come inside you without moving?"

Lexie froze in place, her croissant halfway to her lips. She blinked once. Twice. She placed the pastry on the table. "Hon, you better start at the beginning and don't leave anything out."

Angellica took a fortifying sip of coffee, then told Lexie everything from the time they quit work until Sean drove off like a mountain lion was chasing his ass. "And that was the last I saw of him."

"He hasn't called this morning?"

She shook her head. "Nope."

"You sure he didn't say anything after he came?"

"Not a word unless you count him saying that he had to answer his phone. In his defense, it was ringing off the hook."

"And you're sure he didn't," she made an in-and-out gesture, "at all?"

Angellica nodded, then sipped at her coffee that had gotten cold during the telling of her story. "I was high on endorphins, but not that high. When a guy like him is inside you, you'd know if he moved."

Lexie stuffed another bite of pastry in her mouth and chewed. Her gaze remained fixed on Angellica, as if she was hoping an answer would flash across her forehead. She swallowed, then got up and went to the refrigerator. She came back with a bottle of orange juice. "You got any champs around here? It's not too early to drink mimosas."

Angellica located a bottle in the wine rack underneath the island. It would have been better chilled, but neither one cared. The women worked together with practiced efficiency. Once seated at the table, they clinked glasses, then took healthy sips of the breakfast cocktail.

Lexie finally broke the silence that had fallen around them. "He's that big, huh?"

"Yeah, and thorough. He made sure I was ready before…"

"A considerate lover," Lexie nodded, understanding where she was going with her comment. "And you came first?"

"Yeah. The next thing I knew he was, you know, pulsing inside me, and he had this look on his face. Sort of surprised and blissful at the same time. I don't think he meant to come. Then his phone started ringing, and he ignored it the first couple of times."

"Wait. The first couple of times?"

"Uh, huh. It quit ringing, then it would start right back up again. Like someone really wanted to speak with him instead of leaving a voicemail."

"Did he say anything while this was happening?"

"While he was coming?"

"No. After. While the phone was ringing."

Angellica shook her head. "No. Not a word. It was…different from anything I've ever experienced. We just stared at each other, and I swear we were connecting on some other level. Not just physical. It was like…"

"Like?"

"This is going to sound crazy, but for me, it felt

mystical. He was still hard, and I was more than satisfied. I'd already come twice, but I never wanted him to pull out of me. It was like he belonged there. When he pulled out, I felt like he'd taken a part of me with him. I ached to have him back inside me. I still ache for him."

Lexie drained her mimosa, then poured herself another one. After taking a sip of the newly filled glass, she summed up their conversation in one word. "Damn."

Angellica nodded and finished her drink. Earlier, she'd noted the pain in her eyes, and wondered at the source. Now she knew. Every molecule in her body craved Sean. She needed him. Physically needed him.

"Who was on the phone?"

"Huh?"

"You said his phone was ringing. That's why he pulled out. Who was it?"

"Oh. It was Wade—his brother—I think. He didn't really say, but I figured from the one side of the conversation I heard, it must have been him."

"Why didn't he leave a voice message instead of calling repeatedly?"

"Sean didn't say, but I gathered that someone, maybe their younger brother Ian, had been injured or something. Ian's in law enforcement. I overheard him ask if he was going to be okay."

"That doesn't sound good. And it would explain why he beat it out of here like his ass was on fire."

Angellica agreed. "It does, and I want to give him the benefit of the doubt for the way he just left me sitting there and took off into the night without a word. I even asked him what to do about the wine and he said to do something with it. He didn't care. That right there tells me it was something serious with Ian or someone else in his family because Sean has been all about the wine ever since he got here. That's why he bought Capello's. To just blow if off like this doesn't make any sense."

"Like blowing you off does?"

"No. It doesn't. I still don't get why he came so quick."

"Maybe that's why he spent so much time making you come—twice. He's got no stamina once he gets inside a girl."

Lexie's explanation made sense, but she hadn't been there. Angellica had been, and she'd bet her special blend in the cellar that Sean had been more surprised than she was when he came. Judging from his expression, the moment had meant something to him, like it had meant something to her. But he'd run off before they could talk about what had happened, much less try it again.

"I don't think that's it, Lex. He was stunned, just like I was. If his phone hadn't interrupted us, I think he would have gone another round. Or two." She stared at her almost empty crystal glass. "Maybe I'm reading more into it than was there, for him anyway."

"I just don't want you to get your heart broken, Jelly."

"I know, and thank you for that." She reached out, and the two locked hands together across the table. "You've always got my back, and I've got yours."

CHAPTER TWENTY-EIGHT

"What's with you?" Wade asked as Sean paced the aisle for what felt like the millionth time since they'd taken off from the regional airport two hours ago. "Sit down. You're making everyone else nervous."

Sean plopped down in his seat across from his brother. A glance around the small private plane confirmed everyone else was asleep, reading, or watching a movie on their phone. Only Wade had been watching Sean's every move. "By everyone else, you mean you."

His brother shrugged. "So, sue me. You're my brother and your behavior is worrying me. Dad's going to be alright. And even if he isn't, wearing the aisle carpet out isn't going to change anything."

"It's not that. I mean, it is. I'm worried sick about dad and want to find out who did this to him, but I've got something else on my mind. You got a minute? I need to pick your brain."

"If it's about that blend you want to make, you need to wait and talk to dad."

He prayed he'd have a chance to talk to his dad about the blending process, but that wasn't what had him pacing like a caged animal. "It doesn't have anything to do with my plans to blend wines from both coasts. It's something personal."

Wade raised an eyebrow. "Okay. I'm listening."

"Not here. Can we go to the bedroom?" There was a small bedroom at the back of the plane for long, overnight trips. No one had taken advantage of it on this trip, probably because they were all worried about his dad. A couple of them had fallen asleep in their seats, but he knew it was a restless sleep.

His brother unfastened his seat belt and stood, giving Sean a concerned look as he stepped into the aisle. "Let's go," he said. Sean followed him to the back of the plane.

Once inside the tiny room, Wade took a seat on the bed while Sean leaned his shoulders against the closed door. "Promise me everything that's discussed inside this room will stay here."

The look of concern on his brother's face deepened. "Okay, but if it's something the rest of the family needs to know, I'm not going to keep that promise."

"It's nothing anyone needs to know. Not even you. But I'm dying here. I've got to tell someone."

Wade was on his feet faster than a Jack-in-the-box. "You're dying? What the hell, Sean?"

Sean held both hands up like stop signs. "Whoa. Whoa there. I'm not sick, but I am dying. I screwed up big time with Angellica, and it's killing me. I don't know what to do."

His brother collapsed back onto the bed. With his arms spread wide, he stared at the ceiling. "You fucking moron. You scared me half to death. If I wasn't so relieved, I'd kill you myself."

"Would you cut out the dramatics, asshole? I need your advice."

"About what? If you screwed up, send some flowers, and apologize. What else is there to do?"

"It's not the kind of thing flowers will fix."

Wade sat up; his interest piqued. "What kind of thing is it?"

Sean sat beside his brother, more so he didn't have to look him in the eye when he asked the question. "Promise me you'll never say a word about this for the rest of your life."

"Already been there, dude. You know how this works."

"Okay, but I will murder you if you breathe a word of this to anyone. And that includes Serenity."

Wade made a show of zipping his lips and throwing away the key. Sean nodded, took a deep breath, and spilled his guts. "Have you ever come inside a woman—without moving? I mean, not even once? Just put it in, then come?"

Raucous laughter filled the tiny room as Wade flopped back on the bed, rolling around laughing. Sean jumped to his feet and grabbed a pillow off the bed, and pummeled his brother. "Shut the fuck up. I'm serious. I need to know if it's normal."

"You're serious?" Wade sat up, all traces of humor gone from his face. "You're telling me you didn't last long enough to satisfy her?" He shook his head. "That's seriously messed up, bro."

"I *know* it's messed up. I *told* you it was messed up. But it wasn't like that. She'd already come once." He wiggled his fingers. "Magic lips and hands, you know?"

"TMI, brother. TMI."

"Would you shut up and listen?" He waited until Wade agreed before continuing. "I made sure she came, then I put on a raincoat, and we were kissing, and I was touching her." He wiggled his fingers again. "Then I went in for the main event, if you get my drift, and I touch her one more time, and she's coming again. And fuck me, her orgasm sends me over the edge, too. I couldn't breathe, man. But something happened to me. I don't know how to explain it, but I didn't want to move. Didn't want to pull out. Ever. Best fuck I've ever had, bar none, and I didn't do a fucking thing to make it happen. It was all her. And…us."

Silence hung in the air between them for what seemed like forever before Wade finally spoke. "Did either of you say anything? Talk about it?"

Sean shook his head. "No. You fucking called, and the phone wouldn't quit ringing, and I knew I had to answer it, so I pulled out and grabbed the phone. Next thing I know, I'm running out the door with my suitcase and she's standing in the doorway looking well-fucked and asking me what to do with the wine." He hung his head between his knees. "I'm so fucked."

"Took the words right out of my mouth." Wade shifted on the bed. "You think she thinks you're a one-pump chump?"

"What else would she think?"

"I don't know. Maybe she felt whatever it was you felt, too?"

"Whatever that was. There aren't words to describe it. It was like time stood still or some shit like that. I was still hard and *needed* to move inside her, but the damn phone…"

"Yeah, I get I ruined the moment for you, but I didn't know, and even if I had known, Dad getting shot trumps your sex life every time."

"We were staring at each other. Not moving. It was the weirdest thing, but I think I could have fucked her all night and all the next day and it still wouldn't have been enough."

"Promise you won't bite my head off if I say something?"

"Depends on what it is."

"Do you think you could be in love with her?"

Sean's heart beat took off like a racehorse on steroids. Hadn't he himself thought she could be the elusive *one*? His soulmate? "You've lost your mind. I barely know the woman." He stood and tried to pace in the confines of the room, but gave up and pressed his back to the door instead. "Why would you ask something like that?"

"Because that's how I felt about Serenity the first time."

Sean covered his ears and scrunched his eyes shut. "TMI, brother."

"This entire conversation is TMI, if you haven't noticed. Have you even considered that she might mean more to you than a casual and convenient hookup?"

"She's my employee, for god's sake, Wade. Not only have I crossed a big fat line, but I can't fix it because she probably won't let me near her ever again. Not after the way I," he made air quotes, "performed." He wiped a hand over his face. "What am I going to do?"

Wade slapped his thighs. "Send her flowers, dude. Then call her and apologize. Did you even tell her why you were leaving, or does she think she scared you away?"

"Seriously? You think she thinks I left because of her?"

"I think it's a possibility. If you want a second chance with her, you'd better make sure she knows the real reason you tore out of there. By the way. What did you tell her to do with the wine?"

"What?"

"The wine. You said she asked you what to do with the wine. What did you tell her?"

"I have no idea. All I could think about was getting to the airport as fast as I could."

"There's your excuse to call her." Wade stood and stretched. "When you get her on the phone, tell her you love her and that you're sorry you left the way you did. Let her know you want to finish what you started as soon as you get back."

"Are you insane? I'm not telling her I love her."

"Suit yourself. But you're in deep shit here, bro. If I were you, I'd figure out what that feeling was that you were talking about. The one you couldn't name? I think that's the key to all of this."

Wade shoved Sean out of the way and exited the room, leaving Sean there with more questions than he'd had before.

CHAPTER TWENTY-NINE

"How is he?" Sean embraced his brother Ian, who met his older brothers in the hospital lobby.

"Not much has changed since I spoke to you before." Ian embraced his oldest brother, then stepped back. Hands on his hips, he looked tired and worried. "Like I said earlier, he made it through the surgery. Doc said he was lucky no major blood vessels were hit. They removed two small caliber slugs and had to repair a section of his small intestine and remove his appendix. The concern now is infection. They're keeping him sedated and pumping him full of antibiotics. Mom's a wreck. She'll be glad to see both of you."

"Any word on who did this?"

"Yeah. It was Shillingford. Caught everything on the security cameras outside the bank."

"The banker?"

"Former banker. He got fired a few weeks ago. Someone ratted him out to his superiors, and they launched an investigation into his shady foreclosure practices. Best guess is he thinks you," he pointed at Wade, "are the one responsible."

"Then why didn't he come after me? Why Dad?"

"He saw Dad get out of your Range Rover and assumed he was you. From a distance, the mistake is believable. You're about the same height and you have the same mannerisms. Dad was wearing a Nightingale polo shirt and chinos, not your usual suit, so Shillingford missed that detail."

Wade let out a heavy breath and shook his head. "Why was Dad driving my vehicle?"

"That old truck of his was in the shop for new brake pads. You were out of town, so he took your car."

"Shit. This is all my fault, then."

Ian placed a hand on Wade's shoulder. "No. It's not. We all know you weren't the one to contact Shillingford's bosses. Besides, the blame rests solely on Shillingford. He's scum and his dirty deeds finally caught up with him."

Sean caught Ian's attention. "So, Shillingford really was working a shady deal to steal the Granger farm out from under Serenity and her dad?"

"Yeah. And it wasn't his first time doing something like that. That place on the other side of town? Where the big box store is now? He foreclosed on the Walker family so fast they didn't have a chance to save their home. Then he sold the land to the giant retail group and pocketed a huge finder's fee." He used air quotes on the finder's fee part. "All of it was illegal as all get out. The Walkers are suing the bank and the retailer, and they'll win. They won't get their land back, but they'll have enough money to buy land somewhere else and start over."

"Any idea who squealed on him?"

"I have an idea, but no proof. Whoever did it, despite what happened to Dad, did the town a service. We don't need scum like Shillingford holding the purse strings."

"You're right about that," Sean said. "So, what do we

do now?"

"We get Dad well," Ian said. "Doc said he's going to be on bed rest for at least a month."

"Shit." Wade rubbed both hands over his face. "We've got hundreds of barrels of wine from this year's harvest fermenting and more that need to be bottled."

Sean didn't even think about it. His decision was the only logical one. "I'll take care of it. All I've got back in California is one IBC container fermenting. Angellica can take care of that. I'll stay here and keep things running until Dad is back on his feet."

Wade gave him a questioning look, but Sean shook his head. "Who else is going to take over for Dad? You? Ian?"

"Uncle Stephen might be able to," Wade said, though his tone said otherwise.

"He's got his hands full preparing the vineyard for winter. It's me or nobody. The wine is already fermented. We don't have time to hunt up a temporary vintner. We'll lose this year's entire harvest."

"He's right," Ian jumped into the conversation. "I might not know the first thing about what Dad, and Sean do, but I know this time of year is critical."

"Then it's settled. I'll stay and take care of the winery. Wade will do whatever he does. What was that again?" Sean said, trying to inject a bit of levity into an otherwise gloomy conversation.

"Fuck you." Wade punched Sean in the arm. "Don't think you're going to get a paycheck for this."

"Never crossed my mind," Sean said, truthfully. "Let's go see Mom. Are we allowed to see Dad?"

Ian nodded. "Yeah. He's still in the ICU, but the doctor said you guys could go in as long as you keep it down and don't disturb the other patients."

The three brothers took the elevator up to the ICU unit on the top floor. Ian led the way to the nurses' station, where he introduced his brothers to the caregivers on duty.

Moments later, Sean and Wade entered their dad's room.

The first thing Sean noticed was how pale his dad looked. Then he noted the various tubes and monitors keeping tabs on his father's vitals. He'd had hours to prepare for this moment, but as he watched his dad's chest rise and fall, he knew nothing could have prepared him for this. "Sean. Wade." His mother rose and embraced them both like they were still toddlers. "I'm so glad you're here."

"Couldn't keep us away," Sean said. "How's he doing?"

"Doc says he's going to be okay. It's going to be a long haul, though."

Sean stepped up to his dad's bedside and peered down at the man he'd admired his entire life. "We'll get him through this."

His mother caught one of his hands in hers and squeezed it. "I know. He's going to need all of you to step up."

Wade stood on the opposite side of the bed. "We've already discussed that, Mom. Sean's going to stay and oversee the winery until Dad is back on his feet. I'll keep doing what I do, and Ian will make sure they put the bastard who did this away for a very long time."

"What about your vineyard?" she asked Sean. "Who's going to run it?"

"I have someone. She's been running the place for the last three years. A few more months won't hurt."

"That's good." She nodded. "But you let me know if you need to go back. We'll figure something out. I can do a lot more than just HR, you know. It's been a while, but I used to help with the blending." She placed her free hand on his dad's. "Paul always said I'd make an excellent vintner, but I was more useful in the office, so I concentrated on that part of the business."

Sean shared a mystified look with his brother. "You helped with the blends? When was this?"

"When Wade was little. Admittedly, it's been a while, but I still consult with your dad now and then when he can't decide which iteration to go with. So, if you need another opinion, just ask."

His mother's history in the blending room immediately made him think of Angellica and her insistence that she was going to be part of the blending process. Not that he'd have much of a choice in the coming months. He needed to be here, which left the small amount of wine he had fermented in California, not to mention all the wine Wade had shipped out to him sitting there. His gaze met Wade's once again. His brother raised one eyebrow, questioning Sean's thoughts. Sean shook his head. This wasn't the place to discuss his situation with Angellica Capello or his newly acquired vineyard. "Thanks, Mom. If Dad trusts your palette, then I do, too."

Wade offered to sit with the elder Nightingale, so Sean drove his mother home to get some rest. As soon as he turned down the long drive leading to the house, he felt the weight of responsibility descend upon his shoulders. As the head of the marketing department, he'd felt it before, but not like this. Selling the product was one thing. Being entirely responsible for the development of said product was different. Misjudging the appeal of a blend could cost the family millions in lost revenue and damage the brand's reputation in the marketplace.

As if she sensed Sean's reticence, his mom reached over and placed a hand on his arm. "You can do this, Sean. Dad will tell you himself when he can, but he trusts your judgment."

"Does he?" His dad had initially been the most vocal about his move to California. Sending the lab equipment was a nice gesture, but one that wouldn't have happened if Wade hadn't orchestrated the remodel of their dad's lab.

"How can you doubt that? Honey, he's always been in your corner. Of all our boys, you're the only one who inherited the discerning palette necessary to make fine wines. You don't think your dad sees that?"

Sean sighed as he braked to a stop in the wide area next to the garage. Staring out at the vineyard stretching to the horizon, he shook his head. "I don't know, Mom. He never let me have any input into the development of the wine. He'd make sure I was familiar with each vintage, but that was after it was bottled, and only so I could speak knowledgeably with the buyers."

"How do you think he realized you had the gift of a winemaker? It was through those tastings. Think about it, Sean. He never told you what flavor notes to expect. He let you experience them for yourself. Remember? He'd give you a glass, and then he'd ask you to describe it. He'd come in after every one of those sessions, beaming. He was so proud of you. He'd go on and on about how you picked up the most subtle notes and how you were the real deal—a Nightingale, through and through."

"Then why was he so dead set against me buying the Capello vineyard?"

"Because you're the future of Nightingale Wines. Who else is going to take over when he retires? Wade? Ian?"

She had a point, but so did he. "The new vineyard *is* the future of Nightingale's, Mom. We're losing market share every year. If we don't adapt to the changing market, we'll end up selling grape juice to our competitors in a few years."

"Your dad knows that, but he can't help thinking that you're abandoning your family and turning your back on your heritage."

"I'm not, Mom. I promise you I'm not. I'm trying to ensure Nightingales will be there to hand down to another generation. I don't know how to make Dad see that."

"He will, Sean. He will. Give him time."

Sean's eyes filled with tears. "We almost lost him, Mom."

"I know. Believe me, I know, but he's still with us, and there's plenty of time for you to show your father that you're the legacy he believes you to be."

Sean felt the weight of generations, past and present, on his shoulders. "I'll try, Mom. I promise I'll try."

"That's all I ask, son." She reached for the door handle. "Now, I need a hot shower, a cup of tea, and a nap. In that order."

Sean joined her outside the car. "Go ahead. Get your shower. I'll fix us some tea, then while you're resting, I'll go check out the new equipment in the blending lab."

CHAPTER THIRTY

Angellica hadn't heard a word from Sean since he'd told her he didn't care what she did with the wine he'd left for her to ferment over three weeks ago. Through a wine blogger she followed, she'd found out about his dad's close brush with death. Word was that Paul Nightingale would be okay, but that he would be out of the blending lab for an extended period. His son, Sean Nightingale, was rumored to be at the helm now. The wine world was full of speculation about this year's vintage under the unproven Nightingale offspring. Had he inherited the palette that had made Nightingale's one of the premier American wines for over two hundred years? Or would the brand suffer the fate of others who had lost their vintner and wither into obscurity?

Angellica scrolled through the latest blog post, which featured a photo of Sean in a tuxedo with a supermodel on his arm. She hadn't seen that one before, which probably meant he'd slid right back into his old life. "So much for making California his home," she muttered to the computer screen.

"What did you say?" Lexie asked from the kitchen doorway. Angellica's best friend had the weekend off and had come to visit. They'd spent the previous evening eating ice cream and binge-watching Sandra Bullock movies.

"Nothing." Angellica carefully shut the laptop, hoping her childhood friend wouldn't question her further. If she never spoke of Sean Nightingale again, she'd be a happy camper. In the weeks since he'd been gone, she'd cried a million tears, and thoughts of that last evening with him had played in her dreams until she dreaded closing her eyes. *It's time to get over him. Time to move on.* Which meant looking for a new job and finding a place to live. "Just looking at the job postings." It wasn't a complete lie. She'd started out surfing the wine industry association site's help-wanted section. Returning to the front page of the site, an article about the troubles that had befallen Nightingale Winery in New Jersey. That led her down the proverbial rabbit hole. But she wasn't going to let Sean ruin the day. She'd given the memory of him enough of her time already.

"Did you find anything?"

"Nope. But all isn't lost. Yet. If I can't find anything by the end of the year, I'll start looking for a retail job. I hate starting out in sales, but that might be the only way to get my foot in the door."

Lexie opened the refrigerator. The leftover pastries from the harvest were long gone, so she set out a carton of eggs and a package of breakfast sausage links. "Orange juice?" She held the plastic container up for Angellica to see.

"Sure." Angellica pulled a mixing bowl from the cabinet and set it beside the egg carton. After breaking the first egg into the bowl, she asked, "What do you want to do today?"

"How about we go down to San Diego? I think the

Padres are in town. We could catch a game. Baseball players have the best butts." Lexie laughed as she hip-checked Angellica. "Afterward, we can bar hop in the Gaslamp. The area will be crawling with single guys."

"I don't know." She dragged out the last syllable.

"Come on, Jelly. You need to get out of the house. Heck, you need to leave the property. There's a whole wide world out there. You can't sit here pining away for the jerk. What if he never comes back?"

"He's not coming back, but besides a couple of part-time high school kids, I'm the only person on the payroll. There's a lot to be done."

Lexie put a hand on Angellica's arm, stopping her before she cracked another egg on the rim of the bowl. "This isn't your vineyard anymore, Jelly. None of this is your responsibility. Sean Nightingale is just another celebrity who bit off more than he could chew. One of these days, he's going to realize that and either sell to someone else or hire a stranger to come in and run the place for him. At best, he's always going to be an absentee owner. There's no reason for you to be breaking your back to keep this place running."

Angellica thought about her secret blend with a pang of regret. Everything Lexie said was right. She knew it in her heart, but she couldn't help hoping she could score an interview for a position in a blending lab. Somewhere. The barrel hidden away in the cellar was her ticket to a new life. One where she was respected. One where she could put her talents and her years of education to work. "I hear you, but until I find a job, I can't afford to go anywhere. I need to save as much as possible to afford a security deposit on an apartment. I know I can't continue to live here forever. I get it. It's time to move on. I just want to find the right position."

"I'll help you with the money, Jell. I'm doing great. The show's been good to me, and we're already locked in for at least two more seasons."

"That's fabulous!" She was genuinely happy for her friend. She'd worked hard to earn her position on the production team, and she knew her experience would open all kinds of doors for her when the show finally shut down. Whenever that would be. It was one of the most popular shows on TV, and it seemed their audience grew every season. "But I can't take your money, Lex. Don't worry about me. I'm far from destitute, but I don't want to stretch myself too thin."

Lex found a skillet and arranged sausage patties in it. "You always were the most stubborn person I'd ever met. But I hear you. You want to do this on your own, but just know I'm there for you. Anytime. Always." They worked side-by-side preparing breakfast. After plating the meal, they sat at the small table in the breakfast nook. "So, if we aren't going to San Diego today, what are we doing?" Lexie asked as she speared a bite of sausage.

Angellica shrugged. "I need to test the barrels in the cellar. The oldest vintage needs to be bottled soon. I guess I need to contact Sean and see what he wants to do about that. We'll need to order bottles, labels, and corks." She chewed a bite of egg and then washed it down with orange juice. "I need to call and schedule the mobile bottling truck to come out—if we're going to bottle this year."

"I'm all for testing the barrels."

Angellica rolled her eyes. "It's not day drinking, Lex. All I need is a tiny sample to determine if it's still good. All the barrels should be fine, but if one isn't, we'll mark it and go on to the next."

"Are you going to call Sean?"

"After I test the barrels. I'll need facts and figures for that conversation."

"What if he doesn't want to bottle this year?"

"Then he's more of an idiot than I thought."

They finished their meal and then cleaned the kitchen

before going to the cellar. Lexie had been there before, but only to satisfy her curiosity. Today was different, as they had a job to do. Angellica showed her how to withdraw a sample, then taught her how to evaluate it based on several simple factors. Basically, if it hadn't turned to vinegar, it was going to be bottled. They worked through the oldest vintage quickly. Angellica was surprised that none of the barrels had been compromised. It was approaching lunchtime when they finished cleaning the equipment they'd used. Tired, they sat in the newly cleaned office on the ground floor of the building to rest.

"I'm hungry," Lexie complained.

"Why don't you go into town and pick us up some burgers and fries while I call the boss man?"

"In and Out Burger?"

"Absolutely. Get my usual and a chocolate shake."

"God, a chocolate shake sounds good." Lexie pushed out of the chair she'd sunk into. "Okay. I'm going, but don't let Nightingale give you any shit. It's a business call. Nothing else."

"Right." Angellica attempted a smile at her friend's pep talk. "Just the facts, ma'am." She waited until she heard Lexie's car rumble down the driveway before slipping her phone from her pocket. Pulling up Sean's contact information, her finger hovered over the call button as she braced herself for hearing his voice. She thought his voice might just be the sexiest thing about the man, and he'd cornered the market on sexy. Shaking the unwelcome thoughts from her head, she pressed the call button, then placed the phone on the desk and activated the speaker function. Wringing her hands in her lap, she listened while the phone rang. And rang. And rang.

CHAPTER THIRTY-ONE

"Are you going to answer that?"

Sean jumped at the sound of his brother's voice and jerked his gaze away from the phone ringing on the counter beside him. "No. I don't think so." He glanced back at the device just as the ringing stopped. *Thank God.* He breathed a sigh of relief, and his shoulders dropped. Angellica had him twisted up in knots. The last thing he wanted to do was talk to her. Hearing her voice would be a kick to the gut and would surely have him on the next flight back to California. As it was, concentrating on his job here was a monumental task. Every time he closed his eyes, he saw Angellica's face, heard the sounds she made when he pleasured her and envisioned doing it over and over again. *If only I could.*

He glanced back at Wade. "I'm busy. What do you want?"

"Sen wants you to come to dinner with us tonight."

Sean raised an eyebrow. "Who's cooking?"

His brother guffawed. "Not my fiancée, that's for sure.

I was thinking we could go into the city. It's been a long time since we've done anything special. What say you? Want to come along?"

"I don't want to be a third wheel."

"It's just dinner. Not a date. We'll eat, walk around a bit, then come home. It'll do all of us good to get out of town for a few hours."

He wasn't wrong about that. They'd all been sticking close to home since their dad had been shot in front of the bank a few weeks ago. He was finally out of the hospital but had been moved to a rehabilitation facility where he had around-the-clock care until he could take care of himself. "Okay, but nowhere fancy. All I brought with me were T-shirts and jeans."

"Gotcha covered, bro. You can borrow one of my suits." Wade clapped him on the back, then hustled out of the blending room so fast Sean didn't have a chance to argue with him. The brothers were close enough to the same build and height that borrowing clothes from his brother wouldn't be a problem. What was a problem was dressing up in the first place. Part of the allure of living in California was the laid-back lifestyle. He hadn't had a suit on since moving to the Golden State. The closest he'd come was a dress shirt and slacks, and that had been for a meeting with his new bankers. As soon as he'd gotten back to the vineyard, he'd put on shorts and a T-shirt and swapped his Italian loafers for hiking boots.

Decked out in one of Wade's designer suits, Sean stuffed his hands in his pockets and strolled down the busy sidewalk a step behind his brother and his fiancée. Once upon a time, he'd loved New York City. Loved the lights, the noise, and the rush of people. Loved the nightlife. Maybe he was getting old, but all it did was annoy him now. He'd awoken before dawn that morning with another dream about Angellica fresh in his mind, and he'd been going full blast ever since. Other than the phone call he'd ignored, he'd stayed so busy with the blends he was working on that he hadn't thought about Angellica more than a million times. No matter what he was doing, thoughts of her were always swimming in the back of his mind, ready to resurface at the slightest break in brain activity. Like now.

Sean pulled his phone from his pocket and activated the screen. Why hadn't she left a voicemail? Surely, if something was wrong, she would have left a message. Right? Right. So, if there wasn't anything wrong, why had she called? Had she wanted to hear his voice as much as he wanted to hear hers? Did dreams of him keep her awake at night and haunt her thoughts during the day? He was so caught up in his own head that he failed to notice Wade and Sen had come to a stop. Sean barreled into his brother, almost knocking him into the woman they'd stopped to talk to.

"Hey! Watch what you're doing," Wade admonished. "Are you crazy? Put your phone away. They call that distracted walking, you know."

After one more look to see if he'd missed a voicemail from Angellica, Sean pocketed his phone and turned his attention to his brother. "Sorry. I thought I heard it ding." Wade smirked at Sean's lame excuse. The asshole. "Why'd you stop?"

"We're here." Serenity waved a hand at the elegant door to her right. He knew the place. It was hellaciously expensive and exactly the sort of place he brought his A-list dates when he was living a playboy lifestyle. He stifled a groan as his future sister-in-law and former best friend continued to drive the speeding train down the track. "And this is Sheila. She's a friend of mine from the party planning firm I worked for before I moved back home. She's going to join us for dinner."

A spark of rage ignited in his gut, but being the gentleman his mother raised him to be, Sean plastered a fake smile on his face and offered Sheila his hand. "Nice to meet you. I'm Wade's brother, Sean." *I'm going to kill them both. With my bare hands.*

"Oh, I know who you are," the woman gushed. Was she blushing? "Sen talked about you all the time when we worked together. Sean this, and Sean that." She giggled. *Giggled.* "I never dreamed I'd actually get to meet you, much less have dinner with you. I follow you on Snapogram."

Shit. He hadn't shut the social media account down, figuring he might need it in the future to promote the new blends and his west coast winery. He hadn't posted to it in over a month and had no plans to anytime soon.

"Shall we go in?" Serinty asked, causing Sean to shift his gaze to her. If looks could kill, she'd be melting into the sidewalk right about now. She pretended she didn't know exactly what he was thinking and smiled her innocent, I'm not up to anything smile. "Our table should be ready."

"I'm starving," Wade interjected as he reached for the door handle. "Ladies." He ushered the women forward.

Sean closed the distance between them. As he brushed past his brother, he murmured low so only Wade could hear him. "I'm going to kill you."

The evening was pure torture. Sean had never met a more annoying woman than Sheila. He hated the way she tapped her index finger on the side of her wineglass. He hated the way she giggled at everything. He hated she asked if the wine Wade ordered was Nightingale wine. He hated she pointed out every celebrity in the place, and there were plenty of them. A few even stopped by the table to say hello to Sean. He would have given his right kidney to leave with any of them, but he was stuck. Trapped in exactly the scenario he'd left behind when he bought the Capello Vineyard and moved to California.

Thinking about his new home brought to mind the woman he'd left behind there. He shot his brother a look that couldn't be mistaken for anything but murderous. Wade smirked and lifted his glass in a silent toast. The bastard had done this on purpose. And it worked. *Damn it.* Sean glared at his brother. "Okay. You made your point, asshole." Scooting his chair back, he glanced at the women. "If you'll excuse me, I have an important call to make. I'll be back shortly." Or not. It would serve his brother right to be stuck with the giggling idiot for the rest of the evening.

Leaning against a lamppost listening to Angellica's phone ring, Sean missed phone booths. He could use a little privacy, but short of renting a hotel room, there was none to be had on the city streets. *Come on. Come on.* He held the phone away from his ear, checking the timestamp. Given the time difference, it was still relatively early there. Angellica should still be awake. Now that he'd called her, he was eager to hear her voice.

"Hello?" an unfamiliar female voice answered.

"Angellica?"

"She's busy right now. Can I take a message?"

"Who are you?" Yeah, he realized that came out sounding hostile. But damn it, he'd finally accepted that he needed to hear Angellica's voice and apologize for running out on her the way he did—and other things. "Put Angellica on the phone."

"Sorry. No can do, Mr. Nightingale."

Sean waited for her to say something else, but all he heard was silence. Pulling the phone away from his ear, he stared at the home screen. "She hung up on me!" What the actual fuck? Who was this woman, and what right did she have to screen Angellica's calls? Sean hit redial, and after the first ring, the call went to voicemail. "Fuck!" he screamed at his phone. A couple walking past gave him a wide berth. The guy even looked over his shoulder to make sure the weird man yelling obscenities hadn't followed them.

Collapsing against the lamppost, Sean ran his free hand

over his face as he dealt with the disappointment stabbing at his chest. Or was it fear? Where had this woman come from? It didn't escape his notice that she hadn't given him her name. Did Angellica even know her? She'd called him by name, but she could have gotten that off the caller ID. Had some random psycho invaded the vineyard and done something to Angellica? *Fuck!* He shouldn't have left her there alone. Anyone could have come onto the property when she was outside and done who knew what to her. Should he call the police? What did Ian call that? A wellness check? How long would it take for someone to get out there? Did they make those things a priority, or did they send someone when they had nothing else to do?

He was staring at his phone when it rang. *Wade.* The evening was getting better and better. He answered right before it went to voicemail. "What?"

"Where are you? Are you done with the call?"

"I'm outside, and no, I haven't talked to her yet."

"Why the hell not? Quit being an idiot and make the call."

"I made the call, not that it's any of your business. Some woman I don't know answered and told me Angellica was busy and couldn't come to the phone. Then she hung up on me. I called back, and it went straight to voicemail."

Wade dropped into his I mean business voice. "Who was it? Did you recognize her voice?"

"I have no idea. She didn't give her name."

"Could she be one of her friends from college? One who came out to help with the harvest?"

"I met all of them, and no, I don't think it was anyone I've met."

"Send me Angellica's number. Let me call."

That was a good idea. His name wouldn't come up in the caller ID. If that woman was a friend of Angellica's that he hadn't met, she wouldn't have any reason to keep

Angellica from talking to Wade. "Okay, but if that woman answers, do *not* tell her your name. I guarantee she'll hang up on you."

"Maybe Serenity should make the call. Another woman might be less threatening. She could say she's calling about a problem with a shipment or something."

"This late in the day? It's earlier there than it is here, but it's still way past business hours."

"Give me the phone." He heard Serenity in the background and could imagine her grabbing the phone. A second later, her voice came through loud and clear. "What's going on, Sean? Where are you?"

He told her the same thing he'd told Wade, ending with the suggestion that she make the call.

"I've never talked to Angellica. How would I know if it's her I'm talking to or some other random woman?"

"If someone comes on the line and says they're Angellica, hand the phone to Wade. He'll recognize her voice."

"Okay. But I'm not doing this here. Wade's getting the check. We'll be outside in a few. Oh, and don't worry about Sheila. When you didn't come back, she said she thought you were a jerk. She's at the bar talking to some other dude right now. I got the impression she knew him because he kissed her cheek when she walked up."

Sean sighed. "Sorry about that, Sen. Angellica is messing with my head and there's no room left in there for anyone else."

"She's not messing with your head, buddy. She's messing with your heart."

The line went dead. What was with women hanging up on him tonight? He put a hand over the ache in his chest. Could Wade and Sen be right? Was he in love with Angellica?

CHAPTER THIRTY-TWO

"It's ringing." Serenity glanced at Sean over the back of the front seat. They'd opted to retrieve their car from the parking garage before making the call. If they determined something sinister was going on in California, they wanted access to wheels immediately. Not to mention, the inside of the car was quiet and private. Two things a New York City sidewalk could never be. "Still ringing."

"She's not going to pick up," Sean stated. "I wouldn't if I didn't recognize the number." Sen held up a finger, shushing him. Her eyes flashed as she listened to someone on the other end. Sean mouthed, *Put it on speaker*. Sen nodded, but didn't immediately comply.

"Good evening. I'm sorry to call so late. My name is Lucy Granger, and I'm with *Wine Enthusiast* magazine. I'm looking for Angellica Capello." She held her finger up again. "Yes. I'll hold." She pulled the phone from her ear, then tapped a button on the screen. When she was done, she handed Sean the device. "I muted it. She went to get Angellica."

"Thank you." He unmuted the call and pressed the phone to his ear. He tapped his fingers on the knee of his borrowed slacks while he waited. If the next voice he heard wasn't Angellica's, he was calling the police because *no one* in the wine industry would refuse a call from *Wine Enthusiast* magazine. That idea was a stroke of genius on Serenity's part and one he'd thank her for later.

"This is Angellica Capello. How may I help you?" Sean almost wept as relief washed over him. "Hello? Is anyone there?"

Wade's gaze caught his in the rearview mirror while he twirled his right hand in a get on with it gesture. Serenity leaned over the seat and swatted at him. Sean ducked his head. "Angellica. It's me." Silence. "Sean."

"Sean? Nightingale?"

"Yeah. It's me. Are you alright? Who was that woman who hung up on me earlier? Tell me you aren't being held hostage or something."

"Uh."

"Angellica?" She'd either covered the microphone with her hand or stuffed the phone underneath something. He heard people talking, but the conversation was muffled, and the words indistinguishable. Panic was a knife to his heart. He shouted into the phone. "Angellica! What the fuck is going on?"

"Sean." She was back on the line, her voice calm and reassuring. "Everything is fine. That was Lexie. She's my best friend. Say hello, Lexie."

"Hello, Lexie."

Yeah, that was the same woman who had hung up on him.

"Say you're sorry."

"You're sorry."

Sean stifled a laugh. The Lexie person clearly wasn't sorry, but she was making nice because Angellica wanted her to. That was something, he guessed.

"I'm sorry I missed your call," Angellica said, returning to the conversation. "I was…indisposed."

"Is everything okay? Why is Lexie there?"

"She has a few days off from work. She works in L.A. and came down to keep me company. We've been best friends since third grade."

"I don't recall her from the harvest."

"She couldn't get off work, but she's been helping me get ready to harvest the Pinots."

"Crap! I forgot about the Pinots. Did you call the co-op? Can they send day laborers?"

"All taken care of. This isn't my first rodeo, cowboy. It shouldn't take more than two days to get the entire crop in. I spoke with the buyer yesterday to let them know to expect shipment by the end of the week."

"You have enough help? I don't think you should run the crusher on your own."

"No worries, boss. Everything is under control here."

Sean pinched the bridge of his nose. "That's great," he said. Truthfully, he hadn't given the vineyard a thought. He'd been too focused on his dad's recovery, his new responsibility in the Nightingale blending lab, and above all, he'd thought of Angellica. "Look. Can I call you back in about an hour? I'm in the car with Wade and Serenity."

"That was Serenity who called?"

"Yeah. Lexie kept hanging up on me. Anyway, I need to talk to you about…well, something personal. Can I call you later?"

"Sure. But really, Sean, there's nothing to talk about. Is there?"

It took a moment for him to process what she'd said, but once he had, he had a hard time breathing. "You're wrong, Angel. We've got a lot to talk about."

He focused on making his lungs function while he waited for her answer. When she finally agreed to take his call, he felt every muscle in his body relax.

"Okay. I'll call you in about an hour." Closing his eyes, he rested his head on the back of the seat.

"You've got to tell her," Wade said just as they exited the GW bridge and headed west toward home.

"I know. But I'd rather not say it over the phone."

"Yeah," Serenity chimed in. "Something like that needs to be said in person."

"Maybe I should fly out there tomorrow."

"Have you settled on the blends for this year?" Wade caught his gaze in the rearview mirror.

"You know I haven't." He narrowed his eyes, letting his brother see his frustration. It was one thing to blend wines for fun. Blending them to get the closest match possible to vintages already on the market was something entirely different.

"What's the holdup?"

"The percentages Dad used last year aren't working this year. I've spent every minute working on the whites since they need to be bottled soon. The Cayuga is the only one ready to be bottled. Everything else is going to take a while."

"Why are the percentages off?"

"For one thing, Uncle Stephen left the Pinot Grigios on the vine too long. Dad usually blends them with the Chardonnays, but that's not going to work this year. I'm going to transfer the Chard from the stainless-steel tanks to oak barrels for a few months. I think it will be fine on its own then. No blending needed. The Pinot Gris though?" He shook his head. "I'm working on blending them with a small amount of the Sauvignon Blanc to bring the acid level up. We've never put out a sweet white, and I'm not going to be the one to start. Dad would kill me."

"You know that sounds like gibberish to me, right?"

"Then why did you ask?"

"Had to do something to get your mind off your woman."

"That's mean," Serenity said as she playfully slapped Wade on the arm. "Don't you want your brother to be happy?"

"You're the one who tried to match him with your friend, so don't talk to me about Sean's happiness. I told you he's hung up on Angellica and wouldn't give another woman a second glance."

"Okay. I admit you were right, but if I hadn't taken the initiative and introduced him to Sheila, he never would have called Angellica tonight."

"I'm right here," Sean said, leaning forward to wave his hand between the front seats. "I can hear every word you're saying."

"We know!" they said in unison before turning to smile at each other.

"Okay, you two. Cut it out. I don't need your help."

"All evidence to the contrary," Wade said.

Sean caught his brother's gaze in the rearview mirror, then made a rude gesture Wade was sure to see. "Can you drive this thing any faster? I'm not getting any younger back here."

Serenity craned her head around to look at him. "You're worth waiting for, Sean. If she feels the same way as you do, she'll wait for your phone call."

"I appreciate your sentiment, Sen, and I hope you're right."

"Well, if I'm not, then she doesn't deserve you." She turned to face forward. He didn't miss the warm gaze his brother cast at his fiancée. Serenity really was one of the good ones. It was a shame she'd always had eyes for his brother, or Sean might have made a move in that direction himself.

"Thanks, Sen."

They made it out of the densely populated eastern side of New Jersey and were winding up into the higher elevations where farmland alternated with bands of untamed forest. Even in the darkness, he could see that everything was still green, but that would change soon enough. The leaves would put on their show of fall colors. Once that happened, winter wouldn't be far behind. His thoughts immediately went to his rental property in La Jolla, where winter meant sunny and seventy degrees. He could count on even warmer temperatures inland, where his vineyard hugged the hillsides of Temecula Valley. He'd only lived there for a few weeks, but he missed the dry air and the feeling of pride and anticipation that washed over him every time he stood amid the vines.

Thoughts of the vineyard inevitably drifted to Angellica, and the evening he'd left. No matter how many ways he tried to analyze what had happened, he still came up empty. He knew two things for sure. One, being with her meant something. It hadn't been casual sex. Not for him, and if Angellica's guard dog was any indication of her feelings, it had been important to her as well. And second? There was no doubt in his mind that he wasn't done with Angellica Capello.

"Almost home!"

Serenity's cheerful exclamation jolted Sean back to the other occupants of the car. They passed the familiar green sign marking the freeway exit. "Drop me off at the blending room," he instructed. "I've got work to do." *And a phone call to make.* Unlike his parent's house where he was staying, he'd have privacy in the empty facility. His family meant well, but they were a nosy bunch.

"Whatever you say, brother," Wade said, catching Sean's gaze in the rearview. "You know I wasn't pushing for results earlier. Right?"

"Yeah. I know. I'm really close on two blends. If I can get a couple of them settled, then I might take a few days off and go home."

They made the last turn onto the gravel road leading to the blending room. A knot of anxiety over the impending phone call formed in his stomach and the enormous pressure of taking over for his father settled onto his shoulders once again. For the first time ever, he questioned his decision to change the course of his life.

The car came to a stop and Sean opened his door. Before he exited the car, Wade turned and spoke over the front seat. "Hey, bro. The jet is yours whenever you need it. Whether or not the blends are ready."

His throat clogged with emotion, Sean simply nodded his understanding and thanks, then slipped out of the car and into the dark building. Without turning on the lights, he disarmed the security system, then pressed his shoulders against the closed door. It was now or never. Sinking to the cold floor, he pulled out his phone and placed a call to the woman who had him twisted up in knots.

CHAPTER THIRTY-THREE

Angellica stared at the ringing phone. She didn't have any photos of Sean, so the screen simply displayed his name and phone number. The blankness of it emphasized just how little she knew of the man who had somehow become important to her.

"Are you going to answer that?" Lexie asked from her spot on the other end of the sofa, where they'd been watching a popular program based on a series of historical romance books. "You know, you don't have to talk to him if you don't want to."

"I still need an answer about bottling this year, remember?" She grabbed the phone and headed for the stairs. She waved the device in the air. "I'll take it in my room."

"I'll pause this." Lexie aimed the remote at the television. "We can watch the rest later."

Sensing she'd let it ring as long as she could, she answered when she hit the first tread. "Hello?"

"Angel. It's me." He sounded tired, and her heart

immediately went out to him. She couldn't help it. He and his family had been through so much lately.

"How's your dad? Did they catch the guy who shot him?" she asked as she reached the top step and had to stop as a wave of fatigue washed over her.

"They caught the guy almost immediately, thanks to the security cameras outside the bank. Thanks for asking about Dad. He's going to be okay, but it's going to be awhile before he's cleared to work. He can't take the pain meds *and* sample wine. Plus, he needs to heal. It was a nasty wound."

Just thinking about it made her stomach queasy. She continued down the hallway to her room. After shutting the door, she sat on the bed, her back to the headboard. "Please give him my best wishes. The incident is the talk of the wine industry."

"So I hear. Sales have gone through the roof. I guess what they say about all publicity being good is correct."

"I don't know about that. Maybe people just want to show their support any way they can."

"I suppose. I'd rather think of it as support than monetary gain from a senseless tragedy. Thanks for putting that spin on it for me. You're a good person."

"You're welcome." She paused, then plunged on. "Hey, I tried to call you earlier today. We need to bottle this year or risk losing an entire vintage. Should I arrange for the mobile bottling trucks myself? And we'll need to order supplies."

A long sigh filled the line. "I'd forgotten." He really did sound tired and stressed.

"I can handle it. You don't need to do anything."

"I'd appreciate it. I'm swamped here. Since my dad is out of commission, I've been put in charge of blending this year's vintage. It's an enormous responsibility and everyone is breathing down my neck to announce the new blends as soon as possible."

"No wonder you sound tired."

"I do?"

"Yes. You need to take care of yourself, Sean. Is there anyone who can help?"

"My mom has some experience. I'm thinking of bringing her in to taste test some blends I think are contenders. A few of the wines won't need to be blended at all. That helps."

"Sounds like you have it under control. When do you think you'll be back?" She held her breath while waiting for his answer. Was he coming back at all? Or had he become one of those absentee owners when he promised he wouldn't?

"I'm going to come back soon, at least for a few days. Maybe I can help with the harvest? Or the bottling? Then I'll need to get back here. With any luck, I won't be here for more than another month or two."

Angellica fought the urge to cry. Why, she didn't know. She'd never been the type to dissolve into tears. It wasn't like she needed his help. She was capable of running the entire business. It's what she'd wanted from the beginning, so why was she getting teary-eyed at the prospect of Sean being in New Jersey for a couple of months? "No worries." She forced the words past the lump in her throat. "I'll take care of the bottling and the harvest. I might need to hire some temporary labor. Is that okay?"

They spent the next few minutes discussing the business. Angellica was surprised at how much responsibility Sean was giving her, but she knew better than to argue. "Okay. I guess it's all settled then," she said as the conversation wound down.

"I'm sure the vineyard is in excellent hands," he said. "The best." His voice had dropped an octave and was even sexier. "But that wasn't the actual reason I called."

"Oh?" She hated how her voice shook on the single syllable.

Sean cleared his throat. "I called to apologize for the way I left. And to tell you what I should have told you that night."

"There's nothing to say," she said in a rush.

"Yes, there is." He cleared his throat again. "What we did…it meant something, Angel. I think that's why it's taken me so long to apologize for my behavior. I've never felt the way I did with you, and it stunned me. Took me by complete surprise. I don't know what, exactly, I felt, but I know what we had wasn't just sex. It was more. So much more."

Angellica closed her eyes and dropped her head back against the headboard while she tried to process what he was saying. The way he said those last few words, *so much more*, sent a wave of warmth through her body and made her fingers and toes tingle.

"Angel?"

"I'm here," she whispered. "I—I don't know what to say."

"Say it meant something to you, too. Tell me I wasn't the only one who felt like we'd made a genuine connection."

Her heart raced, hearing his confession. The image of his face the moment he realized what he'd done flashed into her mind, and with it, a tsunami of doubt washed over her. Whatever that expression had been about, it had been the opposite of what she'd felt. She'd given Sean Nightingale everything that evening. Her body. Her heart. And in return, he'd shut down. The phone call had been a convenient excuse for him to leave—albeit a tragic one— but an excuse all the same. If his father hadn't gotten shot, he would have found another reason to run. As sure as she was that she was in love with Sean, she was equally sure he wasn't in love with her.

Taking in a deep breath, Angellica did the only thing she could do to protect her heart. She lied. "Connection?

What are you talking about? We had sex. It was great sex; I'll give you that. But then, you've had lots of practice, haven't you, Sean? I guess I should be grateful I was the beneficiary of your experience once, but that's all it'll ever be. A one-night stand." She drew in another steadying breath before ending the call. "There's really no need for you to come back. Just make sure I have full access to the accounts, and I'll keep Capello's running for you. At least until I find another job."

She dropped the phone away from her ear. Before she could press the button to end the call, she heard his voice calling out to her. "Angel. Angellica!" She pressed the button anyway.

There wasn't anything more to say.

Angellica woke the next morning with a headache and an upset stomach. Lexie was lying on the bed next to her. They were both still wearing the clothes they'd had on the night before—minus their shoes. She vaguely recalled her best friend coming to check on her and plying her with ice cream and wine. Angellica had eaten the ice cream but, for once, had rejected the wine. Judging by the empty bottles on the nightstand, Lexie had taken up the slack left by her indifference.

Sitting up, she brushed a lock of unruly hair out of her eyes and bent to pick up an empty ice cream carton from the floor. Remnants of the frozen treat swirled in the bottom of the container. Her stomach cramped, sending Angellica stumbling toward the ensuite. She kneeled in front of the toilet just in time to empty the contents of her stomach into the bowl.

"Jelly?" her friend called from the bedroom. "Are you okay?"

"I'm fine," she said before dry-heaving over the bowl again.

"You don't look fine." Lexie crouched beside her and brushed her hair back to look at her face. "If I didn't know better, I'd think you drank too much last night."

Angellica sat up and scooted across the floor until she was leaning up against the bathtub. "Must have been the ice cream. I think I ate most of the carton."

"I ate as much as you did." Lexie took a washcloth off the stack of clean ones on the shelf next to the tub and wet it in the sink. "Here. Clean your face, then put it on the back of your neck. Are you running a fever?" She pressed the back of her hand to Angellica's forehead. "Nope. No fever."

"I cried buckets last night. I probably swallowed as much snot as I blew out my nose."

"That *was* a lot of snot. You went through an entire box of tissues. That's probably what has your stomach upset." She joined Angellica on the floor.

The cold cloth felt good on the back of her neck, and her stomach was feeling marginally better. She wished she could say the same for her heart, but it was irrevocably broken. Sitting on a cold bathroom floor after having cried herself to sleep over a man was a rude wake-up call. She'd known Sean's reputation from the get-go. She should have stayed as far away from the man as possible, but like so many other women, she'd fallen for his false charms, and look what it had gotten her. "I'm pathetic," she cried as she reached for a wad of toilet paper and blew her nose.

"You're not pathetic. He is. Who does he think he is, anyway? God's gift to women? Did he think he could fu—I mean—have sex with you once, and you'd fall in love with him? Men. They're all the same. They think having an extra appendage makes them irresistible. Mark my words. One of these days, the man is going to find a woman who will bring him to his knees. He'll get what he deserves, then. You'll see."

The photo she'd seen of Sean with that supermodel flashed across her brain. He had his choice of women. No doubt he'd been seeing his share since returning to New

Jersey. She'd never been there, but she knew his family's vineyard wasn't far from New York City. He'd probably been partying every night. The very thought of Sean doing to another woman the things he'd done to her twisted her stomach and sent her heaving over the bowl again.

"You'd better take it easy today, Jelly.

"You think?" She couldn't hide the sarcasm in her voice.

"Hey, don't take it out on me. I'm not the one who fu—screwed you over."

Angellica pressed the wet cloth to her forehead. "I know, and I'm sorry. You're a good friend, Lex, and I should have listened to you and not taken his call." She sat up a little straighter. "And I know I shouldn't care about the vineyard any longer, but this is my home. A hundred years of my family's blood, sweat, and tears went into this place. There's no internal switch to turn that off. I won't sit by and let everything my father and grandfather worked to build crumble just because I exercised poor judgment in my personal life."

Lexie brushed a strand of Angellica's hair off her face and tucked it behind her ear. "I get it. I think. At any rate, I'm here for you. I have to go back to work tomorrow, but I'll only be a phone call away."

"I appreciate that, Lex. I really do."

CHAPTER THIRTY-FOUR

Sean woke up face down on his desk with a construction crew hammering inside his head and a sour taste in his mouth. He wanted to blame it on that last blend he'd sampled the night before, but he knew that wasn't the source of his discomfort. The blend had been awful. A total reject, but it was the whiskey he'd consumed afterward that was responsible for his present condition and the fact that he'd passed out on his desk. Rather, his father's desk.

He was still wearing Wade's suit, the whereabouts of the jacket unknown, and the tie had disappeared before the jacket had gone missing. A quick sniff of his armpit confirmed he needed a shower before he got near anyone else. He thought about sneaking into his parents' house, but decided against it almost as quickly as the thought had come to him. His mother was home, and if she caught him, he'd never hear the end of it. Didn't matter how old he was. She'd lecture him and probably try to ground him. That didn't change the fact that he needed to get cleaned up. He could find his car and drive into town and crash at Ian's apartment, but doing so at this hour of the morning might get him shot. Ian was a light sleeper, and he had a gun. That left Wade.

Sean pushed to his feet and, once he felt steady enough, walked out into the pre-dawn morning. The chill went a long way to waking him, and the walk through the vineyard to the Granger farm where Serenity had grown up helped sober him up. The sun was tinting the horizon a deep pink when the old farmhouse came into view. The last time he'd seen the place, it had looked one good gust of wind away from collapsing. Even in the dim light, he saw that was no longer the case. Wade had obviously put a lot of money into fixing the house up so he and Sen could make it their home. The porch no longer sagged, and the siding was bright white. The window on the second floor that had been boarded up a few months ago appeared new, as did all the windows. Sean smiled at the sight. It was good to see the old house getting a new lease on life. He couldn't wait to see what they'd done with the inside.

Wade was not happy to see him. He deduced this from the way his brother slammed the front door in his face. Sean couldn't blame him. If one of his brothers rousted him out of a bed he shared with his fiancée, he'd probably do more than shut a door in his face. All things considered; he'd made out okay. No one shot at him, and there was a cozy-looking quilt on the refurbished porch swing. He'd be okay out there until the couple were properly awake and maybe downed a cup of coffee or two. Wrapping the quilt around his shoulders, he curled up on the swing and closed his eyes.

"Hey." Something poked him in the shoulder. "Asshole. Wake up." Sean cracked his eyes open. His brother wore his standard suit and tie get-up. He held a travel mug in one hand and a briefcase in the other. No doubt he'd used the briefcase to prod Sean awake. "You look like hell. What happened last night?"

Sean pushed to a sitting position and rubbed both hands over his face to wake up. "No clue." He'd taken Wade and Sen's advice and called Angellica. He'd thought the conversation had gone pretty well—until it took a turn he hadn't seen coming. "All I know for sure is that I'm screwed."

"I wish I had time to listen to your love life woes, but I don't. I have a meeting in a few minutes with the state agricultural commission about preserving the Granger homestead."

"Butch Granger is okay with that?" It would mean he couldn't sell or develop the land. Having the property remain agricultural was a good thing for Nightingales since the two properties adjoined.

"It was his idea. Once he found out the state would pay him to designate the property as preserved agricultural land, he was all for it."

"I don't suppose he's going to invest any of that money in making improvements to the house."

"Nope. That's all on Sen and me." He shrugged. "I've got the money, and it makes Sen happy to see the old place fixed up. You know what they say. Happy wife. Happy life."

"She's not your wife yet."

"She will be. Go on inside and have some coffee. She'll be down soon. You can tell her your sob story, and she'll fill you in on the wedding plans."

"Can I borrow some clothes? I didn't want Mom to see me like this."

Wade shook his head. "This woman has you all messed up. Never thought I'd see the day. Go ahead. But wait until Sen comes down. Take whatever you need, but I want my suit back. Dry-cleaned."

"Thanks, bro." Sean stood and dropped the quilt on the swing. "Good luck with the meeting," he said as he shuffled toward the front door. He stopped short just inside the door. The living room sported a fresh coat of paint, and the original hardwood floors gleamed like new. A new rug and furnishings brought life to the room. Recalling the layout of the house from all the times he'd visited as a kid; he made his way to the kitchen. *Wow!* This was nothing like what he remembered. Everything from the floors to the cabinets to the appliances screamed modern farmhouse. If he didn't know better, he'd think he'd stepped into a magazine layout. He zeroed in on the coffee bar they'd put in on the opposite wall. Leave it to Wade to have a fancy coffee maker when a simple one would do. He was still trying to figure out which buttons to push to make the confounded thing spit out a plain cup of coffee when his future sister-in-law joined him.

"Wade said you were still here," she said as she hip-bumped him out of the way. "Let me do this. I think I've got it figured out."

"How long did it take you?"

"We've had it for three weeks. The first two were a disaster, but last week I finally figured out how to get it to do what I want."

Sean leaned his hips against the counter and crossed his arms over his chest. "Sorry to barge in on you. I spent the night in Dad's office and didn't want Mom to see me straggling in this morning."

Sen smirked as she pushed a couple of buttons, and the space-age device sputtered to life. "No problem. You're always welcome here."

"The place is looking good."

Her gaze swept the newly decorated kitchen, and her smile was brighter than the fancy overhead lighting. "It is, isn't it?" She handed Sean the first cup of coffee and then put another mug beneath the spout. "We're going to be happy here. I can feel it."

"It's a great place, but Wade would be happy anywhere as long as you're with him."

"Ahh, that's so sweet," she said. "And I'd be happy anywhere as long as I'm with Wade. We owe it all to you."

Sean shrugged. "I just nudged you together. Left to your own devices, no telling how long it would have taken for the two of you to see what was right in front of you."

She grabbed her mug and led the way to the new island. "I like to think we would have eventually found each other."

"Have you *met* my brother?" Sean teased. "He was married to his job until you came along."

Serenity smiled and then took a sip of her coffee. When she set the mug down, her expression turned serious. "What happened last night? Did you call Angellica?"

"I did." He filled her in on the conversation. "I don't know what happened, Sen, but I know I'm screwed."

"You're in love with her, aren't you?"

"I think so." Sen raised one eyebrow at him. "Okay. Yeah, I am, but she doesn't want to see me or talk to me."

Sen sipped her coffee but didn't respond. "That's all I get? I just told you I'm in love with a woman, and you don't say anything? Not a word?"

"Quiet. I'm thinking." She took another sip.

Sean waited, drinking his own coffee until the mug ran dry. "You keep thinking. I'm going to go upstairs and take a shower. Wade said I could borrow some clothes."

Serenity stood. "I'll fix some breakfast." At his raised eyebrow, she retorted, "Don't worry. I won't burn the place down."

"Better not," he said as he left her alone in the kitchen. He showered as fast as he could, barely taking time to admire the newly remodeled bathroom. Wade's clothes were easy to find in the dresser he recognized from his brother's old apartment. He chose a pair of jeans and a Nightingale Vineyard T-shirt. After pulling on socks, he rummaged around in the only closet in the room until he found a pair of Wade's running shoes. They were ancient but looked better with jeans than the dress shoes he was wearing when he arrived. A quick glance in the mirror revealed disheveled hair and an excess of beard. He ran his fingers through his hair and then shrugged at the mess left behind. It wasn't like he was meeting the public today. The hair and beard could wait another day.

He found Serenity in the kitchen with an open box of Pop-Tarts and a box of sugary cereal. She was munching on one of the iced pastries and sipping from the same mug she'd had when he left. "You didn't have to go to so much trouble," he deadpanned, as he took a stool and reached for the cereal box. "Got any milk?"

"In the fridge. Help yourself. If I'd known you were coming over for breakfast, I would have picked up pastries from Dott's yesterday."

"I'll try to give you more notice next time." She directed him to the bowls and spoons, then he looked around, confused. "Where's the refrigerator?"

"There." She pointed to a wall of cabinets. "It's disguised as a cabinet."

He tugged on the cabinet handle she'd indicated and found a fully stocked refrigerator behind it. "Nice," he said as he grabbed the milk carton and returned to his seat at the island. "Did you come up with a solution to my problem while I was gone?"

"Nope."

They ate in silence, except for the crunching of Sean's cereal. When he'd finished his first bowl and poured another helping from the box, he asked, "Are you going to, or am I completely screwed?"

"I've been trying to put myself in her shoes, and I can't do it. Not without knowing what happened between you two."

"Have I ever told you details about my sex life? The answer is no, and I'm not going to start now."

"Ah, so you *did* have sex with her. I knew it! What

happened? Don't tell me she didn't come. If that's the case, then man, you really are screwed." She took a giant bite of Pop-Tart and chewed.

Sean sighed and shook his head. "I always make sure the woman comes first." He put the emphasis on the word, always. "And in this case, she came twice, so she can't accuse me of being an inconsiderate lover."

"You didn't call her by someone else's name, you know, when you were doing it?"

He stared at Sen. "No. And I'm offended that you would even ask."

"Then tell me what actually happened, or I'm going to keep asking questions until I get to the bottom of this."

He lifted a spoon full of cereal to his mouth. "You'd never guess in a million years," he said before stuffing his mouth full and crunching down.

"Oh. My. God!" Serenity leaned over and got right in his face. "You came too soon. Holy shit! Is that a problem you have often?"

Sean choked on his cereal and ended up coughing it all over the island. When he finally got himself under control, he drank straight from the milk carton to wash the rest down before turning to face his soon-to-be sister-in-law. "I did not come too soon," he growled. "Not really, anyway."

Serenity tapped a finger on the countertop. "You either did, or you didn't, Sean. Which is it."

So, he explained as best he could about what had happened. When he was through, Sen stared open-mouthed at him. "Then my phone started ringing, and it wouldn't stop, so I, you know," he used both hands to demonstrate how he'd pulled out of her. "It was Wade. And the next thing I knew, I was running out of the house with a suitcase, and she was asking about the vines, or the wine, or something. It's pretty much a blur."

"Then you waited how many weeks to call her?"

"Three?" He'd sort of lost track of time since he'd

been here.

Serenity propped her elbows on the counter, then, with a groan, dropped her head into her upturned hands. "Sean Nightingale. You're an idiot."

CHAPTER THIRTY-FIVE

"Tell me something I don't know, Sen." Sean went to the sink and wet a sponge to clean up the mess he'd made on the island. "In my defense, I was in shock. Double shock, I guess. From the phone call, and from…the other thing. Nothing like that had ever happened to me before, and as wrong as it sounds, it felt right. I know that doesn't make any sense, and maybe that's why I put off talking to her about it for so long." He wiped down the counter and then returned the sponge to the sink. He stayed there, his hips resting against the counter and his arms crossed over his chest. "She's it for me, Sen. I think I knew that all along, but when you tried to fix me up with what's her name last night—"

"Sheila."

"Yeah, her. When I saw what you were doing, all I could think about was that I didn't want anyone but Angellica. She was excellent, by the way. That night. Responsive—"

Serenity held up both hands, palms facing him. "Stop!

I got the message. No need to go into any more detail."

Sean nodded, then continued. "Angellica is intelligent and beautiful. Not like any of those models and actors. She's real. You know?"

"I know what you mean."

"She's a hard worker, too. She can drive a tractor, and she can run the crusher. She knows grapes, too. Did I tell you she's got degrees in enology and viticulture? She's the exact opposite of all those society women, and God help me, she's perfect for me."

"Oh, Sean," Sen said. She slid off her stool and approached him, arms spread wide. Her hug felt good, even if it was a pity hug. He squeezed her tight. "I know what you need to do."

Sean pushed her away and bent so he could look her in the eye. "You do?"

"I do."

"Well, don't keep me in suspense. Tell me."

Another hour had passed by the time Sean and Serenity walked through the vineyard to their respective jobs. Sean was still thinking about what Serenity had said. There were a million details to work out if he was going to implement the plan. Ideas swirled around in his head so fast that he found it difficult to latch onto one long enough to think it through. The closer he got to his dad's blending lab, the more he felt the weight of that responsibility settling back on his shoulders, too. This was not the life he'd imagined when he handed the marketing reins over to Serenity and moved to California.

They were about to part ways when Sen brought up her new job. "I've got a conference call in a few minutes with those cruise ship guys you talked to. We're still trying to work out an agreement with them. I'm pushing for featured status on all our wines in both locations. Am I shooting too high with them?"

Sean had done the initial legwork on the account. It

had been his last official duty as the marketing director for Nightingales and the account that convinced him he'd made the right decision when he purchased Capello Vineyards. "Honestly, Sen? If they won't give us featured status, then walk away. Richard and Ryan are nice guys, and I get that they're trying to elevate their business, but it has nowhere to go but up. They own a floating sex den and are opening the same type of facility on their private island. We don't need their business. The only way it makes sense for us is if we get the top spot on every menu in every restaurant they operate. And that includes room service."

"I was thinking the same thing. Thanks for confirming my thoughts. We could use that market share, but it won't break us."

The sooner Sean perfected his new blend and introduced it to the Nightingale product line, the better. It alone would make up for losing an account the size of the one they were talking about. But first, he had to finish up the blends he was working on here. "You're welcome," he said, pulling her in for a quick hug. "I knew you were the right person for the job."

Serenity extricated herself from the hug. "I wasn't so sure, but I love it. The clients all ask about you, but they've been nothing but nice to me."

"Like I said, you're the right person for the job. So go do it. Don't second-guess your judgment. There's nothing to be gained from doing that."

Serenity playfully poked him in the chest with her index finger. "You should take your own advice, Mr. Nightingale. Listen to your gut, and don't second guess yourself."

"Wise words, soon-to-be Mrs. Nightingale."

They wished each other a good day. Sean went one way, and Serenity went the other. As Sean covered the distance to the blending room, her words stuck with him. He'd done nothing but second guess himself since he'd temporarily taken on his dad's role as head vintner. Instead of listening to his own instincts, he'd tried to create exactly what his father would create if he were there. "Listen to your gut," she'd said. *Not my gut. My palette. I need to trust my judgment, just like I told Sen. I'm not Dad, and I never will be. But I am a Nightingale, and I know wine. Especially these wines. I grew up on the same soil that grew these grapes. Winemaking is my heritage. It's in my blood. It's who I am.*

Sean entered his workplace without the burden of responsibility weighing him down and set to work. In a matter of hours, he'd accomplished more than he had in weeks. A couple more days like this one and he'd have the answers Wade needed, and he'd be free to return to California for a few weeks. Nightingales employed people to do the work of blending the massive vats of wine according to the specifics established by the head vintner. If they had questions, they could call him, and he could be back here in a matter of hours if need be. For once, the corporate jet would be put to good use instead of ferrying him to parties.

Exhausted, Sean walked to his parent's house with a satisfied smile on his face. His mother had left a note on the kitchen counter for him saying she'd gone to the rehab facility to have dinner with his dad. He warmed up some leftovers he found in the fridge and sat at the breakfast table to eat. In the silence of the house, he let his mind wander to the one place it always wanted to go. To Angellica. Before he thought better of it, he picked up his phone and dialed her number. The call immediately went to voicemail. Not a good sign. He remembered his conversation with Serenity that morning, and when the beep sounded, he left a simple message. "I'm thinking about you tonight. Remembering the day we got soaked, running back to the house. It was cold outside, but your smile felt like sunshine on my soul."

He hung up and placed the phone face down on the table. *That was what Sen said to do. Right?* "You haven't known each other for very long," Sen had said. "Your hasty withdrawal and lack of communication probably convinced her it was nothing but sex to you, and bad sex at that. You can't blame her for not wanting to talk about it." He'd wanted to argue that it had been the best sex ever—for him, at least—but Sen didn't want to hear it. Instead, she'd laid out a plan of action. "You need to convince her it wasn't just sex, and to do that, she has to believe you were developing genuine feelings for her *before* you did the deed."

Step one was to open up to her. Tell her how he fell in love with her in a way she could relate to. Feed her snippets of information she wasn't privy to. His private thoughts. Things he would have shared with her over time if they'd taken the time to actually date. "That's what dating is for," Sen had said. "You skipped that part entirely, so now you have to go back and fill in the blanks."

Easier said than done, he thought as he put his dishes in the dishwasher. He might be grown, but his mother would read him the riot act if she came home to a dirty kitchen. That thought reminded him of how he'd ended up having sex with Angellica that night. If he'd left her to clean the kitchen on her own, none of this would have happened. But even though the evening had ended badly, in more ways than one, he couldn't regret what they'd done. That night had proven to him that Angellica was the one. The elusive unicorn he thought he'd never find. The person who made him feel whole. The person he wanted to spend his life with. The woman he wanted to be the mother of his children. His partner in every way.

He dreamed he was making love to Angellica that night. This time in a soft bed with the morning sunshine highlighting her features as they came in perfect unison.

Sean woke with a start, immediately slinging his arm

over his eyes to block the sunlight streaking across his bed. Damned curtains. Why the hell couldn't they stay together in the middle? But it wasn't the sun that had woken him. It was the dream. It had seemed so real that he'd come in his briefs like a horny teenager. Eyes closed, he recalled every second of the dream. How warm her skin had been. How she looked up at him with love and wonder in her eyes as he moved inside her. How she'd dug her fingernails into his ass cheeks and cried out his name as she'd come, her inner muscles milking his dick, spinning him out of control.

And just like that, he was hard again. Aching to be inside her, to give her everything. To mark her as his. He palmed his erection through his damp briefs and willed it to go away. After several minutes, he gave up and planted his feet on the floor. The house was quiet, which he hoped meant his mom was still asleep. He hadn't heard her come in last night, but then he'd gone to bed earlier than usual.

Rising, he crept to the door and opened it enough to see the hallway was empty and that no light was visible beneath the door to his parents' room. One of the many problems with a two-hundred-year-old house was the lack of ensuite bathrooms. Before he was born, his mom and dad had remodeled the old house, so their room had a private bath. That left one bathroom for all three brothers to share, and it was across and down the hall from Sean's room. As a teenager, he'd grown adept at dashing between his room and the bathroom without being seen. With his mom still asleep, there was no need to hurry, so he gathered his clean clothes and made the trek down the hall. In a matter of minutes, hot water cascaded over him, and he took his cock in hand.

Sitting at the kitchen island later with a cup of steaming coffee in front of him, he pulled his phone out of his pocket. It was too early on the west coast to call Angellica, so he opted for a text message instead. *I dreamed of you last night.*

He slipped the phone back into his pocket and reached for his coffee just as his mother came in through the back door. "Whoa, there, Mom. Out past curfew?" he joked.

She sat her purse on the corner of the counter that was always covered in junk—mail, car keys, stray tubes of lip balm, and other things that had no particular place they belonged. "Hush." She smiled as she admonished him. "I fell asleep in the recliner next to your dad's bed. We watched that show, the one where the bachelor dates a bunch of women at the same time? Anyway, we both fell asleep, and no one bothered to wake us."

The mention of the popular reality show sent Sean's mind back to the night he'd tried to call Angellica and hadn't gotten an answer. He'd been out of his mind with worry, though he tried his best to play it off as simple concern for an employee. Why he hadn't been upfront with Angellica then, he didn't know. He'd been half in love with her by then. Maybe all the way in love with her. Once he'd seen the lack of security at the cottage, there was no way he was going to leave her there. If she hadn't agreed to go back to the house with him that night, he had been prepared to sleep in his car in front of her place.

"How's Dad?" he asked as he pulled his phone out of his pocket, intent on sending another text message to Angellica.

"He's getting better every day. A few more days, and he should be able to come home."

"That's good news."

His mom set about making herself a cup of coffee. "He won't be cleared to work for a few more weeks, but I doubt that'll keep him from doing it anyway."

Sean glanced at the dark screen on his phone, then back to his mother. "I'm sure you're right." He was having a hard time concentrating on their conversation. He held up the phone. "I need to return a couple of emails."

"You go ahead. Do what you need to do. I'm going to

take this cup upstairs with me."

He slid off the barstool. "See you later, Mom." As soon as he was out the door, he pulled up his text thread with Angellica and typed. *Do you remember the night I came to the cottage to check on you? If you hadn't gone back to the house with me, I planned to sleep in my car outside your house. I dreamed about you that night, too.* His fingers hovered over the keyboard. Should he tell her he was already in love with her then, or should he wait?

Sen's advice echoed in his memory. "Whatever you do, don't tell her you love her over the phone or in a text. She deserves to hear it from you in person. She needs to see it in your eyes when you tell her."

He hit send and pocketed the phone. The stakes were too high. He couldn't mess this up again.

CHAPTER THIRTY-SIX

Angellica glanced at her phone as it chimed with another text message. She'd woken early, her stomach rolling. She'd never been under so much stress in her life. Not even in college, when exams loomed over her head. She'd always felt confident then. The weight of everything that was going on in her life was taking a toll on her body. She'd been sick to her stomach off and on for the last few days. Had to be the stress. But what could she do?

She looked at the list she'd made the night before. There were bottles, corks, and labels to be ordered, and she had to schedule the mobile bottling truck and confirm the late harvest date with the co-op. The list went on and on. She didn't have time to be sick, and she especially didn't have time for whatever game Sean Nightingale was playing now. He'd made his feelings clear the night he left.

Glancing at her phone on the corner of the desk, she sighed as she reached for it and opened the messaging app. Another message had come in from Sean. The first had come in while she'd been puking up her guts long before dawn. She'd forgotten all about hearing the chime while she'd been sitting on the bathroom floor and had only read the message after she'd showered and dressed for the day. So what if he'd dreamed about her? She hoped it had been a nightmare. And why had he told her in the first place? His dreams weren't any of her business.

Swiping the app open, she groaned when she saw another text from Sean. Her finger hovered over the button that would delete the message. On the off chance it was something business related, she clicked to open the message.

Do you remember the night I came to the cottage to check on you? If you hadn't gone back to the house with me, I planned to sleep in my car outside your house. I dreamed about you that night, too.

What? Why was he telling her this? Despite the long list of things she needed to accomplish that day, she let her mind drift back to that night.

It had been hotter than hell in the cottage, but she'd been determined to stick it out. What choice did she have? She was basically a squatter on the very land she'd grown up on at that point. Were the conditions ideal? No, but neither was living out of her car. Then he'd shown up, acting like he cared about her safety, and then practically forced his way into the house. She still didn't know what to think about the time they'd spent together. Had he genuinely been interested in her mother's painting? And why had he told her that story about knowing the contestant on the reality show? She'd kept her mouth shut about her best friend's position with the production company. *She* didn't have anybody to impress. He'd been right about the cottage, though. It wasn't safe. Anyone could access the property. So, she'd given in and returned to her former home with him. *I dreamed of you that night.* Angellica sighed. She'd dreamed about him that night, too.

Setting the phone aside, she forced her thoughts back

to her list of things to accomplish. She used a highlighter to prioritize the various tasks and then gone to work. It was her phone signaling a new text message that drew her attention to the time. Right on cue, her stomach grumbled, this time with genuine hunger, as she realized it was nearing dinnertime, and she'd worked right through lunch.

Turning the phone over, she slumped into the desk chair and flipped to the messaging app. No surprise. The incoming text was from Sean. Blowing out a frustrated breath, she opened the message. *I'm wearing my hiking boots today. I'll never forget the day I met you. You pretended to be concerned about my safety and suggested I rethink my footwear. You showed me your boots. I'd never seen anything sexier.*

"Whoa." Angellica read the text twice more before tossing the phone onto the desktop. He couldn't be serious. Women in hiking boots weren't his thing unless a supermodel was wearing them for a photo shoot. And she was far from being a supermodel. "What are you doing, Sean Nightingale?" she asked the empty office. "What are you trying to prove?"

The days passed in a blur of stress-induced stomach problems and worrisome text messages from Sean that had her revisiting every in-person encounter she'd had with the man. To hear him tell it, he'd been drawn to her from the first time they met. But he still hadn't addressed what had happened the night he left. Not a word.

She thought maybe he *did* find her attractive, but attraction wasn't enough. Not when she'd fallen so hard for him. She'd given him everything and gotten a blank stare in return. That moment still hurt, and probably always would.

With the final grapes being harvested tomorrow, Angellica had spent the day on the tractor, hauling crates to the field. The part-time high school kids Sean had hired were once again cleaning the crushing equipment. They'd been good hands to have around, and they learned quickly.

Because of them, the previously harvested vines had been trimmed, and the rows weeded. The barn was more organized than she'd ever seen it, and she'd had them move her mother's paintings from the cottage to the house where they rightfully belonged.

She barely slept that night, worrying about the harvest. It wasn't the first harvest she'd been in charge of, but it was the first time she didn't have her father, standing in the wings, ready to lend a helping hand if need be. She was up before dawn, nervously checking the weather forecast and double-checking everything else. Assured all the moving parts were aligned for the day, she filled an oversized insulated mug with coffee, and pulled on an old sweatshirt from her high school days. Walking out onto the back patio, she took a moment to enjoy the peace and quiet as the sun painted the eastern sky with vibrant brush strokes. It wasn't long before the sound of vehicles coming down the long driveway had her shoulders tensing. *Time to go.*

Angellica rounded the house in time to see half a dozen vans park and discharge their passengers in front of the blending room. As she was walking over to greet the migrant workers who the co-op had assembled to pick the grapes, her phone vibrated in her pocket. Without breaking stride, she pulled the device out and glanced at the screen. At the sight of Sean's name on the home screen, her heart did a somersault, and her feet became cinder blocks she couldn't budge. *What does he want now? Doesn't he know I'm busy?*

Huffing out her frustration, she opened the messaging app.

Have a great harvest today. You've got this.

Her world narrowed to the words displayed on the small screen in her hand. *You've got this.* The figurative pat on the back was so unexpected that she didn't know what to think. Rooted to the spot, she stared at the words, trying to make sense of them. Was he being genuine? Did he believe in her ability to run a successful harvest? The phone vibrated in her hand with another incoming text.

I've seen you in action. You're a natural leader. The workers will do anything you ask of them.

Another bubble appeared.

I'll do anything you ask of me.

"Ms. Capello?" A heavily accented voice demanded her attention. She closed the app and pocketed the phone. She'd analyze Sean's troublesome texts later. Or never. Never was good.

"Yes. That's me. Is everyone here?"

"Yes, ma'am," the stout farm worker said with a smile. "Just point us in the right direction, and we'll get to work."

The next eight hours were a blur of activity as two-dozen skilled laborers picked the grapes. Angellica transported the filled crates to the barn where the crushing machine was set up. She was more than exhausted when the last van full of workers pulled out onto the main road, as the sun was just beginning to set. After taking one last look at the tons of grapes stacked in the barn, she locked the giant doors. The farm hands would be there the following day to help her render the juice, and a tanker truck would arrive the following day to deliver the product to the buyer.

CHAPTER THIRTY-SEVEN

As she climbed the stairs to her room, her phone vibrated in her pocket. A glance at the screen confirmed her suspicion. It was another text from Sean. *I can't deal with this right now.* She placed the phone on the nightstand and then headed for the ensuite bathroom. She needed a shower and food, in that order. She'd had nothing to eat that day other than the cup of coffee she'd had that morning and a candy bar she ate so fast around noon that she barely tasted it. Thinking back on it, she couldn't remember what kind it had been. Not good, she thought as she stepped into the glassed-in shower.

The water felt heavenly, but her stomach had finally realized her neglect and complained, so she took care of the basics and shut off the water. For the first time in weeks, she was genuinely hungry, and the stomach ailment that had plagued her for so long hadn't reared its ugly head for the entire day. It was amazing what stress could do to a person. And lack of stress.

Re-energized, she threw on her oldest sweats and a T-shirt she should have thrown away years ago, but from a comfort standpoint, it couldn't be beaten. Her grocery supply was running low, but she found the makings of a grilled cheese sandwich and a can of tomato soup that might have been past its sell-by date. As much as she wanted a glass of wine, she was too hungry to take the time to get one from the cellar, so she opted for water instead. She'd just settled at the kitchen island to eat when she heard the front door open and close, causing her heart rate to escalate.

Shit. Shit. Shit! Had she locked the door? She'd forgotten to set the alarm, that much was clear as it wasn't going off.

My phone. She patted her pockets and scanned the kitchen counters, coming up empty. Then she recalled placing it on the nightstand before her shower. *The one time I leave my phone in my room! Crap!*

The landline. If she could get to her father's, *Sean's,* office, she could call for help from there, but judging from the sound of the footfalls she'd never make without being seen. Double crap!

Sliding off the barstool, she rounded the island and pulled a butcher knife from the wooden block next to the stove. *Hide. I've got to hide.* Frantic now, her gaze flitted over the room and landed on the door to the walk-in pantry. It didn't have a lock, but it was the only option she had without leaving the room, which would put her square in the intruder's line of sight. Her legs felt like wet noodles as she forced them to propel her toward the pantry. Suddenly, a figure loomed in the doorway. Angellica screamed and jolted back a step. Trembling all over, she tried to raise the arm holding the knife but couldn't get it to move.

"There you are." The familiar voice cut through the haze of her fear. She narrowed her eyes at the man. "Sean?"

"Were you expecting someone else?" He cleared the

doorway, circling the island so they faced each other. His gaze swept her from head to toe, stopping at the weapon in her hand. "Whoa. What are you going to do with that?"

"Sean?" she lamely asked again, though he stood right in front of her. "What are you doing here?"

He cocked his head to one side, a sideways grin on his face. "Well, I seem to recall that this is my home." His glance darted to the knife in her hand, then back to her face. "Can you put that down? I come in peace."

Her arm finally cooperated with her brain, and she lifted the knife. Her breath caught at the sight of it clenched in her fist. The thought of plunging it into anyone, even to save her own life, made her stomach lurch. She tossed the knife on the counter and ran, shoving Sean aside in her haste to make it to the powder room down the hall.

"Hey! Where are you going?" he called out as she careened down the hall. It wasn't far, but with one hand over her mouth and her sock-clad feet sliding on the hardwood floor, it seemed to take forever to get there. Then she was on the floor, emptying her empty stomach into the toilet bowl with Sean Nightingale hovering in the door. Watching.

CHAPTER THIRTY-EIGHT

"Are you okay?" That had to be the stupidest thing he'd ever asked, considering he'd just witnessed Angellica vomiting into the toilet. Her skin was pale, and the hand holding her wet hair back seemed shaky.

"Do I look okay?" If looks could kill, he'd be a dead man. "Go away."

"I don't think so." He stepped inside, practically straddling her to reach a washcloth hanging on the rack next to the sink. By twisting at the waist, he was able to wet the cloth and wring it out. "Here." He dangled the wet fabric in front of her face. She snatched it out of his hand and grumbled her thanks before wiping her face with it. He grimaced as she heaved again. He'd gone to college. Seen his share of people who had overindulged, but for the life of him, he didn't think that was Angellica's problem. Considering it was barely sundown, and he knew for a fact that she'd worked most of the day, she hadn't had time for more than a glass or maybe two of wine. It could be a stomach virus. Those things came on fast and were highly contagious. She could have gotten it from one of the farm workers she'd come in contact with earlier. As much as he didn't relish the idea of catching it from her, he couldn't find it in him to leave her on the cold floor by herself. When she finally sat up, her shoulders hunched and her head lolling forward, he offered her a hand. "Here. Let me help you up to bed."

She swatted his hand away. "Move. I don't need your help."

Raising both hands in surrender, he eased out of the tiny room. Angellica leveraged herself to her knees, then to her feet. She didn't appear too steady, but having been rebuked twice, three times if you considered the greeting with a knife in hand, he backed away. She went straight to the kitchen, where she sat on a barstool. Two seats down, a grilled cheese sandwich, a bowl of soup, and a glass of water sat untouched. Not the dinner he'd planned for the two of them, which he took as rejection number four. Opting to distance himself in case she had a stomach virus, he retreated to the far side of the island and leaned his hips against the countertop. "I guess you aren't up to going out to dinner, are you?"

Elbows on the island, Angellica lifted her head up from where it rested on her upturned palms. Eyes squinted, she deadpanned, "What gave you that idea, genius?"

"Oh, I don't know. The wet hair. The sweatpants. The shirt, or what's left of one, you're wearing." He pointed at the uneaten meal. "The dinner. Or maybe it was the puking." He pretended to give it some thought. "All those are compelling reasons, but I think the puking was the giveaway."

"Ugh." She dropped her arms to the countertop, and her head followed.

Sean crossed his ankles and gripped the counter behind him with both hands. He wanted to touch her so badly, but germs aside, she didn't seem receptive to his help in any way, shape, or form. Orgasms were definitely off the table. "How long have you been sick?"

"I'm not sick."

"Not buying it." Even though she couldn't see him with her head lying on her crossed arms, he still shook his head to emphasize his point. "You're sick. Go up to bed, and I'll bring you some tea and crackers."

Her head rocked back and forth before she raised up and fixed bloodshot eyes on him. "I was fine until you got here. You didn't answer my question earlier. What are you doing here?"

He pushed away from the cabinet and leaned on the island instead, facing her. "Don't you read your text messages? I came to take you out to dinner to celebrate completing the harvest."

The way her brows knit together as she tried to work out what he'd said would have been comical if she hadn't been worshiping the porcelain god a few minutes ago. He hadn't said anything complicated. He thought. He was thinking she wasn't going to respond when she suddenly sat up straight.

"My phone! I left it upstairs." She slid off the stool, presumably intent on retrieving her phone.

"You really didn't get my message?"

"What message?"

"The one I sent when my plane landed. I said I'd be home in about an hour and to be ready to go out to dinner."

Standing in the doorway, she shook her head. "I took a shower as soon as I got home. Then I was hungry, so I came down to fix something to eat and forgot all about my phone."

"Then you didn't know it was me when I came in?"

"I thought you were a burglar."

Sean nodded. "That explains the knife. Sort of. Doesn't explain the puking, though. Does seeing me make you physically ill?"

"Maybe."

He raised one eyebrow, inviting an explanation.

Angellica huffed out a breath. "Okay. Okay. It's stress. I've been under a lot of stress lately. I was feeling better— then you walked in and scared the living daylights out of me."

"So that wasn't the first time you barfed up your guts?"

"It's the last. You're back so you can take over—do things your way."

Guilt at leaving her all alone here for so long ate at him. She was perfectly capable of running the farm on her own. She'd done so for three years prior to him purchasing the land, but her father had been here then. Even though Tomas hadn't taken any interest in the vineyard, he'd been around to lend his advice or to help in a pinch. Sean had left without a word of instruction and left her to figure out everything on her own. No wonder she'd been stressed. He needed to put her at ease, and there was no time like to present to admit he'd been wrong.

"I'm sorry, Angel. I would have been here if I could have. At any rate, I should have communicated with you every day. But I'm glad you were here. Part of the reason I didn't call was that I had confidence in your ability to run the business on your own. You proved that to me during the first harvest." He smiled as he admitted, "When your dad first told me about you, I thought you were a bimbo."

Angellica's mouth dropped open and her eyes narrowed. Sean raised a hand to stall the impending outburst. "I know he's your dad, but he really didn't paint you in a favorable light. He made it sound like you'd need an entire year to find a job and another place to live. I realized he was wrong the moment I met you. I don't know if he truly believes you're the person he described to me or if he had some other motive for building your employment into the sale contract. I *do* know you turned out to be the most welcome surprise I've had in forever, and I don't know what I would have done these past weeks without you."

"You said that was *part* of the reason you didn't call." He found he couldn't look away from her steely gaze. "What was the other reason?"

"Maybe we should save that discussion for tomorrow. You need a good night's sleep, and frankly, so do I." Like Angellica, stress had kept him awake at night. He couldn't wait to sleep in his own bed.

She stared into his eyes for the longest seconds of his life, then, with a slight nod, said, "You win. I'm going to bed. But don't think I'm going to forget."

"I promise we'll talk about it tomorrow." He listened for the creak of the topmost step on the staircase before he set the teakettle to boil and cleaned the dishes Angellica had left behind. Once the tea was ready, he placed it on a tray along with some saltines and carried it up to her room. She'd left the door cracked open enough that he could see that she was fast asleep. Since she hadn't eaten the meal she'd prepared, he tiptoed in and placed the tray on her nightstand in case she woke up hungry in the middle of the night. Soft light from the hallway touched her slumbering figure. For the briefest moment, Sean imagined what it would be like to wake next to her every day for the rest of his life. A few months ago, the thought would have sent him running, but not tonight. She was a timeless beauty, inside and out, and he'd be a lucky man to win her heart.

Not the evening I imagined.

CHAPTER THIRTY-NINE

For the first time in weeks, Sean woke feeling rested. He had confidence in the blends he'd decided on for the New Jersey wines, and being back in the same house with Angellica eased the anxiety he'd lived with since the night his father had been shot. His dad wasn't one hundred percent yet, but he was getting there. He'd spent an hour with him at the rehab facility before boarding the company jet to come home. A smile broke across his face as he recalled their conversation. The two had come to a mutual understanding regarding Sean's continuing role in the family business, and Paul Nightingale had expressed his confidence in the blends Sean authorized in his absence. "I never doubted you, son," were words that stuck with him, and always would. "And if you say we need to incorporate some California grapes, then that's what we're going to do. I've always known you inherited the winemaking genes. When you were a kid, you would only eat one brand of grape jelly. You said they made the others with inferior grapes." His dad had laughed until he winced with pain. "I knew you'd be the next head vintner at Nightingales. Your brothers couldn't tell grape jelly from blackberry much less one grape from another. Not that I'm not proud of them, too. They're the best at what they do, but you? You've got wine in your blood."

Sean had been hesitant to leave, but his father practically insisted he return to California. "What's this I hear about some woman tying you in knots?" he'd asked.

"Who told you that?"

"Your mother. I don't know where she heard it, so don't ask." He adjusted his position on the bed. "Is it true? Are you finally going to settle down?"

The question had stunned him, and his answer stunned him even more. "Yeah, Dad. She's the one. I screwed up, though. She says she doesn't have feelings for me."

"What did you do?"

He gave his dad a truncated version of the last time he'd seen Angellica. "Last time I talked to her, she said it hadn't meant anything to her. She's lying, Dad. I saw it in her eyes. The problem is, I panicked. I'm certain that's what she saw in *my* eyes. Not the love I have for her. Not the future I see for us."

"You're serious about this? You're in love with her?"

"Absolutely." He hesitated a moment, then met his dad's gaze head-on. "Do you believe in Déjà vu?"

"Is that where you have the feeling that you've been somewhere before?"

"Yeah. The other day we were in the kitchen together and I zoned out for a second. I saw us, Dad. Angellica and me, and our four kids—three boys and a baby girl—having breakfast together in that very kitchen. It threw me for a loop, but it felt right. That's my future. Our future. I know it."

"Love is timeless, son. Don't let her get away. Go home and tell her you love her. And for goodness' sakes, get busy on those four grandkids! I'm not getting any younger, and I want to see them before I go."

"But—"

"I'm fine. I'll be out of here in no time, and the staff at the winery know what they're doing. They don't need me or you to blend this year's wines. So, get. Shoo. Go make mes some grandbabies."

Fresh out of the shower, Sean made his way down the hall, pausing at Angellica's door. It was still open slightly, just as he'd left it the night before. He lifted a hand to knock, but the sound of someone retching froze him in his tracks. Not bothering to knock, he strode into the room, past the rumpled bed and untouched tea and crackers on her nightstand. "Angellica?" He paused in the bathroom door. Angellica was on her knees, her upper body bent over the toilet. She glanced his way, then retched again.

Stress my ass. "Why didn't you tell me?" he asked as he wet a washcloth and handed it to her.

"Tell you what?"

"That you're pregnant."

She heaved again, then flopped over onto her butt and glared at him like he'd grown horns on his head. "What are you talking about? I'm not pregnant?"

Sean joined her on the floor. One eyebrow raised, he nodded at her, then toward the toilet. "Really? That's the story you're sticking to?"

"It's not a story," she said, but her expression said otherwise. "I can't be. We used protection."

"Nothing other than abstinence is one hundred percent effective. And we didn't abstain." A horrible thought entered his brain and Sean shot to his feet. "It's not mine."

Angellica narrowed her eyes at him, then they widened, and her mouth dropped open. "What? You think I've been with someone else?"

"You said it yourself. We used protection."

"Who the hell do you think I would have had sex with,

genius? Look around. I've been all alone out here for weeks. Except for Lexie, and if you really aced all your biology classes, you'd know that's not the way it works." She leaned over the bowl and retched again.

Sean waited until she'd sat back again and wiped the spittle off her lips. "What about that Kevin guy? During the harvest?"

"He had his chance years ago. Besides, he's moved on. He told me so himself when he was here for the harvest."

"Then the baby's mine."

"There's no baby!" She retched again. When she sat back up, Sean arched an eyebrow at her. "You think I could be pregnant? Seriously?"

"Yeah. I seriously think you could be." He stood and held out a hand to help her up. "Come on. I'll help you get back to bed, then I'll go to the pharmacy. We'll know for sure in less than an hour."

CHAPTER FORTY

The moment she heard the front door close behind Sean, Angellica hit redial on Lexie's number. The call went to voicemail. No surprise given the time of day. The production schedule for her show was insane. She'd probably been at work for hours already. "Come on. Come on," she chanted as her friend's recorded message played. Finally, the beep sounded, and Angellica broke down in tears. "He thinks I'm pregnant, Lex! I'm not. Please tell me I'm not pregnant! I can't be!" Another beep signaled the end of the recording session. Angellica hit redial again, and wiping tears from her cheeks, left a second message. "Call me ASAP." With the phone still clutched in her hand, she rolled over and closed her eyes. The next thing she knew, Sean was nudging her shoulder.

"Wake up, Angel. I bought three different tests."

"Huh?" She blinked sleep and remnants of her crying jag from her eyes to focus on the brown paper bag Sean held up for her to see. "Oh." Feeling like she was in a nightmare, she allowed Sean to escort her to the bathroom, where he dumped three boxes out on the countertop. She stared at them like they were grenades and pulling the pins would destroy her life.

"I asked the pharmacist. She said you just pee on the sticks. In minutes, you have your answer."

"Minutes, huh?" Her future defined for her in minutes. Seconds if she thought about that night. He'd gone off like a rocket as soon as he was inside her, then regretted it. One mistake, and here they were, buying pregnancy tests. This couldn't be happening. But it was.

"Yeah. Uhm. Have a seat? I'll hand you the first one."

"You'll do no such thing! Get out! Out!" She pointed to the door.

"But—"

"No. You are not watching me pee. No way. No how. I can do this on my own."

His gaze bored into her for a second before he relented. "Okay, but we'll wait it out together. Just let me know when you're through and I'll start a timer." He held his phone up.

"Get out. Now."

"Okay. I'm going." The smile on his face was so at odds with her own feelings that she didn't know what to make of it. Was he happy about this? Did he want her to be pregnant? What guy *wanted* to knock a woman up outside of wedlock? None that she knew, that's for sure. Angellica locked the door then leaned against it. Her gaze landed on the boxes that held the key to her future.

"I'm not pregnant," she mumbled as she picked the first one up and read the instructions. It was as simple as Sean had said. After reading all three, she positioned herself on the toilet and did the nasty deed. "Okay," she called out. "Start the timer. Three minutes!"

She flushed, then washed her hands. She stared at the three sticks lined up on the counter like sentinels. Would they bring good news, or bad? She didn't want to be pregnant. Or did she?

"Are you coming out?" It sounded like he was just outside the door. The doorknob jiggled, confirming her suspicions. "Come on out, Angel. We can wait together."

With one last glance at the sticks lined up on the counter, Angellica unlocked the door and swung it open. "Did you start the timer?" she asked.

"Yeah." He held his phone up. "See? Two more minutes."

Two minutes. Then she could have her life back. *I'm not pregnant. I'm not.* She would know something like that. Right? Though who hadn't heard of women giving birth who claimed they never even knew they were pregnant? *That's not me. I'd know. If I was carrying Sean's baby, I'd know.* She skirted past him to sit on the edge of the bed. He joined her without invitation, but she didn't have the energy to make him leave. Besides, he'd never believe her if he didn't see the results for himself. "I'm not pregnant." She felt the need to say it one more time. "I'd know if I were."

Sean shrugged. "I'm sorry about what happened. I mean…I'm not sorry about what we did. I'm sorry about the way I reacted afterward." He reached for her hand, enclosing it in his much bigger one. "I panicked, Angel. What I experienced with you was unlike anything I've ever experienced before. I know I came like a teenager having sex for the first time, but in a way, I was. Don't get me wrong. I've had a lot of sex, but it was never like it was with you. The moment we connected, I felt like I'd come home. I never wanted to leave. That's why I just sat there, not moving. Then you came, and God help me, I couldn't stop what happened. You had me, Angel. I was yours. I'll always be yours. No matter what those sticks say, I love you. I'll always love you." He squeezed her hand, and her gaze met his. "I know this is going to sound crazy, but you remember when I zoned out that day? Before? You were fixing breakfast and I kind of drifted off?"

"I remember." He'd been daydreaming or something.

"That's the moment I knew we'd be together for the rest of our lives."

"What?" She tried to pull her hand away, but he held on tight.

"I told you it was going to sound crazy," he continued. "I had this Déjà vu moment. I saw us, Angel. You. Me. And our four kids. Three boys and a baby girl. We were all in the kitchen. The one here, in this house, and you were fixing a meal for us. The boys were running around like little monsters, and the baby was in a carrier thing on top of the island. I saw our future, Angel. We were happy. So happy. And I knew I loved you then."

She didn't know what to say—couldn't wrap her head around what he was saying. "But—" Struggling for words, she opened her mouth just as his phone chimed. The time was up.

Sean sprung to his feet, dragging her to her feet by the hand he still held securely in his own. "No matter what, Angel. Baby or no baby, I love you. We belong together."

"I'm not pregnant." For the first time since Sean had placed the thought in her head, she felt a tinge of sadness. She could almost see the vision he claimed to have had, and as scary as it sounded, it felt right. Her. Sean. And four kids. Three little boys who looked just like their father and a little girl to boss them all around. It would be a good life here on the land her ancestors had toiled on for a century.

"I love you anyway, Angel." He tugged her toward the bathroom. "Come on. Let's go see the results."

CHAPTER FORTY-ONE

"I thought for sure…"

I'm not pregnant. Tears clouded her vision. Not the tears of joy she'd expected, but tears of disappointment. No matter his declarations of love and his crazy daydream, she wasn't the kind of woman who could hold a man like Sean Nightingale for long. A child would bind them together in parenthood—if nothing else. Now, there wasn't even that. "I told you," she said, the words coming out in a whisper. "I would have known."

And she would. She was certain of that. If Sean left a part of himself behind, her body would tell her. She'd had one chance and failed. No rambunctious Nightingale boys. No sweet baby girl to bring Sean to his knees. He'd be a great father, but someone else would be the mother of his children. Not her.

She'd told him it was only sex when it had been anything but. He'd move on, but she never would. And now, she wouldn't have anything to show for all she'd given him. No baby. No heart. Five minutes ago, she was certain she didn't want to be pregnant. Now, she mourned the loss of something she never had and never would have.

"What the hell is that?" Sean asked. He moved toward the bathroom door, and that's when she heard it. Someone was banging on the front door. "Are you expecting anybody?"

She shook her head.

"Wait here. I'll be right back." He sprinted out of the bathroom before she could beg him to stay, and somehow, she knew. He wouldn't be back. She'd lost him for good.

Forcing her gaze away from the negative results, she made her way out of the bathroom and down the hallway. Sean stood in the foyer; the door still open to reveal a woman. A very pregnant woman standing on the porch. Angellica inched closer but stayed to the side where she wouldn't be seen.

"Why haven't you taken any of my calls? I've been looking for you for months!" the woman screeched.

"I've been busy," Sean replied with a disinterested air. "How *did* you find me?"

"A friend saw you in New York last week with some bimbo. She overheard you talking about the vineyard you bought in California. I thought she meant in Napa, not this backwater, wanna-be vineyard in…where the hell are we, anyway?"

"Temecula, and it's not a backwater. They've been making excellent wine in this valley for a century." She rolled her eyes at him. "You didn't come here to critique my choice of vineyards, so why *are* you here?"

"Why? You have to ask *why*?" She put a hand on her distended belly. "I've been hunting you down to tell you that you're going to be a father!"

"What? No. Oh, *hell,* no!" Sean took a step back and pointed a finger at her enormous pregnancy bump. "That's not mine. No way in hell."

"It is yours!"

"Jesus, Camilla. You can't be serious. You're about to pop! We were only together once, and that was what, two months ago? Three at most? That," he pointed at her again, "is not mine."

The woman was gorgeous. Tall. Skinny, except for the enormous baby bump. Hair and makeup that looked professionally done. The purse on her arm bore an expensive designer label and matched her shoes. Just the type of woman Sean was known to be seen with. He even admitted to having sex with her!

"It only takes once," the woman shrieked. "This baby is a Nightingale, whether you like it or not. I should have known you'd deny it. How many other women have you fucked, then left them to deal with your by-blow? Well, I'm here to tell you I won't stand for it. I'll take you to court if I have to, but you're going to support this child in the manner it deserves, or the entire world will know what a deadbeat you are!"

The woman took off toward the driveway, and Sean followed, hot on her heels. "Wait! Hey, stop! Let's talk about this!"

And there it was. If he was willing to talk, then there had to be some truth to her statement. Angellica was just one in a long string of women he'd seduced, but no more. *I'm out of here.* She raced back to her room and dressed as fast as she could. She had to leave before Sean came back inside. A quick glance around the room yielded her phone and charger and her laptop. After throwing them into an old canvas tote she'd left in the closet when she moved to the cottage, she slipped on her shoes. She swept through the bathroom, gathering her toothbrush and hair products. As an afterthought, she scooped up the three negative pregnancy tests and dropped them into the bag as well.

Taking the back stairs, she exited through the kitchen door and ran to the cottage where she'd left her car. Sean would probably have a fit if he knew she'd left her purse on the front seat and her keys in the ignition, but it worked to her advantage now. Minutes after leaving the house, Angellica barreled up the driveway and out onto the main road. A few minutes later, she was on the highway, headed north. Lexie would know what to do.

CHAPTER FORTY-TWO

"I don't have a fucking clue where she is, Ian. If I did, I wouldn't be asking, no *begging*, you to help me find her." He'd video called his younger brother out of desperation. After chasing Camilla down, to no avail, he'd returned to the house to find Angellica gone. No note. Nothing. A search of her room and the cottage revealed she'd taken the bare minimum with her. Her phone. Possibly her laptop, but he couldn't be sure about that, and her toothbrush. Inexplicably, she'd taken their test results. He didn't have a clue what that meant, but he aimed to find out just as soon as he tracked her down.

"Have you tried calling her?"

Sean held the camera closer to his face. "Do I look like an idiot, Ian? Of course, I tried calling her. I've left so many voicemail messages that her inbox is full." He pulled the phone away from his face. "I even called her father in Italy. Woke the bastard up. He told me her friend Lexie works for that TV show, *Love at First Sight.* He gave me a last name, but he wasn't sure it was correct. Who doesn't know their daughter's best friend's last name?"

"You think she's with Lexie?"

"I don't know." He hoped she was. The only other friends he'd met of hers were men, and he didn't want to think she'd run to them to get away from him. "It's my best guess. I looked up the production company. There are several Alexas, Alexandrias, listed as employees, and none of them have the last name Tomas gave me. I haven't got a clue what she does for them. She might not be important enough to list on their website."

"Did you try calling them?"

"Duh. They told me they don't give out personal information about their employees."

"I'd be surprised if they did."

"Then why did you ask if I'd called them?"

"Because if you did, it would tell me how desperate you are to find Angellica."

"You're an asshole. Thanks for nothing. I'm hanging up now." He was about to press the red disconnect button when Ian's voice stopped him.

"Wait! Don't hang up! I'll help you find her. Okay?"

Sean lifted the phone back to his face. "How?"

"I don't know but let me make some phone calls. I might know someone in L.A."

"You *might* know someone? How does that work?"

"A guy I went to the academy with. He moved out there a few years ago because of the weather. Let me see if I can find his number. He might be able to help."

It sounded like a long shot, but it was better than nothing. "Okay, but I'm driving up there tonight. If I can find out where they're shooting this show, maybe I can find Lexie."

"Don't you have grapes to process? Dad said you went home to help with the harvest."

"I don't give a shit about the grapes. I've got to find Angellica."

"Look, Sean. I know she means a lot to you. You wouldn't have called me for help otherwise, so let me handle this. I'll call my friend and get him started on finding this Lexie, or Alexa, or whatever her name is. In the meantime, I'll take some time off and fly out there. Finding people is part of my job. You stay where you are. Keep your business running, and I'll find your girlfriend."

He needed to process the last harvest. If he didn't, he'd lose the money he stood to make on the sale of the juice, and he needed that money. He'd gladly sacrifice the vineyard and the investment he'd made in it if it meant getting Angellica back, but that wasn't part of his vision. His and Angellica's future was at the vineyard. He'd seen it himself. "You're right. I need to take care of the harvest. I hate it, but I'll stay here." He met Ian's gaze. "Are you sure you can take time off? I don't want you to lose your job because I fucked up with my soulmate."

Ian pounced on Sean's word choice like a cat on a trapped mouse. "Soulmate? Is that what you said?"

"Fuck off, baby brother. Just find her for me. Okay?"

"Consider it done."

Sean scrubbed his free hand over his face. "I can't thank you enough, bro."

"Don't thank me yet, but once I find her, you're going to owe me, big time."

After promising to focus on keeping the vineyard afloat, Sean ended the call. He fell face-first onto the kitchen island. The day had started out so promising, then it went to shit in a matter of minutes. He'd gone from potentially becoming a father to not being one, to…*absolutely not* being one. Camilla was out of her mind if she thought he was going to accept that kid as his. She had to be at least six months along. He'd never even heard of her six months ago, much less slept with her. "Fucking Brad." The kid had to be his. He'd dumped Camilla a week before Sean met her and that's all she wanted to talk about on their "date." She'd even called him Brad in the throes of her orgasm. She'd been in no shape for a new relationship and Sean hadn't been looking for one, so going their separate ways was the only way to go.

Sean wondered if Brad had found out about the baby, and that's why he left. If so, he was a Grade A scumbag. Any man who would walk out on his child was lower than low. But that didn't mean Sean had to take on a responsibility that wasn't his. Camilla had money. She'd made a fortune modeling and could provide for a dozen children without outside financial help. Which meant she wasn't necessarily after Sean's money, which was a good thing because his cash reserves were dangerously low. No, she was after a name to give her child. Sean would rather give her his last dollar than his name. The money meant nothing. His family name, though? That had meaning, and he wasn't going to be responsible for tarnishing it.

Pushing back from the island, Sean stood and stretched. It had been a long day, and tomorrow wasn't going to be any better. He had a couple of day laborers coming early in the morning to help him run the Pinot Noir grapes through the crusher. Once that was done, he could concentrate on bottling the six-year-old vintage currently stored in the cask room. The sooner he got those out, the sooner he'd be on his way to financial solvency.

He'd slept like crap the night before. Every time he closed his eyes, he imagined all kinds of terrible things that might befall a woman on her own. Feeding grapes into the crusher involved a lot of heavy lifting, and by the end of the day, Sean ached from head to toe. The manual labor had helped keep his mind off Angellica, but now that the hard work was done, she was all he could think about. A quick call to Ian yielded no new information regarding her whereabouts. Ian had arrived earlier in Los Angeles and assured Sean he would find his runaway girlfriend in a matter of days. Sean trusted his brother, but that didn't make the waiting any easier. To make matters worse, Camilla was still hounding him. He'd sent countless calls from her to voicemail and ignored dozens of text messages. As he sat down to enjoy the pizza he'd had delivered, he skimmed through the text messages and listened to the last voicemail she'd left. One thing was obvious. He had to resolve this thing with Camilla before he could get Angellica back. Having another woman's pregnancy hanging over his head wasn't going to help his cause.

After washing a bite of pizza down with a healthy swig of a Capello wine he'd found in the cellar, Sean sat back on the sofa in the family room and dialed Camilla's number. She answered on the second ring. "Sean! I knew you'd come to your senses."

"Whoa! Camilla. Stop right there. I called to tell you that there is nothing between us. Nothing. No relationship. No baby. It's not mine, and you know it."

"But, Sean," she pleaded. He could almost see the pouty face that had launched her career as a cover model. It was sexy, and seductive, and fake.

"No buts. I get that you're scared and that you want a father for your kid, but that's not me. I've met someone. I'm going to marry her and have a houseful of kids with her. Her, Camilla. Not you." There was silence on the other end. Sean sighed. "Where's Brad? Did you tell him you're pregnant?"

"I don't know where he is. We haven't spoken since he left."

"You never told me why he left." She'd gone on and on about the man, and cried buckets of tears over him, but he'd never heard her say why he'd ended their relationship.

"He wanted to get married."

What? "And you said no?" Sean couldn't keep the disbelief out of his voice.

"He wanted me to quit modeling! I'm not the kind of woman who's going to stay at home and mop floors, Sean.

I love my career!"

Sean took a moment to process what he was hearing.

"Sean? Are you still there?"

"I'm here." He let out a heavy sigh. "Look, Camilla. I don't want to be the one to point out the obvious, but you're pregnant! I assume you want this baby, or you would have done something about it a long time ago?"

"What kind of   question is that? Of course, I want the baby! It's Brad's! It's all I have left of him."

"Again, pointing out the obvious, but that's not all you have left. The man asked you to marry him, Camilla! I'd bet money that you can have him back. Call him. Don't tell him about the baby, just ask to see him. If he refuses to see you, then you'll know the relationship is over for good, but if he agrees to meet you? You've got a real chance at happiness. But you have to be strong. Tell him how you feel about your career. My mom worked full time and raised three boys. Lots of women do it. There's no reason you can't do it too. If your career is a deal-breaker for him, then do you really want to spend your life with him? I'm betting the answer is no. In that case, you go on with your life. I know you don't need money. You're a successful model, and perfectly capable of being a single mother. You don't need me or Brad. You don't want me, Camilla. You *want* Brad, so give him a chance to be the man you want him to be."

A long silence followed Sean's lecture, then Camilla's voice, sounding strong and confident, came through. "You're right, Sean. I need to give Brad a chance. If he loves me the way he said before, he'll understand why I want to hang on to my career as long as I can. My agent has some interviews and photo sessions lined up for me, but I have to be married, or at least engaged, or the magazines won't move forward with the project."

And there it was, the real reason she'd tried to sink her claws into Sean. He held his tongue, though. Pointing out her duplicity wouldn't do him any good. "I'm glad to hear that, and I'm sure Brad will be proud to have his wife or fiancée's pregnancy photos on a magazine cover." Personally, he'd rather keep that private, but, again, Camilla didn't need to hear his opinions. "By the way, you look gorgeous. Pregnancy suits you." That, at least, wasn't a lie. Even through the rage she'd thrown his way, he saw her inner beauty shining through. "I wish you all the best. Send me an invitation to the wedding?"

Her laughter filled the line. "Absolutely, and I hope this mystery woman you spoke of knows how lucky she is. Have a good life, Sean."

The line went dead, and every muscle in his body went slack. Camilla's appearance on his doorstep couldn't have happened at a worse time. Undoubtedly, Angellica had overheard their one-sided conversation, and on the heels of finding out that she *wasn't* pregnant, had run. He couldn't blame her. The optics of the situation had been bad. Really, really, bad. Still, he wished Angellica had stayed long enough to hear his side of the story. He couldn't blame her for running. He'd wanted to run, too. Being named daddy to a baby that wasn't his was enough to make his nuts shrivel. Thank God Camilla had listened to reason. He could only hope Angellica would let him explain. If he ever found her

CHAPTER FORTY-THREE

"You need to see a doctor."

Angellica didn't want to admit it, but Lexie might be right. She'd been hiding out in her best friend's house apartment for two days, and the nausea hadn't abated one bit.

"Are you sure you aren't pregnant?" Lex asked as she opened another package of saltines and placed them on the coffee table. "You've got all the classic symptoms. Nausea. Fatigue. Sore boobs."

"I took three home pregnancy tests. They all said the same thing."

"They could be wrong?" Lexie didn't sound convinced. "Even if they're right. No—especially if they're right, you need to see a doctor. Something's wrong, Jelly. This—isn't normal."

"You're right, Lex. I've chalked it up to stress, but all I've done since I got here is lie around and I'm still sick. Who should I see?"

"A GP?"

"General Practitioner?"

"Yeah. You know, someone you go to when you have the flu." She reached for her phone. "I'll call mine, see if I can get you in."

"You think I have the flu?"

"No." She shook her head as she scrolled through her contacts. "I think you're pregnant."

Angellica wanted to argue the point, but Lex pressed her phone to her ear and turned to look out the window, effectively cutting off communication. A few minutes later, Lex was dragging her out the door. Somehow, she'd convinced the person on the phone to let Angellica come in for an emergency pregnancy test. Once they were in the car and stuck in L.A. traffic, she brought the subject up. "Why did you ask for the pregnancy test? I can't be pregnant."

"We've been over this. Those home tests can be wrong. It's uncommon, but not unheard of. You need the test they do at the doctor's office. If that one's negative, we'll book you an appointment to find out what's really going on, but my bet is on pregnancy."

The waiting room was packed, but once Lexie explained who they were and why they were here, they were quickly shown to a small office in the back. A nurse handed Angellica a specimen cup with a sticker bearing her name stuck on it. The woman pointed her toward a bathroom.

"I'll wait here." Lexie sat in one of the visitor chairs facing a desk cluttered with files and empty coffee cups. "Make sure you wash your hands when you're done."

"Yes, Mother." Angellica rolled her eyes. This was a waste of time, but Lexie was right. She had to find out what was wrong with her, and taking a real pregnancy test was the most logical place to start. Once it came back negative, the doctor could concentrate on finding the real culprit for her symptoms.

They'd been sitting in the office for almost half an

hour when a woman wearing a white lab coat and carrying a file folder breezed into the office. She shut the door behind her. "Hi," she said, stopping beside Angellica's chair. "Hey, Lexie. It's good to see you. How's the show going?"

"We've been renewed for two more seasons, so that's good."

The *doctor*? Was all smiles. "Congratulations! That's awesome." She turned her attention to Angellica. "And you must be Jelly." She held out her hand. Angellica automatically shook it.

"That's me," she said, glancing from the newcomer to her best friend, and back. "You two know each other?"

Lexie jumped in while the other woman walked around the desk and took a seat. "Laura, Dr. Winters, was a contestant on season 4? Yeah, season 4. She didn't fall in love at first sight, but she did fall in love." Lex arched an eyebrow at the doctor.

Dr. Winters smiled at Lex, then focused on Angellica. "I married one of the producers, Michael Rhodes. We've been married for three years. Going on that show was the best thing that ever happened to me. I earned enough money to pay off a chunk of my student loans, and I met the man of my dreams." She beamed a dazzling smile at Lex. "So, are you one of the new contestants?" she asked Angellica.

"No. I'm, well, Lex is my best friend. We've known each other since third grade."

"That's sweet." The doctor dragged out the last syllable as she opened the file folder Angellica had noticed earlier. "Well, congratulations are in order. You're definitely pregnant!"

"What?!"

"You'll want to set up an appointment with your OBGYN as soon as possible, but unless you have any immediate concerns, that can wait a few weeks."

Angellica scooted to the edge of her chair. "I took three home pregnancy tests. They were all negative."

The doctor's eyebrows met in the middle. "That's concerning, but not unheard of."

"Um…Laura?" Lexie had also scooted to the edge of her chair. "What kind of things could cause a false negative? Anything Jelly should be concerned about?"

The doctor's gaze landed on Angellica. "Are you taking any drugs, prescribed or otherwise?"

"No."

"Are you sure you peed on the sticks?"

"Yes."

"First thing in the morning?"

"Yes."

"That's when the pregnancy hormones are the most concentrated. Had you missed a period when you took the tests?"

Angellica had to think for a second before answering. "Now that I think about it, yes."

"Okay, then. There's only one thing I can think of that would cause the tests to report a false negative." She chewed her lip.

"And that would be?" Angellica prompted.

"Multiple fetuses."

Angellica shot to her feet. "What?"

"More than one fetus raises the level of Human Chorionic Gonadotropin, hCG, for short, in the mother's body to a level that can sometimes cause a false negative with the home pregnancy tests. It's rare, but the mistake is well documented. Of course, you'll need to see your OBGYN to confirm, but given your answers to my other questions, it's a safe bet that you're having twins. Or more."

"But she's definitely pregnant?" Lexie asked.

"Oh, yeah. Our tests don't lie."

Angellica didn't recall leaving the doctor's office. She didn't recall the car ride back to Lexie's apartment. At some point, she'd changed into her pajamas and tucked herself into the corner of her best friend's couch. "Have some tea." Lexie stood over her with a mug in one hand and a sleeve of saltines in the other. "It's herbal. No caffeine for you, little momma. Oh, and some crackers. You need to eat. You're eating for three now. Or more. You've got to take care of yourself."

Angellica looked past the meager meal being offered and met Lexie's gaze. "Tell me I just woke up from a nightmare, and none of what you're saying is real."

"Nope. You're pregnant. Probably with multiples. The sooner you get used to the idea, the better. Want me to call your doctor and make an appointment?"

"No."

"But…you need to see a doctor."

"I know, but if I go back to Temecula right now, it won't be long before everyone in town knows. You know how the town is. It's grown in the last few years, but it's still a small town at heart. The receptionist's first cousin is Carmen Sanchez—the editor of the town newspaper."

Lexie set the mug and crackers on the table, then plopped on the sofa next to Angellica. "I'd forgotten about that. Neither one can keep their mouth shut." They digested the information for a few seconds before Lexie broke the silence. "I'll call Laura and ask for a local recommendation. She won't refer you to a quack."

"Thanks. I'd appreciate that." She placed a hand over her abdomen. "It doesn't seem real, but at the same time, I feel like I have to protect…them."

"Them," Lexie repeated. "You really think there's more than one?"

She nodded. "Yeah, I do. I know it sounds crazy. A few hours ago, I was certain I wasn't pregnant at all, and now that I know I am, it's as if I knew all along. It's twins,

Lexie. Two boys."

Her friend shifted on the sofa to face her, one eyebrow raised. "That's awfully specific. Do you know something medical science doesn't?"

"No, but I know what Sean told me." She explained about the daydream, Déjà vu, that Sean experienced. "I thought he was, I don't know, wishful thinking? Dreaming? Hallucinating? But now, I think he might have been right."

"If he saw that, and you're carrying twin boys, then you know what that means, don't you?"

"That we'll have two more kids and live happily ever after?" Angellica scoffed. "I'm not willing to go that far. He got a supermodel pregnant, Lex. I saw her with my own eyes. He chased after her when she left! He didn't chase after me."

"Did he see you leave?"

"Well, no, but still. It's been days. Why didn't he come after me?"

"He called and sent you text messages. None of which you answered. Is it possible he doesn't know where you are?"

"He knows you're my best friend. How hard could it be to find me?" She reached for the tea Lex had prepared for her and brought the mug to her lips for a sip. "He quit calling and texting. He's with her. I know it." She took another sip. "You should have seen her. Even pregnant, she was gorgeous. Not a hair out of place. Perfect makeup. And I was upstairs in my ratty pajamas with dried barf on my chin and red eyes from crying over three sticks I'd just peed on. Hardly a glamourous scenario. I grow grapes, Lex. She…smiles for cameras and wears designer clothes that are probably given to her because they look better on her than on a mannequin. I wear steel-toed boots, and I buy my work shirts at the farm supply store. Sean's a millionaire who attends galas all over the world. It doesn't take a genius to figure out who he'll choose."

"Yet you didn't get knocked up via immaculate conception."

Angellica snorted. "Same difference. I've been on the pill for years, and he wore a condom. Some might call that a miracle."

"Or fate."

A shiver raced down Angellica's spine. She stared into the cooling tea, recalling the night she'd become pregnant. It certainly hadn't been an immaculate conception. She'd welcomed Sean into her body and given him her heart that night. Having him inside her had been the most beautiful experience of her life. Mind-blowing. Life-changing. In more ways than one, it seemed. She'd known he'd had exponentially more lovers than she'd had, but none of that had mattered when he drove deep inside her. If she closed her eyes, she could still feel his heart beating against hers and his life force pulsing inside her as her body rhythmically clung to his. They'd been one at that moment.

And now she was three.

CHAPTER FORTY-FOUR

Ian didn't have to be as brilliant as Sean to see the appeal of Southern California. At noon, the sun beat down from almost directly overhead like a sunlamp on its highest setting. According to the information he'd read online, this was an almost daily occurrence, year-round. He could get used to it. His friend, Tony, had.

As he drove his rental car along the Pacific Coast Highway, he cast furtive glances at the ocean waves. Every now and again, a dark speck stood out in the water. A surfer, no doubt. The houses lining the small strip of land between the road and the beach kept him from seeing the waves roll up on the beach, but he hoped to catch a glimpse soon. Tony had given him an address where they were taping the latest season of *Love at First Sight* and assured him he could find the person he was looking for on the set. The set being one of the multi-million-dollar homes blocking his view of the beach.

He'd had some concerns about locating the exact house, seeing as most of them didn't have any visible house numbers, but his concerns were unfounded. As he rounded a slight curve in the road, his destination became clear. Half a dozen white trailers, and as many box trucks lined the mainland side of the road. Production trailers. He'd seen them a time or two in New Jersey. Their lack of markings was supposed to make them appear discreet, but the blank white sides screamed, production in progress! More cars lined the road ahead of and behind the trucks and trailers than Ian could count, making it difficult for him to find a parking place. He ended up turning up a small road that led away from the beach. About half a mile up, he found the turnout for a fruit stand selling strawberries picked from the field behind the stand. Ian pulled in at the far edge of the parking area and cut the engine. Judging from the traffic coming and going, the place did a good business. Climbing out of the car, he stretched his arms over his head and twisted his torso around one way, then the other. Travel could be a bitch, even in the family jet. A walk in the sunshine would do him good.

After purchasing a half-flat of the fresh berries, Ian set off on foot down the hill toward his target. The berries, if there were any left when he got there, would serve as an excuse to get close to the house. "Delivery for food services," he practiced as he chomped down on another plump berry. The damn things were addictive, and you sure didn't get them that fresh where he lived. Yeah, California was rapidly growing on him.

It turned out he didn't need an excuse to approach. People scurried all around, but no one paid any attention to him. Following a guy carrying what appeared to be a heavy light, Ian waltzed right into the house. The first thing that caught his attention was the stunning view of the beach—if he cocked his head just right to see beyond the lights and umbrella-like thingies placed around the main room of the house. The second thing that caught his attention was a woman. Magnificent was the first word that came to mind.

Not because of her beauty, though that wasn't in question. She was gorgeous in that sun-kissed Southern California way that so many women seemed to come by naturally out here. What drew Ian's attention was her confidence. Every man, and most of the people in the room were male, jumped at her every command. And she had plenty of commands. "Move that over here. Tilt that this way. Get that the fuck out of here!"

Someone off to Ian's right yelled out, "Clear the set!" People scampered like cockroaches running from the exterminator. Not knowing where to go, Ian stood his ground, which earned him a glare from the woman. Her gaze met his, and for a fraction of a second, he couldn't breathe. Fuck, she really was beautiful. High cheekbones. Full lips, and deep blue eyes he could drown in. She eyed him up and down, then slowly approached, her hips swaying as she carefully skirted chairs and ottomans scattered around the room. The place had grown deathly quiet, so much so that Ian could hear her footsteps on the plush rug as she grew nearer. She stopped a scant foot in front of him and cocked her head to one side, examining his face.

"Who the fuck are you?"

"Uh." He held the half-eaten box of strawberries a little higher. "Delivery for food services?"

Her lips rose on one side. Not really a smile, but close. Ian flashed her his pickup line smile. "Wait here, delivery man. Don't move a muscle. Don't even breathe until I tell you to."

Okay. I can do that. As she returned to the spot where he'd first seen her, he leaned to one side and placed the box of strawberries on a small table. When he straightened, she frowned at him. A shake of her head told him that even his slight movement had displeased her. Fuck it. He wasn't about to hold those damn berries all day long.

"Hey, Lexie!" someone called out. "You ready for the

girls?"

The woman he'd spoken to shot him a glance, then lifted her chin and called out, "Yeah. Send in the first one." She took her place behind a camera mounted on a tripod and, if his ears didn't deceive him, muttered, "Let's get this fucking show on the road."

So, that's Lexie; he mused as she worked through a series of about ten women, one after the other, as they sat on the sofa and gave their impressions of the bachelor they'd met for the first time the night before. More than a few cast lascivious glances his way, but as attractive as the contestants were, they weren't Lexie Hanson.

Ian had never been on a set before, and he found the whole process fascinating. Lexie was clearly in charge, and everyone, including the contestants, jumped to do whatever she said, and she had a lot to say. Most of her commands were in a vocabulary he didn't understand but found easy to pick up as he listened and watched. After an hour had gone by, his legs and back were aching from standing in one place for so long. He shifted slightly, earning him another glare from Lexie. He shot her one right back. If he were back at home, he'd flash his badge and insist she stop what she was doing to talk to him, but he had zero authority to question her in Los Angeles. That he was trespassing wasn't lost on him. She had every right to have him thrown out of there, and he'd gone to too much trouble to locate her to risk it. So…he stood there like a statue and hoped she'd finish up soon so he could ask her where Angellica was hiding.

He'd tuned out the interviews long ago. Every single woman said basically the same thing. It was like they all shared one brain and didn't have an original thought between them. He felt sorry for the bachelor and hoped he wasn't really expecting to find the love of his life among that assemblage of women, but then again, he hadn't met the bachelor. Maybe the guy wasn't the catch these women seemed to think he was. Maybe he was just as shallow as they were. He was ruminating on the personality traits of the kind of guy who would go on a show like this when suddenly Lexie yelled out. "Cut! That's a wrap! Let's get the room staged for tonight's charm ceremony." The lights abruptly shut off, and people scattered like someone had kicked their ant hill. Ian blinked as he tried to adjust his eyes to the new light level in the room. When he looked up, Lexie stood in front of him, wearing the same frown she'd flashed him before.

"Come on," she said, nodding for him to follow.

He fell into step behind her, admiring the sway of her hips and the shape of her legs beneath her pencil skirt. She led the way out onto the deck, then down to the beach, where she kicked off her sky-high heels before trudging out onto the sand. Ian stopped for a moment to admire the view—of the beach and of her bending over to remove her shoes—then scrambled to catch up to her as she walked toward the surf. He caught up to her on the wet sand. "Hey! Give me a second, will ya?"

Lexie paused long enough for him to remove his shoes before hauling off down the beach again. He had no idea a woman wearing a skirt that tight could move so fast. "What's your hurry, anyway?"

As she glanced his way, the wind whipped a strand of her hair loose from the tight bun at the nape. She reached up to tame it, and there was something about the light, and the position of her body in that moment, that nearly made Ian swallow his tongue. Jesus. Effing. Christ. The woman was a goddess. Someone out of Greek mythology. Aphrodite came to mind, but he wasn't positive that was the one he was thinking about. The name seemed to fit, though, so he went with it. Then she opened her mouth and broke the spell. "What are you doing here?"

Ian pointed a finger at himself. "Me?"

"You," she said, getting right up in his face. His gaze

drifted to her lips, and it was all he could do to look away. "What. Are. You. Doing. Here?"

"Looking for you."

"Why me?"

"Because you know where Angellica Capello is."

She studied his face for a heartbeat, then without saying a word, took off down the beach again.

"Wait up!" he called out as he hustled to catch up again. "Just tell me where she is. Sean is worried about her."

Ian took two steps before he realized she'd stopped. He turned around to find her scrutinizing him from head to toe.

"You can tell him she's fine."

Then she was heading back the way they'd come, and once again, Ian chased after her. "That's good to hear, but he needs to speak to her. Can you at least tell her to answer her phone?"

"I could, but I won't. He hurt her. She gets to decide when or if she wants to speak to him."

"He told me what happened, and suffice to say; it wasn't what it looked like. If nothing else, tell Angellica that the woman admitted that Sean isn't her baby daddy."

Lexie stopped and faced him. "Is that the truth?"

Ian made an X across his chest with his finger. "Cross my heart. They had a long talk, and she's going to tell her ex that she's pregnant with *his* kid. I don't know why she caused that scene with my brother. Maybe she was just scared that she was going to have to raise the kid alone? I can see how that would be intimidating."

She narrowed her eyes at him. "Which brother are you?"

"I'm sorry. I didn't properly introduce myself. I'm Ian Nightingale." He held out his hand to shake but dropped it after she pointedly ignored the offer.

"You aren't the one that's engaged, are you?"

"No. That's our older brother, Wade. Why?"

"No reason." Then she was off again, practically sprinting across the wet sand.

"Hey! Wait up!" He caught up to her again. "Geez, what's the rush? Can't we sit down and talk?"

"No time. Gotta set up for the charm ceremony." Once they were back at the production site, she gathered up her shoes, then pointed to a wooden staircase off to the side of the house. "Go. Tell Sean I'll pass on the message, but not to call her. If she wants to talk, she'll call him." She narrowed her eyes at him again. "Got it, Officer Nightingale?"

Ian nodded. "Got it, and it's Deputy Nightingale."

She waved her hand dismissively. "Whatever."

He watched her fine ass ascend the stairs to the deck before trudging the long staircase up to the road. He wasn't looking forward to the hike back to his car, but thoughts of Lexie Hanson were there to keep him company. *Damn. What a woman!*

CHAPTER FORTY-FIVE

"She said not to call Angellica? Really? What the hell am I supposed to do? Just sit here and hope she calls?"

"That's exactly what she meant," Ian said as he scrubbed a hand over his face. He'd moved his rental car to a new location, one where he could see the beach house without being seen. What he was doing was sneaky and borderline stalking, but not strictly illegal. He had a home address for Lexie, but when he'd gone by there earlier, it didn't appear anyone was home. That didn't mean Angellica wasn't there, but on the off chance she wasn't, he'd tail Lexie when she left work. If she ever did. A glance at the digital readout on the dashboard confirmed he'd been sitting there for hours. It was a wonder someone hadn't called the cops on him by now. "I'm pretty sure your girl is staying with Lexie, but I want to make sure before I go stalking around her house. If she's got one of those doorbell cameras that alerts her every time someone steps on the porch, if she's not home, she'll probably have me arrested before I get out of the neighborhood. If she's home, I have a chance of talking my way inside. Even if Angellica's not there, I might learn something about where she's hiding out."

"You said Lexie wasn't talking."

"She wasn't. She's very protective of Angellica, but there might be pictures of the two of them in some other location or something like that. Maybe your girl left something behind on the coffee table. Or maybe she's there, and she'll hear my voice and agree to talk to me."

"I feel useless sitting here just waiting for her to call."

"Waiting is hard. I get it. But chasing her when she doesn't want to be chased will only drive her further away."

"Sending my brother to hunt her down doesn't count as chasing?"

Ian chuckled. "Nah. It just smacks of desperation, and that could work in your favor."

"I *am* desperate, Ian." There was a pause and Ian imagined he could see the cogs turning in his brother's brain. "Hey. Give me Lexie's address."

"Why?"

"I'm going to send Angellica some flowers. If she's not there, Lexie will take them to her, or Angellica will come and get them. Either way, you can see for sure if she's there."

"It's not an awful idea. But, hey. I've got an even better one."

L.A. traffic was a nightmare. Even the freeway off ramps were congested—a fact he ran across while trying to exit near Lexie's house in what the Malibu florist had called, The Valley. The term conjured up something more picturesque than street after street of strip malls and tract houses, all of which were older than him. As he made a final turn onto Lexie's street, he reached out and grabbed the vase he'd seat belted into the passenger seat to keep it from tumbling over. A couple of the expensive blooms had already suffered some damage because of his driving, which tended to be on the aggressive side. With any luck, Lexie would be dazzled by the size of the arrangement and not notice the battered roses on one side. He had to admit; it was an impressive bouquet. When the florist had asked him what the purpose of the arrangement was, he'd told her it was an, "I'm sorry. I fucked up bouquet." She whistled low and quoted him a price that made his butt cheeks clench. Nevertheless, he'd plopped down his credit card and waited. And waited.

It was going on eleven p.m. when he parked in front of what he believed to be Lexie's house and got out. He went around to the passenger side and freed the flowers before crossing the tiny front lawn to the even smaller porch. The light came on as he reached the top step, revealing a heavy metal security door, and one of the fancy video doorbells he'd mentioned to his brother. Above it was a cutesy sign that warned solicitors would be fed to the dragon in the backyard. He hoped that wasn't code for giant guard dog, but when he rang the doorbell and didn't hear any snarling or barking from inside, he shrugged it off as a passive-aggressive way to say fuck off. Knowing he was on camera; Ian hid his face behind the arrangement. After a few seconds, Lexie's voice sounded through the speaker. "What do you want?"

"Delivery for Lexie Hanson." Saying the flowers were for Angellica would raise suspicion right away, so he'd opted to use her name instead.

"It's kind of late for a delivery."

"The buyer paid extra to have it delivered tonight." That wasn't exactly a lie. He'd paid extra to get the florist to make up the arrangement while he waited.

"Who's it from?"

"How would I know? I just drive the truck." *Shit.* He shifted to block her view of the car he'd arrived in. As a law enforcement officer, he'd kick her ass if she fell for his ruse. Women living alone couldn't be too careful. A few seconds later, the front door opened, then Lexie barreled out. Ian had to step back or be hit by the metal security door.

"What the fuck do you think you're doing?" She parted the roses with both hands, so they were face to face. "I told you, she's not here."

"I don't believe you."

"I don't care what you believe." She moved her hands, and the flowers snapped back into place. Ian moved them to the crook of one arm so he could see her face. "Go. Away."

"Sean sent these for Angellica." He held the giant bouquet out to her. When she didn't take it, he tucked it back into the crook of his arm. "He loves her, and he's worried about her. Did you know she's been sick? He thinks she needs to see a doctor."

Lexie exhaled as she leaned against the security door that had slammed shut. Arms crossed; she met Ian's gaze head-on. "I know she's been sick. She saw a doctor. She's fine. There's nothing for him to worry about."

Sean was going to be relieved to hear that. "Thanks. I'll let him know, but I'd feel better if I could see for myself."

"I'll tell you what, Ian Nightingale. I'll let you in to see her tonight under one condition."

The smirk on her face was a warning, one he knew he should heed, but he'd made a promise to his brother, and he wasn't about to go back on his word. Sean needed to know his girl was okay and he would do whatever it took to get him that peace of mind. Ian shifted the vase to his other arm. "Name it."

CHAPTER FORTY-SIX

"She's fine." Ian dropped onto the couch in his brother's family room. The house reminded him of the one they'd grown up in, only newer. Not to say that Sean's new residence was new. It wasn't. Judging from the solid construction and the overall workmanship, the house had to be close to a hundred years old. The structure appeared to have been well kept, and the furnishings were a mix of antiques and newer pieces that blended the old with the new. It was the kind of place he could see his brother purchasing, even if it didn't come with a world-class vineyard. That was a nice bonus, or in Sean's case, the house was the bonus. Sean was all about the grapes. "I talked to her myself."

"How did she look?"

"Maybe a little pale? Hard to tell, since it was the first time I'd met her. She asked a lot of questions about you."

"Like?"

"She wanted to know if you were here. I told her you'd never left. That seemed to surprise her."

"I'm not leaving. Not for any length of time, anyway. With or without her, this is my home now. It's her home, too." He took a sip from the crystal tumbler in his hands. Sean was a wine drinker, so Ian found it odd that his brother had opted for whiskey. Since he preferred whiskey, he wasn't about to complain. "Did she say anything about being ill?"

Ian shook his head. "No, and I didn't press the issue. None of my business." He sipped from his own tumbler, then held it up to the light, examining the amber liquid. Damn, that was good. "What is this? It goes down smooth."

"Maccallan single malt." Sean shrugged. "Thirty years old, I think."

"Fuck, Sean. That stuff costs a fortune."

"I didn't buy it. Or maybe I did, in a roundabout way. It was in the liquor cabinet when I moved in. A new, unopened bottle. There wasn't any dust on it, so I figured the old bastard probably bought it with the money he made from the sale of the property. My money, so either way, I paid for it."

"We shouldn't waste it then," he said as he tipped the glass to his lips.

Sean also took a sip, then set his glass aside. "What else did she say?"

"She wanted to know about the other woman. I told her that the issue had been resolved, but if she wanted details, she needed to talk to you." He lifted his glass in a half-hearted toast. "Again, none of my business."

Sean nodded. "Anything else?"

"She wanted to know if you got the Pinot Noir shipped out. I told her I thought so, but that she needed to ask you."

"I think I'm seeing a trend here," his brother deadpanned.

Ian tucked his chin and raised both eyebrows to peer at his brother. "You think?"

"Yeah, I think. And I owe you. Thanks for taking time

off and coming all the way out here to help me. I didn't know where to look for her."

"Anytime, Sean." Ian studied the dwindling liquid gold in his glass. "What do you know about her friend, Lexie?"

His brother was quick to respond. "Nothing. I've never met her, and the few times we spoke on the phone, she nearly bit my head off. If I had my guess, I'd say she's a dragon lady. There must be something redeeming about her, though, or she wouldn't be friends with Angellica. Why do you ask?"

"No reason." The lie fell easily from his lips. "But you're right about one thing—she's a piece of work." Gorgeous. Accomplished. Loyal. Sexy. Fuck, was she sexy. And manipulative. She'd cornered him, left him with no choice but to agree to her demands. He'd deal with that later. Right now, he was more concerned about Sean. "How's the new business venture going?"

"I guess Wade told you I almost lost this year's harvest, which would have been a disaster I couldn't recover from. He stepped in and saved my ass."

"Your troubles might have saved his life. If he'd been at home, he would have taken the deposit to the bank instead of Dad. Shillingford confessed to shooting Dad, but he said he thought it was Wade. Once he realized he'd shot the wrong person, he quit shooting. He had plenty more rounds in the magazine. I got the impression he intended to use all of them on Wade."

"Seriously?"

Ian dipped his chin in a silent acknowledgment. It had been weeks since the enraged banker had shot their dad, but thinking about how much worse it could have been never got any easier. "Questioned him myself. He blames Wade for him losing his job and because he's facing criminal prosecution for his shady dealings." He finished his drink in one gulp. "It's not like Wade made him do those things. He got greedy and forgot the bank's mission is to aid the community, not destroy it."

"I never did like that guy."

Ian smirked. "Me, either." He set his empty tumbler on the side table. "So, when do I get to see the new Nightingale West vineyard?"

Sean stood. "How about now? I've got something I want to show you."

"Lead the way." Ian got to his feet and followed his brother out into the early evening light. The drive down from L.A. had been brutal, and it felt good to stretch his legs, even if it was in a vineyard. He knew just enough about grapes and wine to know winemaking wasn't for him. Thankfully, he had two older brothers who lived and breathed the industry, so his lack of interest was more or less accepted. He couldn't imagine what his role in the family business would be. Just look at Sean. He'd moved three-thousand miles away to establish a place for himself. Ian wasn't cut out for that sort of thing. He was a man of action. Even as a kid, he hated sitting at a desk. His IQ was almost as high as Sean's so learning had come easily for him. He'd whizzed through college, hardly cracking a book. Once that was done, he'd considered joining the military, but then he saw a recruitment ad in the local paper for the Sheriff's department and went that route instead. He was still helping people, with the advantage of staying close to home.

"Are you listening to anything I'm saying?"

"Huh?" Ian realized Sean had stopped in front of a stone building some distance from the main house. "Yeah. Those are grapevines." He swept his arm out to encompass the vineyard that surrounded them. And this is…," he gave the building a once over, "I don't know what this is."

"This is the blending room. The casks are stored in the cellar beneath it."

Ian nodded. "As dad would say, this is where the magic happens."

Sean chuckled. "Yeah, but it's not magic. It's science." He entered a code into the electronic keypad. There was a hum and a click. Sean grasped the door handle and pulled it open. "Come on. Even you'll appreciate this. If not, then I'll know for sure you were adopted."

"I was not adopted! I know enough about winemaking to know I'd never be good at it. That's it."

As impressive as the vineyard was, the cask cellar was even more so. "Whoa! I wasn't expecting this." Ian turned in a slow circle, taking in the racks of barrels that went on as far as the eye could see.

"It's something, isn't it?"

"Are all these full?"

"Yep. But this is the one," he led the way to a barrel set off to the side, "is the reason I brought you down here."

"What's in it?"

"This," Sean said, as he removed the bung, "is the wine that's going to keep Nightingale Vineyards in business."

Ian tucked his hands in his front pockets and rocked back on his heels. "Seriously? You've already come up with the blend you were telling us about?"

"Want to try it?"

"Hell, yeah." He glanced around. "Got a pipette and a glass around here somewhere?"

Sean produced the equipment from a plastic crate stashed on the other side of the barrel. About the only wine-related gene Ian had inherited was the ability to discern a good wine from a bad one. Beyond that, he was lost. So when his brother handed him a glass, he accepted it with mixed feelings. He believed in Sean, but if he was counting on Ian to discern the subtle notes of his new concoction, he was going to be disappointed. Nevertheless, he went through the tasting ritual he'd learned as a kid by watching his parents and been instructed in as an adult. Certain things were expected of a Nightingale, and wine rituals were one of them.

He held the glass up to the light. "The color is rich." He swirled the liquid around the bowl of the glass, allowing it to breathe before he brought the rim to his nose and inhaled deeply. "Wow! The bouquet is…slightly sweet, but robust."

"Good job, Ian." *You might not be adopted after all.*

"Screw you," he said as he tilted the bowl, then watched as the wine coated the glass. "It's got legs. Nice legs." His gaze met Sean's. "How does it taste?"

"You tell me."

Ian lifted the glass to his lips and took a tiny sip. As soon as the wine hit his taste buds, his eyes popped open, his gaze instantly locking with his brother's. He hastily swallowed. "Holy shit, Sean! This is…it's…fuck, we're going to be rich!"

Sean smiled wide. "Have another sip and tell me what you really think."

Ian did as he was told, savoring his second taste before swallowing. He stared into his glass as the last flavor notes burst on his tongue. With a smack of his lips, he once again met Sean's gaze. "People will pay hundreds of dollars for a bottle of this."

"Yeah, they will."

"You're a genius, Sean. Of course, you can't base anything on my opinion, but wow. This is above and beyond anything we've ever produced."

"I agree."

"I guess the question is, can you replicate it?"

"I don't know about long-term. I've got to brush up on my Italian," he held a hand up, staving off Ian's question before it left his lips, "before I can say for sure, but I can do it once, maybe two or three times, depending on how the younger vintage Cabernets blend." His hand swept out to encompass the vast number of barrels lining the walls around them. "I estimate we can cork around two-hundred thousand bottles this year alone if I can talk Dad and Sean out of some Nightingale Merlot."

"I don't think you're going to have any trouble doing that." Ian took another sip. He wasn't exaggerating. The blend was spectacular. "Is Wade coming out here to try it?"

Sean shook his head. "Nope. I bottled a case for you to take home with you. If it passes the taste test, I'll have Wade ship more Merlot, and I'll bottle the blend here. That way, I can put the Nightingale West logo on it."

Ian couldn't help but smile. "You're really doing this, aren't you?"

"I really am."

"Good for you, bro. It takes a lot of guts to go against the family's wishes and do what's right for you."

"You should know. I thought Dad was going to have a coronary when you told him you were going to the police academy after college, but he came around once he saw it was the right decision for you. He's coming around to my decisions, too." He motioned to the barrel containing the new blend. "This should end all doubt."

"Hey, what's in that one?" Ian pointed to a smaller barrel set apart from the rest.

"Something I found hidden at the end of one of the racks. I'm not sure how long it's been back there. I hope Angellica knows because if you think my blend is good, you need to taste that one."

"Really?" He held out his empty glass. "Fill it up. I can't imagine anything being better than what I just sampled."

"I didn't say it was better," Sean said as he removed the bung and used a pipette to withdraw a few ounces of the dark liquid. "I just said you need to taste it."

Ian took the offered glass and went through the ritual ingrained in his brain. One sniff told him his brother wasn't exaggerating. He closed his eyes and let the liquid slide over his tongue. He swallowed, then went back for another sip, holding the wine on his tongue a little longer than was necessary.

"Well?" Sean prodded.

"This is some good shit. What the hell is it?"

"It's a Pinot Noir blended with Syrah and maybe a little Grenache. That's my best guess. Like I said, I'm hoping Angellica can solve the mystery of who blended it, and what the ratios are. If we can blend this on a large scale, I'd introduce it as a Capello Private Reserve. Estate Bottled—if that applies."

"When you figure it out, save me a couple of cases."

"To hide in your private wine cellar? The one you don't want anyone to know you have?"

Ian shared a smile with his older brother. "Yeah, that one, and if you tell a soul about my wine collection, I'll tell everyone why I really came out here."

"Okay." Sean held his hands up in surrender. "My lips are sealed, and yours better stay that way, too. The last thing I need is Mom finding out I'm having woman troubles. She'll have every friend she knows hunting up single women on the west coast to send my way."

"I saw a few on the set of that TV show that I wouldn't mind getting to know," Ian said as they walked back to the house.

"You could stay a few more days and maybe ask one of them out."

"No can do. I'm taking the jet home tomorrow. I don't want to be anywhere near here when your woman comes home. There are some things a brother doesn't need to see or hear."

"You'd make an excellent witness if she tries to kill me."

"She won't. She loves you, man. I saw it in her eyes when she asked about you and that other supermodel. She was genuinely afraid she'd lost you."

"Never. Angellica Capello is my destiny."

CHAPTER FORTY-SEVEN

"Are you okay?" Lexie joined Angellica on the sofa after showing Ian Nightingale out.

"I'm fine." Now that he was gone, she allowed herself to relax a little. She hated hiding things, and knowing Ian was a deputy sheriff put her on edge. Sure he'd use his powers of observation or his interrogation skills to pry information out of her, she'd tensed in his presence. "He wasn't anything like I expected. He seemed genuinely interested in my health, and he didn't pry into my personal business."

"Are you sure talking to him was the right thing to do?"

Angellica shrugged. "No idea. At least he'll go back and tell Sean that I'm okay, and that should buy me some time to figure out what I'm going to do."

"You have to tell Sean."

"I know. And I know I'll have to go back. I can't stay with you forever."

"Sure you can. I've got plenty of room."

Angellica rolled her eyes. "No, you don't. But it's nice of you to offer, given my circumstances."

"Maybe we could add on a room. Or two? Others on the block have."

"Neither of us can afford to renovate your house." She sighed and tugged the blanket throw tighter around her. She was physically exhausted and mentally tired of skirting around the real issue. "I love him, Lex. I don't know if there's a chance for us as a couple, or not, but I have to find out, and I need to do that before I tell him I'm pregnant."

"You think Sean would want a relationship because you're pregnant, even if he doesn't love you?"

"I don't know, but it's a risk I'm not willing to take. I need to know he loves me, that he wants to be with me, baby, or no baby."

"Babies," Lexie corrected.

"Ugh!" Angellica dropped her head to the back of the sofa and stared at the ceiling. "Don't remind me."

"You're going to be an awesome mom, Jelly. And if Sean Nightingale knows what's good for him, he'll drop to his knees and propose the moment he sees you."

"I can't see that happening." Ian had said Sean was more worried than pissed off, but she had run out on him without giving him a chance to explain. She had some apologizing to do.

It took her nearly a week to gather the courage to face Sean, but as she drove past the sign bearing the Nightingale Vineyard logo, she felt her courage waning. Keeping the pregnancy a secret was going to be hard, but she had no intention of entering a relationship with Sean for any other reason than love.

Hoping he'd be at the house, she stopped there first. Since he only inhabited a small portion of the home, it didn't take long to realize he wasn't there. Which meant he was probably in the blending room or the cellar getting ready to bottle the last of the Capello vintages. Her heart sank at the thought. Once those wines were gone, Capello Vineyard would cease to exist.

Future wines would bear the Nightingale name. She brushed tears away as she trudged the short distance to the blending room. It didn't take much to make her cry these days. Yesterday, she'd burst into tears over a television commercial touting a dog food brand's donation to animal shelters across the country. Seeing the caged puppies happily chowing down on the donated kernels was all it took to open the floodgates. *No crying in front of Sean. He'll know something's up, for sure.*

Once she found him, though, tears were the last thing on her mind. She stopped on the bottom step. "What's going on down here?" she demanded as her gaze landed on a wine barrel sitting in the middle of the cellar floor. "That's…"

At the sound of her voice, Sean spun around to face her. Of all the expressions she'd imagined seeing on his face when she returned, anger wasn't one of them. "So, you came back." His voice was about as welcoming as a rattlesnake's rattle. "It's about fucking time." He rested his hands on his hips and glared at her. "Were you going to tell me?"

Her gaze darted to the barrel, then back to Sean. "Uhm." Was he talking about her special blend or…something else?

"Did you think I wouldn't find out?" He swore, then dropped his gaze to the floor. "Seriously, Angel? Do you hate me so much that you'd keep something this important from me?"

She blamed it on the hormones raging through her system, but she didn't have a clue what he was talking about or how to answer him.

"We're in this together," he said, his voice sounding more hurt than angry. "Did you think I'd take credit for something I didn't do?"

Was he talking about that other woman's baby? Her head spun as she tried to make sense of the one-sided conversation. "What?"

"Did you do this on your own?"

She shook her head. "No." If he was talking about the babies, she most certainly didn't do that on her own. Maybe he hadn't aced biology after all.

"Have you thought of a name for it? Tell me you've at least decided what to call it."

"Call it?" Dear god, he *was* talking about a baby.

"Not Nightingale. Capello Private Reserve?"

Angellica narrowed her eyes at him. *Private Reserve? Who the hell names their baby Private Reserve?* Then she had a moment of clarity and asked, "Are you talking about the wine?" She motioned to the barrel behind him. "Or something else?" He couldn't possibly know about the…

"What the hell else would I be talking about?"

A wave of relief washed over her, clearing the fog out of her brain, and making her knees tremble. "Nothing." She took another step, bringing her down to the same level as Sean. She pointed to the barrel. "I see you found the Pinot Noir blend."

Sean's gaze swept her from head to toe, then landed back on her eyes. "Yeah, I found it. Did your dad blend this?"

"No."

"Then who did?"

"I did."

"Who helped you?"

Okay, that was insulting. She gritted her teeth and forced the answer out. "No one."

"You just said you didn't do it on your own. Which is it, Angel?"

She replayed their conversation in her head. "I thought you were talking about something else." She motioned to the oak cask. "I did this all by myself." She couldn't keep a hint of pride out of her voice. The blend was good. Beyond good, and she knew it. Now that the cat was out of the bag, so to speak, she damn sure was going to take credit for her work.

"Why the hell didn't you tell me you were sitting on a gold mine? Is there more? Can you make more?"

Gold mine? Once again, her brain scrambled to keep up with his questions. She opened her mouth, then shut it as she tried to decide which of his questions to answer first.

"Well?"

His sharp verbal prod shocked her brain back into action. "I didn't tell you because I was going to use it as my resume to find another job—at a winery that would appreciate my talents as a vintner. Some place that wouldn't treat me like a farmhand." She hoped he choked on that bit of truth. "Then shit happened, and I had other things on my mind. No, that's all I made, and yes, I can make more. But I won't."

"What the fuck? This is exceptional, Angel. You have to make more."

"And sell it as a Nightingale wine? A Capello grew those grapes. A Capello blended that wine. I'm the Capello who did that, Sean. You said yourself you wouldn't put your name on something you didn't do."

He stared at her like she'd grown two heads. Technically, she was growing two heads. Two—or more, little bodies, but she wasn't inclined to tell him just yet. At the rate this conversation was going, he'd be ordering her off his property any minute now. She held her ground, her body tense as she waited for him to respond verbally. At last, a giant smile broke across his face, and before she could move, he closed the distance between them. She gasped as his work-roughened palms encased her head, forcing her to look up at him.

"Didn't you hear a thing I said? We'll call it Capello

Private Reserve. Estate Bottled. It'll be huge, Angel! No way am I letting you go to work for any other winery. Fuck no. You're mine. All. Fucking. Mine." His gaze met hers and held. Angellica felt like they were back in the kitchen on a cold, rainy night. Just the two of them, experiencing something momentous. Life changing. "I love you, Angel. I let you slip through my hands once, but never again." His thumbs stroked her cheekbones, and his gaze dropped to her lips, which, to her dismay, quivered. "I need you. In my life. In my bed. In our winery. A partner in every way. I can't imagine my life without you."

Her heart threatened to beat out of her chest, and for a fleeting moment, she wondered if that was good for the babies. Then he lowered his head, and his lips touched hers in a featherlight kiss that spoke of respect and timeless love. She wanted both things, but she wanted…needed more. She parted her lips, inviting him in. He responded, plunging his tongue past her teeth. She wrapped her arms around his neck and lifted onto her toes, straining for more.

Sean tore his mouth away from hers. His lips skimmed her jaw, then he bit the lobe of her ear and tugged. She cried out as white-hot heat shot straight to her womb. "I need you, Angel. I need you so fucking much."

"I need you, too." If she wasn't puking, she was horny. Pregnancy was a demanding bitch.

"Let's go to the house," he said as he bent to pick her up.

"No." She undid the button on her jeans and pushed them and her panties past her hips. "Here. Now."

Sean's eyes lit up, and a smile broke across his face. "You naughty girl. Fucking in the cellar." He kneeled to help her with her shoes. "I like it."

When she was naked from the waist down, he lifted her and set her bare ass on the cask containing her special blend. She held onto his shoulders as he unfastened his shorts and freed his cock. She scooted forward, eager to feel him inside her again. He suddenly exclaimed, "Shit!" and backed away. Angellica let out a strangled cry and forced her gaze from his cock to his eyes.

"What?"

"No condom."

She almost told him then but decided that twins would be the ultimate cockblockers. Instead, she lied. "I'm on the pill."

The light returned to his eyes. He gazed at her crotch, then up at her face. "You're okay with that?"

She nodded. "Fuck me, Sean. Please?"

"I'm clean. I swear to God, I'm clean."

"Me, too. So, hurry the fuck up."

The top of their heads touched as they both watched him drag his cock through her wet folds until the head glistened in the low light. It was, possibly, the most erotic thing she'd ever witnessed and fueled her need to have him inside her. Lubricated with her juices, he notched the head at her entrance. "I'm not going to last long," she warned.

"Challenge accepted." He rocked his hips forward in a powerful thrust that hurt so good it forced a gasp from her lips. Deep inside her, he paused, his chest heaving like he'd run a marathon. "You," he whispered in her ear. "Only you make me feel this way. Like time doesn't exist."

He flexed his hips, retreating, then filling her again. And again. Every slippery slide of his cock sent waves of pleasure through her body. She couldn't get enough of him. Risking a splinter in her ass, she rolled her hips, taking him deeper. He cradled her butt in his hands and crooned into her ear as he withdrew and thrust again. "Easy baby, let me do the work."

In response to his command, an unladylike sound escaped her lips, but she clung to him as he set a steady rhythm that drove her wild with need. He wound the coil inside her tight. Tighter. *So close.* She dropped her head back, her mouth open as she teetered on the edge of orgasm. Then…nothing. Sean nipped at her earlobe, his cock buried to the hilt, he growled, "Not yet, Angel." He squeezed her ass cheeks. "I'm going to give you the orgasm you deserved the first time. Trust me?"

Unable to form words, she bit her lip and nodded.

"That's a good girl." He slid his cock almost all the way out, then back in so slowly that she wanted to scream at him to pick up the pace. "Slow this time. Feel it building." His hands on her ass kept her from accelerating the motion, but that didn't stop her from trying. He simply gripped her harder and admonished, "Shh, Angel. I've got you. Let me lead this dance."

"Feel it? The way we fit together. We've got all the time in the world. Just the two of us. Together forever."

Her skin tingled as his words washed over her like warm ocean waves. He moved within her in a dance as old as time and, so slowly, took her up to the peak of pleasure again. She dropped her head back as she'd done before, and this time, his words gently nudged her over the edge. "Let go, Angel. I've got you. Always."

Angellica's screams echoed off the cellar walls as she let go, anchored to the real world by Sean's solid presence inside her and his arms banded around her. "That's it. Ride me, baby." Somewhere in the haze of the most intense pleasure she'd ever known, she realized he'd let go of her ass, and *she* was riding *him*. He held perfectly still, holding her tight as she rocked herself on his cock. Embarrassment took a back seat to pleasure. To need. She rode him hard, taking what she needed. Desperation clawed at her as she moved over him. Her body craved the feel of him inside her, craved another orgasm, craved the pleasure only this man had ever given her. She rode him like a wild woman, unable to stop herself as the coil tightened until it became unbearable. Poised on the cliff again, paradise beckoned, but no matter how hard she tried, she couldn't reach it alone.

Sean grunted. A low, guttural sound that cut through the roar of blood rushing past her ears. "God, Angel. I can't…stop it." His arms tightened around her, holding her like a drowning man clinging to a lifeline. His body shuddered, and his cock pulsed, jettisoning his life force against her womb. Angellica flew over the edge, rocketing into space until she touched the stars, then she was free-falling toward Earth with dizzying speed. Through it all, Sean anchored her, their bodies locked together. Two merged into the eternal one.

Spent, she dropped her head to his shoulder, and knowing she was safe in his arms, she closed her eyes.

CHAPTER FORTY-EIGHT

Angellica woke with a start. She ignored her rolling stomach as she took in her surroundings. She recognized her parents' bedroom, now belonging to Sean Nightingale. He'd made some changes. A king-sized bed where a queen-sized one once sat was the biggest change. Sean lay on his stomach beside her, his chiseled body on display in the early morning light streaming through the window. His head faced away from her, his breathing slow and steady as he slept.

Memories from the night before flitted through her mind. She'd fallen asleep on Sean's shoulder after the most intense orgasms of her life, only stirring when he'd laid her in the bed and crawled in beside her. She still wore the T-shirt she'd had on when she arrived from L.A. Below that, she was totally naked, the rest of her clothes discarded in the aging cellar along with Sean's shorts and underwear. She glanced at his backside again, admiring the muscles on display. He'd carried her up the stairs from the cellar to the blending lab, across the parking area, into the house, and up the stairs to the bedroom. Naked. She felt her face grow hot at the image they must have made. Thank goodness only the two of them lived on the property!

Her stomach twisted, the now familiar feeling of impending doom forcing her from the bed. She made a mad dash for the ensuite, snagging a towel from the towel bar and wrapping it around her waist as she dropped to her knees and heaved into the toilet. Light suddenly flooded the room, nearly blinding her. She sat back on her heels and wiped her mouth with the back of her hand. Sean, naked as the day he was born, boasting a huge boner, stood in the doorway, his arms crossed over his chest.

"Got something to tell me, Angel?" He raised one eyebrow, inviting an answer.

She thought about lying, but figured there was no way he'd believe her. Not after what he'd just witnessed. "I'm pregnant."

He didn't respond, just reached around the open door to grab a terrycloth robe hanging from a hook on the back. He shrugged into it, tightened the belt, then leaned against the marble countertop. He crossed his ankles and his arms, a defensive position if she'd ever seen one. Her stomach rebelled, and once again, she bent over the toilet. When she looked back up, Sean's face was a mask of concern and something else she couldn't readily identify.

"What about the three pregnancy tests? Did you even pee on them?"

Angellica recognized his expression. Betrayal. Her heart sank as she rose to her feet and flushed the toilet. "I did. I swear I did." He didn't seem convinced, so she rambled on. "It's a long story. Let me brush my teeth, and I'll explain."

He straightened. "I'm going to make some coffee."

"Decaf for me!" she shouted as he left the room. Alone, she braced her palms on the countertop and let her chin drop to her chest. "Shit." She'd wanted to ease into the conversation, maybe feel him out about where he saw their relationship going. Did he see himself getting married and having kids? That sort of thing, but her traitorous stomach had put an end to that plan. Last night, he said he loved her. She could only hope he'd meant it.

Angellica returned to her own room, where she took the time to shower and dress before going downstairs. Still wearing the bathrobe, his feet bare, Sean sat at the island, a mug cradled in his hands. He looked up, his face devoid of emotion, when she walked in. He'd set out a mug for her, but it was empty. He remained silent as she fixed herself a cup of herbal tea and a slice of dry toast.

She took the seat next to him and sipped from her mug. "I didn't lie to you. I took the tests. I followed the instructions to the letter."

"Then what happened? How did they all come up negative?"

Angellica sighed. "I asked the doctor the same thing. She said high levels of the hormone they test for can produce a false negative result."

"Does that happen often?"

She shook her head. "No. But it's more common with twins."

"Twins?"

Unable to look him in the eyes, she felt his gaze boring into her.

"What do you mean, *twins*?"

Angellica forced herself to look at him. "Multiple fetuses. I could be pregnant with twins, or more, but I'm definitely pregnant."

"Are you for real?" She'd been prepared for almost anything, but nothing could have prepared her for the giant smile that broke across his face. "We're having twins?"

"I don't know for sure. I've got to see my OB to confirm, but yeah, it's highly likely."

Sean shot to his feet. "I'll go with you. When? Have

you made an appointment? We need the best doctor. Who's the best?" He froze. "Are you okay? You were puking again. Is that normal? Do you need to see someone right now?"

"I'm fine, Sean. Morning sickness is common. It's getting better. I was puking all day long there for a while. Now it's just mornings. Mostly." She had to admit, his concern moved her.

"I'm sorry." He reclaimed his barstool. "This morning…I saw you in the bathroom, and I the first thing I thought was that you lied to me. I didn't know the tests could be wrong."

"No need to apologize. I didn't think there was any way I could be pregnant, but Lexie insisted I see a doctor. She was convinced I'd somehow messed up the tests, too."

"So, she thought you were pregnant all along?"

"Yeah. I wasn't, even after the test at the doctor's office came back positive. Then she started listing other symptoms of early pregnancy, and I had to admit I had them all. I was in shock. That's why it took me so long to come back here. You have to admit, it was practically an immaculate conception. I was on the pill, and you wore a condom."

"It was meant to be," he said, reaching out to take her hand in his. "How long has it been? Five? Six weeks?"

"Something like that."

"Do you have an appointment with your doctor?"

"This afternoon. It's just to confirm the pregnancy."

"I want to come."

"That's not necessary. I'm a big girl."

"I want to be a part of the process, Angel. I want to be there for you, every step of the way."

She nodded. Reaching for a paper napkin from the holder in the center of the island, she dabbed at the corners of her eyes. "Damn hormones. I cry at the drop of a hat."

Sean scooted off his stool, and closing the distance

between them, he enfolded her in his arms. His terrycloth robe felt cozy and warm against her cheek. The heat pouring off his body melted her tense muscles. She wrapped her arms around his waist and breathed in his familiar scent. "I love you, Angel. I know we haven't known each other very long, but I feel like I've been searching for you all my life." He squeezed her tighter. "I'm so fucking glad I found you."

She chuckled as fresh tears leaked from her eyes. "I love you, too." She didn't want to let go of him, but the other major side effect of her raging hormones stirred inside her. She tried to extricate herself from his arms, but he refused to loosen his hold.

"I'm not ready to let go," he said, shifting his weight to draw her closer still. As he did, she felt the heavy ridge of his erection and smiled to herself.

"Umm…Sean?"

"What, baby?" He kissed the top of her head.

"Do you think we could…" She reached between them, her hand closing around his erection. "You know?"

"Now?" He sounded horrified.

"It's the hormones. They make me horny."

He leaned back to look into her eyes. "Seriously?"

She bit the corner of her lip and nodded. "Seriously. We could…you know…recreate that night?" She glanced at the spot on the island where he'd first made love to her. His gaze followed hers.

"We have a bed upstairs."

"I know, but I need you now. Besides, I have fond memories of that night."

His eyes clouded. "I blew like a horny teenager fucking for the first time. Then I ran out on you without a word."

"Yeah, but you had good reason to run out, and the way you came…it was hot. You asked me once if I'd felt something that night, and I told you I hadn't. That was a lie. I gave you my body, but you left with my heart."

He lifted her from the barstool and marched her slowly backward, around to the other side of the island, where he undressed her. When she was naked, he sat her on the countertop and spread her legs wide. "I wish I'd called you sooner. I was embarrassed. I'd never come like that in my life, not even my first time." He cradled her breasts in his large hands. "I thought I'd screwed everything up with you. I fucked my employee and left her without so much as a thank you."

"You made up for it last night."

His gaze met hers. "Did I?"

"Yes." She drew the word out as he brushed his thumbs across her nipples.

"Sensitive?"

"Uh huh," she said.

"They're bigger."

"Are you complaining?"

"Fuck, no! Just observing. I thought so last night, but we never got around to taking your top off."

"It's off now."

He arched an eyebrow. "Are you begging me to suck your tits, Angel?"

She grabbed his head with both hands and drew his face to her chest. "Suck me, Sean."

"Your wish is my command."

It turned out Sean had an excellent memory. He recalled everything about that night and recreated it to perfection. Only this time, he moved confidently inside her until they both found their pleasure. Instead of running out the door, he carried her upstairs, where they repeated every move in the shower, then again in the bed.

By the time they showered for real, dressed, and had something to eat, they were almost late for her doctor's appointment. She felt a little weird introducing Sean as her baby daddy, but he beamed with pride and took it all in stride. Until the moment the doctor confirmed *three* heartbeats.

Angellica shot up on the exam table as Sean's eyes rolled back in his head and his knees gave way. The doctor barely managed to get out of the way before he hit the floor. The attending nurse yelled for help and before long, Angellica had switched places with Sean. He lay on the exam table while she stood by, watching as the doctor carefully stitched a gash in his head. "You've got a long road ahead of you," she said as she placed another careful stitch. "But you're both young. I don't foresee any problems with the pregnancy, but we'll keep a close eye on you, just in case." She tied off the last stitch, then applied an adhesive bandage. "There's a prescription for pre-natal vitamins waiting for you at the desk. The nurse will give you some paperwork on what to avoid eating, as well as the things you'll want to make sure you have in your diet." She patted Sean on the shoulder, then stepped back, removing her latex gloves. "Exercise is important. Get plenty of it, but I wouldn't start up any kind of exercise regime you haven't already been doing. Sex is great exercise and helps scratch an itch, if you know what I mean?"

"I have been super horny."

"It's the hormones. Like I said, do what feels good. The babies are well insulated. And if their mom is happy, they'll be happy." She gathered up her tablet and placed her hand on the door handle. "Again, congratulations." She smiled at Sean. "Take your time. The room is yours as long as you need it." With a wink for Sean, she was gone, leaving them both shellshocked.

Sean pointed at the closed door. "Was she hinting that we could have sex in here? 'Cause if she was, I'm game."

CHAPTER FORTY-NINE

The ride home from the doctor's office was quiet. Sean sat in the passenger seat while Angellica drove. The doc said he didn't have a concussion, but his stomach wasn't feeling so good, so Angellica offered to drive. As he watched her, he was struck anew by his luck. She was his. His! And they were having triplets. Three boys. There wasn't a doubt in his mind. He'd seen it in that Déjà vu moment, then less than twelve hours later, he knocked Angellica up with triplets. It was meant to be.

He followed her into the house, listening to the silence, imagining the laughter that would fill the halls in the years to come. The house had been just that to him, a shelter. A place to sleep. But now he saw it as a home. His and Angellica's. They'd raise a family here and build a legacy to hand down to their children and grandchildren.

"Hey," he called out before she could disappear somewhere in the enormous house. "I want to show you something." He held out his hand, inviting her to walk with him.

"I'm tired, Sean."

She was gorgeous, and he could imagine her heavy with his babies and his heart swelled. "It'll just take a minute, then I'll carry you up and tuck you into bed."

After a moment's hesitation, she took his hand, and he led her across to the blending lab and down the stairs to the aging cellar. "One taste won't hurt, will it?" He pulled the bung from a different cask than the one they'd sampled the night before.

"No. I can have a little wine now and then."

Sean drew a measured amount out with a pipette and released it into a clean glass. He held it out to her. "Here. Try this."

Sean waited patiently as Angellica went through the tasting ritual every vintner and wine connoisseur knew. Then she let the slightest bit swirl over her tongue. When the flavor notes registered, she turned wide eyes on him. She swallowed and asked, "What is this?"

"It's the new Nightingale wine. What do you think?"

She brought the glass to her nose again and sniffed delicately. "It's our six-year-old Cab Sauvignon, and Nightingale's Merlot? This year's vintage, if I had my guess. But there's something else." She sniffed again, then took another tiny sip. "Is that our three-year-old Malbec?"

Sean's smiled. How had he ever doubted her abilities when it came to making wine? It was in her blood, and their children would inherit it. Or not. Just look at Ian, but that wasn't really true. Ian claimed he didn't know anything about wine or winemaking, but Sean knew better. Of all of them, Ian had the most eclectic wine cellar. He'd chosen the right path for himself, though, and Sean admired that about him. "I had an idea, and as soon as I tried it, I knew it was right. What do you think?"

"It's extraordinary, Sean. I never would have thought to add the Malbec."

"It's just barely there. It's forty-nine percent Cab Sav

and forty-nine percent Merlot. If we bottle it in California, we can't call it any of those things since it has to contain seventy-five percent of one grape to bear the name." He took the glass from her and set it on the floor next to the barrel where he'd taken her the night before. She looped her arms around his neck as he moved in to enclose her in his arms. "I thought we'd call it our Timeless Blend. Like our love, Angellica. When I'm with you, time doesn't matter. It doesn't matter that we've only known each other for a few weeks. What matters is that I never want to be without you. Every minute away from you is an eternity."

He moved his right hand to her stomach. "We've created something special between us. Three special somethings. You're my destiny, Angellica. Will you be my wife?"

"Sean." Angellica couldn't stop the tears streaming down her cheeks. "Are you sure?"

"Absolutely. I love you so fucking much." He smirked. "Honestly, I think I fell in love with you the day we met. Do you remember? You lectured me on my footwear. I got the biggest boner. It's a wonder you didn't notice and start throwing things at me."

"I remember, and I was too busy telling my ovaries to settle down to notice your boner. I hated you on sight, but I think now that was a defense mechanism to protect my heart. Too little, too late, though. You're my destiny, Sean. I love you. I think I have since the day we met."

"So…is that a yes? You'll marry me?"

"That's a yes."

"I don't have a ring. I'll get you one. Anything you want, but maybe we could seal the deal in another way?" He tipped his head toward the nearest barrel. It was the one where they'd made love the night before.

She smiled at him. "I'm never going to look at this cellar the same way."

"No?" He yanked his shirt over his head. "How *are*

you going to look at it?"

"With fond memories." She kicked off her shoes. "*Very* fond memories."

ABOUT THE AUTHOR

USA Today Best-Selling author Roz Lee is the author of over thirty romances. The first, The Lust Boat, was born of an idea acquired while on a Caribbean cruise with her family and soon blossomed into a five-book series originally published by Red Sage. Following her love of baseball, she turned her attention to sexy athletes in tight pants, writing the critically acclaimed Mustangs Baseball series.

Roz has been married to her best friend, and high school sweetheart, for over four decades. Roz and her husband have two daughters and are the proud grandparents to three adorable grandkids. Roz and her husband live in the wilds of New Jersey with their Labrador Retriever, Bud which is code for Big Unruly Dog.

Even though Roz has lived on both coasts, her heart lies in between, in Texas. A Texan by birth, she can trace her family back to the Republic of Texas. With roots that deep, she says, "You can't ever really leave."

When Roz isn't writing, she's reading, or traipsing around the country on one adventure or another. No trip is too small, no tourist trap too cheesy, and no road unworthy of travel.

Learn more at: www.RozLee.net

* 9 7 8 1 9 6 6 2 2 4 1 5 0 *